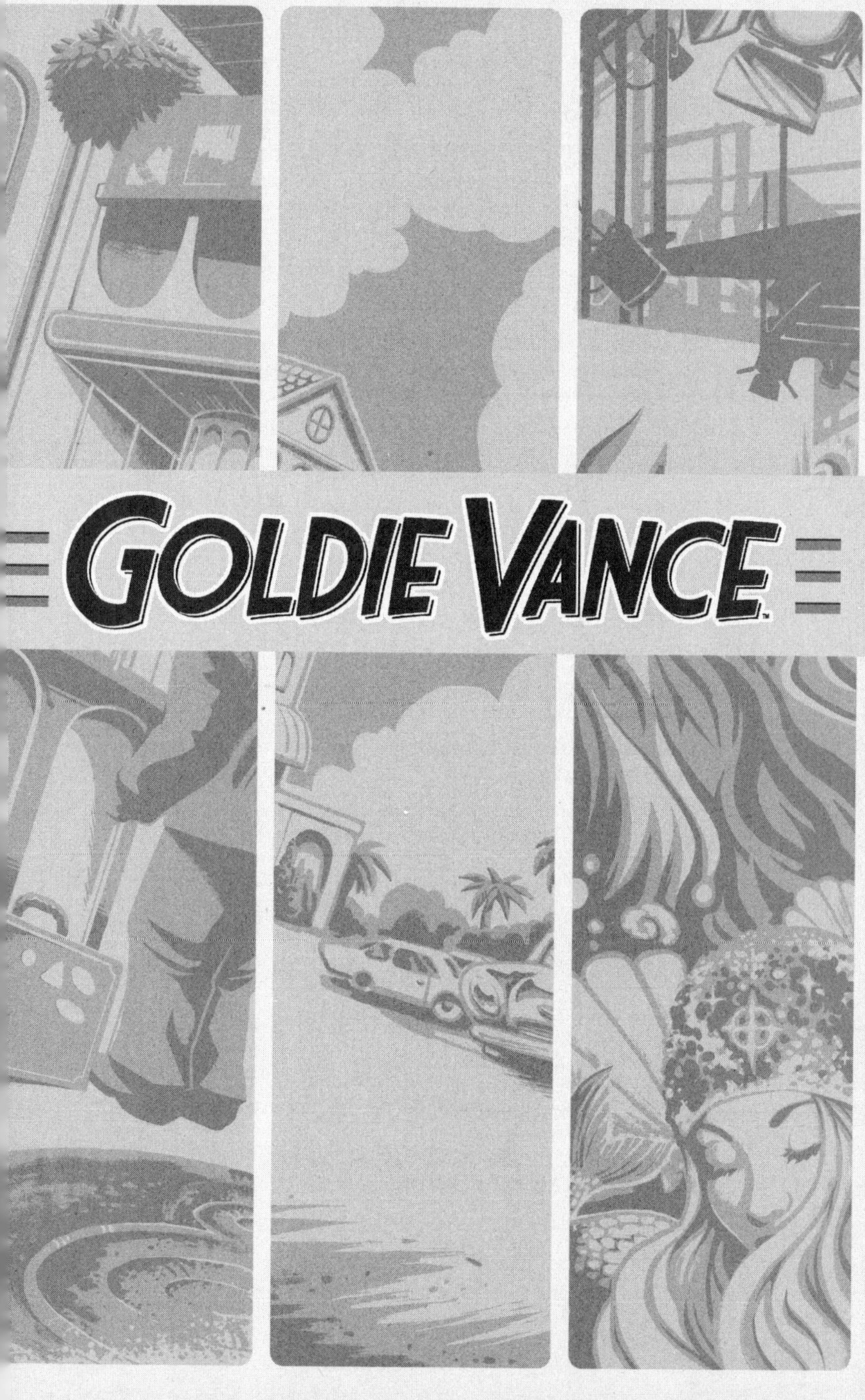

GOLDIE VANCE

Little, Brown and Company
Hachette Book Group
1290 Avenue of the Americas, New York, NY 10104
Visit us at LBYR.com

First Edition: March 2020

Little, Brown and Company is a division of Hachette Book Group, Inc. The Little, Brown name and logo are trademarks of Hachette Book Group, Inc.

The publisher is not responsible for websites (or their content) that are not owned by the publisher.

Library of Congress Cataloging-in-Publication Data
Names: Rivera, Lilliam, author. | Power, Elle, illustrator.
Title: Goldie Vance : the hotel whodunit : an original novel / by Lilliam Rivera ; illustrations by Elle Power.
Description: First edition. | New York : Little, Brown and Company, 2020. | Audience: Ages 8-12. | Summary: In early 1960s Florida, sixteen-year-old Goldie, an aspiring detective at the Crossed Palms Resort Hotel, investigates when a diamond-encrusted swim cap goes missing during the filming of a movie at the resort.
Identifiers: LCCN 2019033910 | ISBN 9780316456647 | ISBN 9780316456630 (ebook) | ISBN 9780316456654
Subjects: CYAC: Mystery and detective stories. | Resorts—Fiction. | Hotels, motels, etc.—Fiction. | Motion pictures—Production and direction—Fiction. | Racially mixed people—Fiction.
Classification: LCC PZ7.1.R5765 Go 2020 | DDC [Fic]—dc23
LC record available at https://lccn.loc.gov/2019033910

ISBNs: 978-0-316-45664-7 (paper over board); 978-0-316-45663-0 (ebook)

Printed in the United States of America

LSC-C

10 9 8 7 6 5 4 3 2 1

GOLDIE VANCE™

THE HOTEL WHODUNIT

An original novel by
Lilliam Rivera

Illustrations by Elle Power

Based on the Goldie Vance
comics created by Hope Larson &
Brittney Williams

Little, Brown Young Readers
New York Boston

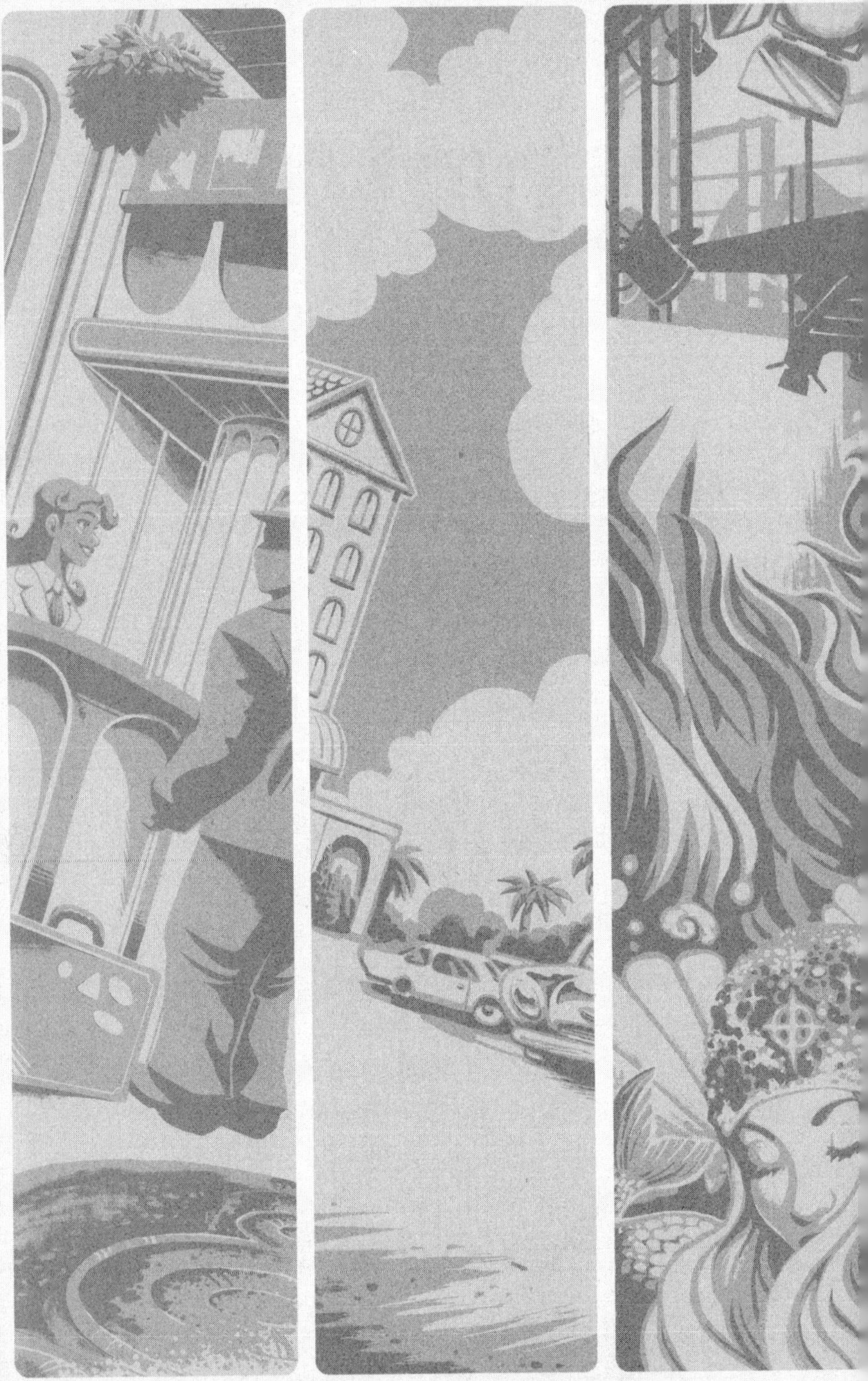

To budding
detectives everywhere!

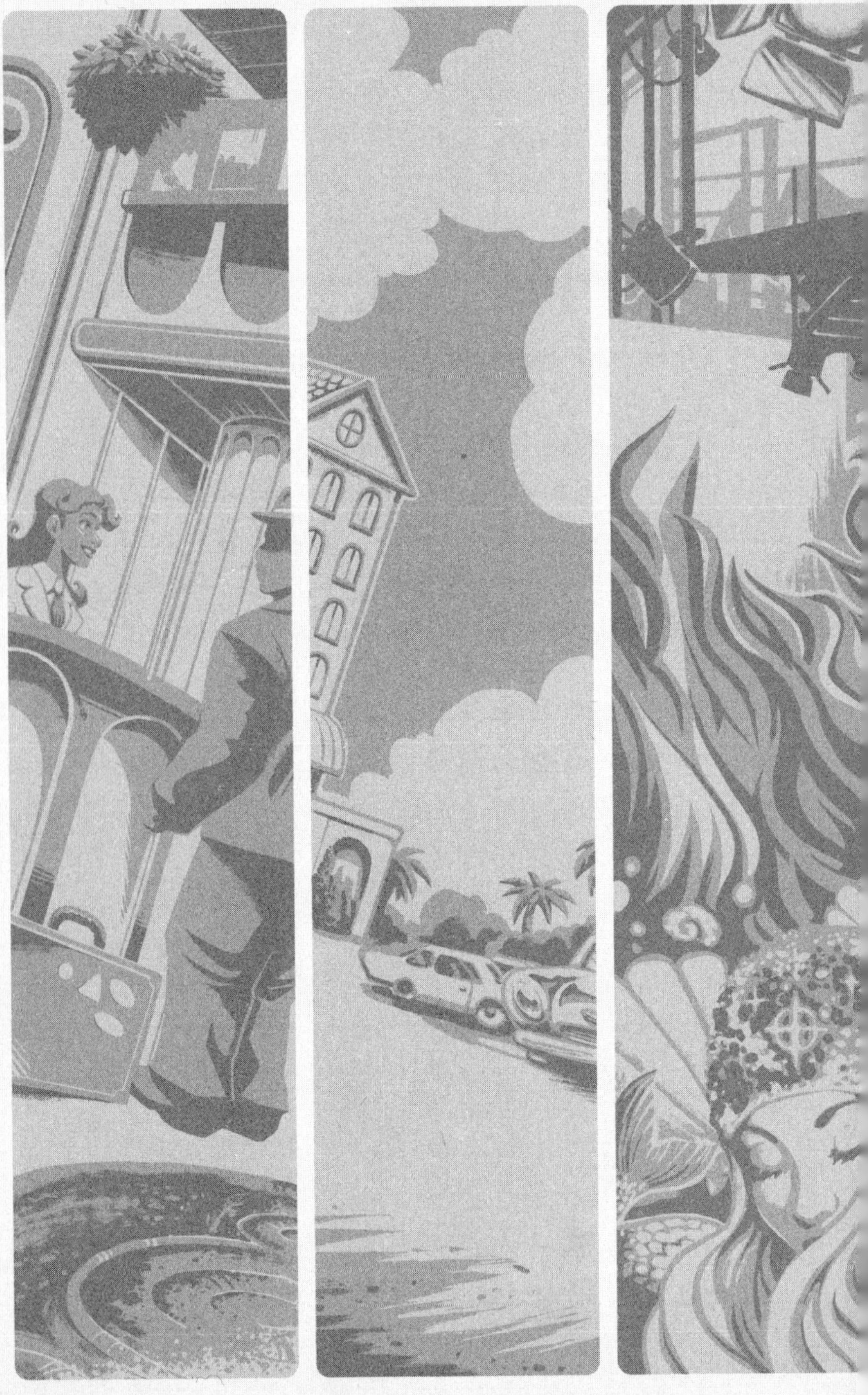

Chapter One

TRIOS OF SWAMP THINGS ARE DEEP IN CONVERSATION over by the lobby's fountain. A man with scaly skin in a slim suit pulls a toothpick from his mouth while a mermaid with long blond hair that practically sweeps the floor follows one of the bellhops into the hotel. The Crossed Palms Resort is being overrun by sea creatures and mermaids.

I pull out my trusty pad and pencil and quickly jot this down: *Mark this day—strange things are afoot.*

"Darling, I simply must have my ring," Miss Dupart whispers. "How will I ever be cast in this movie if I don't have the right accoutrement?"

"No worries, Miss Dupart. I'm on the case!" I open the door to Miss Dupart's mint-green convertible and dive deep into the back seat.

Miss Dupart is a regular at the Crossed Palms Resort. She's been living in the hotel as long as I have. Correction: She's been living here even longer. *Ever since the first palm trees swayed their palms, darling* is what she loves to say. Miss Dupart used to be a big-time actress in Hollywood, but now she waits for the right roles to land in her lap here in St. Pascal, Florida, which means she spends a lot of time by the pool lounging and primping. The thing I love most about Miss Dupart is the way she whisper-talks, like she's about to divulge the most scandalous of secrets.

"My emerald ring was a gift from the ambassador to Spain, or was it the cowboy from San Antonio?" she whisper-talks. "Either way, it's very important to me. You must find it."

"I totally understand, Miss Dupart," I say.

Every morning Miss Dupart likes to drive her vintage green car along the coast. She says the ocean air does wonders for her skin. When she got back this morning, she immediately realized her ring was missing. It's a good thing *I'm* her valet.

"Darling, have you seen the raw talent around here?"

Miss Dupart is dressed head to toe in a mint-green

dress—her favorite color—and oversize sun hat, with Clementine, her tiny poodle, yapping beside her.

"Will you be auditioning?" she asks.

"Oh no, not me, Miss Dupart. I'll leave that for the professionals. Besides, I'm sure Walter needs me to keep my eyes and ears open. You never know what mysteries might unfold."

My official job at the Crossed Palms Resort is valet, meaning I get to park the cars. But what I really want to do, more than anything in the whole wide world, is be the hotel's house detective. I'm already working as assistant to the current house detective, Walter Tooey. I mean, technically, he's not supposed to have an assistant, but there's no way he can handle this whole resort on his own, not when there are always kids running off and getting lost, jewelry going missing, and cars being vandalized. There was also that one time the entire cast of some variety show was sabotaged by a jealous singer. Too bad the singer left her nefarious to-do list written behind some sheet music I found thrown in the trash. Nothing gets past me. Anyway, all this is to say that I've been proving I have what it takes to be a stellar detective. I'm just due for a promotion soon; I'm sure of it.

While I wait for that to happen, I negotiate elbow room with Clementine the poodle, who has decided to join me in the back seat.

"What do you think, Clementine? Do you know where the ring is?" I ask. Clementine answers with a sloppy lick on my face.

"I've never been one for genre ever since I was cast in that horrid vampire movie in the thirties with Bela Whatever-his-name-is, but they say sea monsters are the latest rage," Miss Dupart chimes in.

"Not a problem, Miss Dupart. I'll find it. I have all the confidence in the world!" I yell over Clementine, who is yapping her concern. Clementine doesn't think I've got the chops to perform this miraculous feat. The poodle is forgetting one thing: I'm Goldie Vance, the soon-to-be-renowned house detective of this establishment, and there's no doubt that this mystery will be solved in three...two...

"Sweet Annette Funicello! I found it!"

I leap out from the back seat, my fingers clutching the brilliant ring. A half-swamp thing, half man with sandy-blond hair who's talking to an older woman with severe bangs looks over my way for a second, but they return to their intense conversation totally unfazed. Miss Dupart is elated.

"Goldie, darling, you truly are a godsend," says Miss Dupart while she places the ring on her wrinkly finger alongside all her other rings. "I'd better make my entrance. You never know if they're looking for another damsel in distress."

Miss Dupart hands me a dollar, and I tuck the crisp new bill inside the pocket of my scratchy uniform. This time, Clementine's bark is one of approval.

"Break a leg, Miss Dupart," I say.

The Crossed Palms Resort is a sprawling estate with three—count 'em—*three* pools. There are cabanas, cabana boys, a lounge with a piano, a cigar room, and an extravagant ballroom for weddings and fancy parties. Guests can learn how to cha-cha-cha or be left alone to stroll on the beach looking for seashells. We even have honest-to-goodness pink flamingos roaming around. Anyone who is anyone ends up staying at the Crossed Palms. Starlets, families, and mambo singers straight from Cuba. You name it, I've seen it all.

So that's what you see when you're checking in, but what you don't see is the behind-the-scenes magic that makes this hotel run so smoothly. I know every secret hallway—including the one that will lead me to Chef François (where he will let me sneak a taste of his famous onion soup) or the one that takes me to where a high-stakes game of cards is starting. As a kid I played hide-and-seek in the laundry room and was taught how to Hula-Hoop by a magician. I think I "borrowed" my first golf cart at eight? (Don't tell anyone.) The Crossed Palms Resort has been my home ever since Dad got a job working here ten years ago. Now that I'm sixteen, I get to work here, too. All I need is that one big case to make me an official detective. It will happen soon enough. I can feel it in my bones; just need to keep my eyes and ears open. Actually, I need all my senses working in order to make my private-eye dreams come true!

When Mr. Maple, the owner of the Crossed Palms Resort, alerted us that the Baldwin Movie Studios was planning to shoot their film at the hotel, I had no idea it would mean a full-on convention of movie monsters and serious movie-business types. Mr. Maple warned us to treat every single person arriving at the hotel like royalty. His actual words: "Each demand by these Hollywood types, no matter the case, must be met with expediency and a smile. Understood?" Mr. Maple can be a bit demanding himself, but that's beside the point. Message was received loud and clear. Demands must be met!

A silver Corvette pulls up to the valet tent. What a beaut. A 1951 original. On first impression, the guy pulling up definitely falls in the demanding-movie-business-type category, especially with the large cigar he's chomping on.

"Welcome to the Crossed Palms Resort, the hotel where your every wish is at your fingertips!" I say.

Mr. Very Important barely grumbles.

"Find a shady spot," he says, and tosses me his car keys.

"Of course, sir."

The thing about being a good detective is that you have to pay close attention to details. For example, I notice how his car is immaculately polished. It is as shiny as if it were new. This can mean one of two things: Either Mr. Very Important likes things to be immaculate, or maybe he doesn't want to leave behind any evidence of his recent whereabouts. But next I notice that he collects matchbooks, which reveal exactly where he's been. Aha. I note that one matchbook is from New York, courtesy of the Empire State Building illustration. Another one is from Malibu, Los Angeles. You can tell by the surf. The last item I notice is a small pink handkerchief, smelling of a strong perfume and peeking out from under the front seat. Is it from his wife? Or a movie star? Or is it his? Who knows?

While I let everything percolate in my brain, I'll flex my driving skills in this beautiful silver baby. I pop the clutch and hit the accelerator. I'm sure Mr. Very Important won't mind if I really test his car, make sure it can handle hairpin turns. After a couple of loops around the lot, I finally find the perfect shady space.

What do you know? It's break time.

I head inside the lobby, which is bustling with guests checking in. It's Monday morning and the excitement is simmering.

"Hey, Cheryl," I yell across the lobby. "Can you believe it? You must be in heaven studying these sea creatures."

Cheryl Lebeaux is by far the smartest girl I know. She wants to be an astronaut; that's how smart she is. Who else would read a five-pound science book for fun?

"Ha! If only they were real. Just a bunch of actors in rubber costumes. Anyway, I want to study actual stars, as in hydrogen and helium, straight from the cosmos," she says dreamily, staring up at the ceiling. I try to decipher the diagrams in the oversize science book she has open on the counter. It's so complicated. I don't know how she does it. "And speaking of space, you need to stop using the cars you park as your personal spaceships."

"Well, I figured if I find the right velocity timed with the right pressure and x factor something something, I'll be the first person to land on the moon."

"Be serious, Goldie." She grabs the science book from me. "Don't let Mr. Maple see you or you'll be toast."

"Why? Is he here?" I look around. I must confess: I didn't stop with golf carts. I've been known to "borrow" cars once in a while. I consider each one its own unique tutorial. I mean, if I continue to be a solid driver, then I can only be that much more valuable to the resort. Right?

"No, he's not here, not yet anyway. He's called here at least three times today. I've sat in so many meetings. Who to look out for. Who is arriving early. Who is arriving late. This person has to sleep on this floor.

9

This one wants only firm pillows. I have a headache figuring it all out."

Cheryl's job covers a little bit of everything. She's responsible for finding the perfect activities and adventures for our guests. Anything and everything from scenic tours to pottery or cooking classes to the best restaurants to eat at. Cheryl's like an encyclopedia, which is great for the hotel guests but not so great for her.

"We should totally take a break and go follow some mermaids around," I say. "What do you say?"

"Mermaid shmermaid," Cheryl says. "I want to be a sea creature with extra scales like them."

We stare at a couple of creatures casually walking across the lobby. It's hard not to laugh.

"I can totally see that. Let's go ask them where we can borrow a couple of costumes."

"Uh-oh." Cheryl drops her smile real quick.

"Mr. Maple?" I say, scared to turn around.

"Worse," Cheryl says. She hurriedly puts away her heavy science book and nervously stares at her ledger of hotel activities.

"What are you two chatting about?"

I recognize the voice and it only means trouble for me with a capital *T*.

"Hi, Dad!" I greet him with the world's biggest grin. My lips are practically glued to my teeth.

"Goldie, we've talked about this before. Here, it's Mr. Vance."

Dad has the look, the slight look of stress. It's easy to tell because the vein located right below his left eye pulsates oh-so slightly. If I ever need to gauge Dad's temperature, I need only to glance at the pulsating vein. Right now the vein is a steady tat-tat-tat, which means Dad is about a seven out of ten. Ten being he's about to blow, not that Dad ever blows. He's a calm father, sort of like the dad from *Father Knows Best*, minus the adorable kids. I mean, I'm adorable, but not in the "I wear cute dresses" way, and I'm definitely not a "sit still and be quiet" kid.

It's hard to guess that Mr. Arthur Vance aka Dad is *my* dad. There's a slight resemblance. We definitely have the same nose. But my dad is super tall whereas the tall gene definitely skipped me. The way you can really tell I'm his daughter is by our laugh. Our laugh starts as a timid chuckle and then erupts deep down from the belly until everyone within a hundred-mile radius can hear us. Unfortunately, in this moment, Dad is not laughing. He takes working at the Crossed Palms very seriously, and like everyone here today, Dad is feeling the pressure. Mr. Maple relies on him to keep the resort running smoothly. He's been in early-morning meetings for weeks gearing up for Baldwin Studios's checking in. Oh, I do get one more thing from my dad: my love of work!

"Sorry, Mr. Vance. I was telling Cheryl about the monsters. Isn't it exciting?"

Cheryl refuses to back me up one bit. She's too busy rearranging items on her desk.

"Did you take care of the family in room 12?" he asks Cheryl. "They wanted the scenic tour through the city but were also looking for a romantic dinner without the kids?"

"Yes, Mr. Vance. All taken care of," Cheryl says. "I have them set for tomorrow at nine AM on the city private tour. When the tour is done, I've got the kids set up for the Tree of Wonder dinner and puppet show while their parents have a reservation at Paloma's. I reserved table four, which is tucked away from the main dining room."

"Good work, Cheryl." Dad nods in approval. I nod, too. Cheryl is the best.

"Goldie, you are not to bother Cheryl while she works," Dad says. "Aren't you supposed to be outside?"

And there goes my well-earned break. Dad doesn't mean to be a party pooper, but business is business. His eyes continuously scan the hotel lobby. I guess I also get some of my detective instincts from Dad since he notices everything. But unlike Dad, who's always trying to smooth away the imperfections, I want to dive straight into them. Everyone knows that's where the fun is.

"I still have four minutes left in my break," I say. "Besides, I haven't even checked in with Walt yet."

My dad furrows his brow at me.

"Mr. Tooey, Goldie," Dad corrects me. At that same moment, he notices one of the actresses looking a bit perplexed. Like the perfect hotel manager he is, he starts to walks toward her. I follow.

"Later, Cheryl."

Cheryl mouths the word *good-bye*.

"Goldie, you are not to bother Mr. Tooey."

"So, what I'm getting from you, Dad—I mean, uh, Mr. Vance—is that I should not be bothering anyone?"

"That is correct. Mr. Maple is very excited about the movie being filmed here. It's huge exposure for Crossed Palms, which means everything needs to be perfect and everyone needs to be on their toes. Are you on your toes, Goldie?"

I go up on my tiptoes, which isn't exactly easy when you're wearing stiff, uncomfortable flatties. To avoid keeling over, I grab Dad's sleeves. (Even on tippy toes I still can't reach Dad's height.) Dad pats the top of my head to gently position my feet back flat on the ground.

"You understand what your responsibilities are?"

"Sure do! Parking cars. Right?"

He leans in and gives me a peck on my forehead.

"I know it's hard to contain the energy stirring inside of you. If things slow down, you can go see if Mr. Tooey needs help. Are you packed for your weekend with Mom?"

My mom, Sylvie, works nearby at the Mermaid Club, which is just a quick bike ride away. Mom and Dad are divorced, but they remained best friends after they split. The way they explained it to me is that they are way better at being friends than being married. When they divorced, I was really young, so my whole life has really been between the hotel and the Mermaid Club. Two wondrous places to grow up in.

"Yes, I'm going straight there after I'm finished with my shift. Cross my heart."

One of the bellhops comes over to interrupt Dad's imminent warning not to dally.

"Goldie." Dad doesn't seem to believe me.

"I promise!" I say.

I stride confidently toward the parking lot. As soon as Dad walks off to help quell the bellhop disaster, I take my usual detour.

Dad is busy and I still have two and a half minutes left on my break. Do you know what could happen in two and a half minutes? Just about anything! The day has just begun and the time is right for diving into drama.

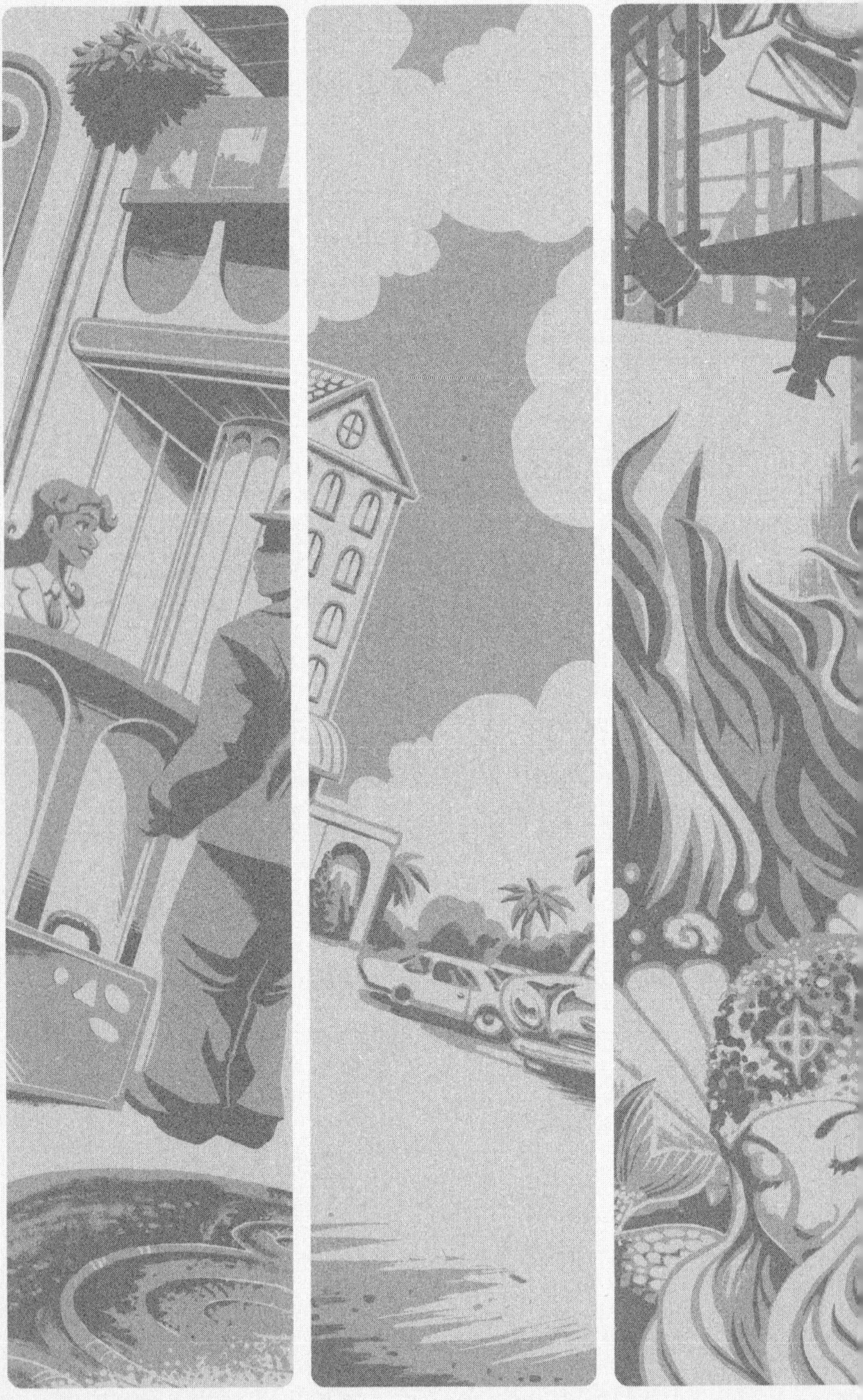

Chapter Two

ȷUST LEFT OF THE SPACIOUS LOBBY ARE MULTIPLE corridors leading to various parts of the resort. To avoid any run-ins with Dad, I continue toward the left wing and enter the library with its oversize chairs and the fluffiest pillows. I can spend hours in this room with floor-to-ceiling shelves filled with books; I love reading anything from mysteries to biographies. I also lead story time for the kids staying at the hotel, but not today. At the other end of the library, I exit a concealed side door to one of the smaller ballrooms. The walls are lined with mirrors upon mirrors that show off my reflection. The dance instructor is about to start a lesson. I wave hello and keep moving.

Crossed Palms Resort has tons of great little nooks. I especially love the Japanese garden with a koi pond.

The pond is a perfect, serene spot for meditating, walking, and just thinking about things. A couple with two young kids smile at the fish. The fish are brilliantly orange this morning. I cross the wooden bridge with intricate carvings and head to one of the pools. Hammocks tied to palm trees hang over the pool for guests to lounge in. I've spent many a day writing in my pad and plotting schemes in so many of these hammocks. And falling asleep, of course.

The flamingos are greeting their morning in pink. The coast is still clear. I press on toward my destination.

Walter Tooey's office is located right by the lobby, off the main hall of the hotel. I, of course, took a roundabout way of reaching the office. You have to be sneaky when you're a detective. It's easy to miss the door marked with a sign that reads DETECTIVE SERVICES, especially since right across from the office is the hotel's flower shop. Before long, the smell of blooming tiger lilies fills the air. I think it's pretty smart to have the office located across from the floral shop. Guests feel reassured when such potent fragrances blanket the air.

I greet Ada the florist. She holds out a red carnation,

as if she somehow knew I was bound to appear at that very moment.

As any true budding detective would, I was only eight years old when I discovered Walter's office. It was on one of my daily expeditions to the flower shop. Once a day—before I got too busy with my job as valet—Ada would give me a red carnation. "*Una flor para la niña*," she would say. Ada is the sweetest person.

"*Buenos días.*" I tuck the red carnation into the lapel of my uniform.

"*Buenos días*, Goldie," Ada says. She returns to arranging an oversize bouquet.

I motion toward Walt's door.

"I wouldn't go in there if I were you," Ada says. "He's not alone."

I help Ada by handing her a couple of roses, careful to avoid the thorns.

"Who's in there with him?" I ask.

"*No sé.* A man in a very expensive suit," she says. "*Muy importante.*"

To be a great house detective you have to pick up as many languages as possible. Lucky for me, there are so many different people who work at Crossed Palms.

I'm always adding a new word or two to my repertoire. Practice is key.

"*Muy importante* people always wear suits."

Ada shakes her head. "You can always tell by the watch. His watch is not on his wrist but tucked in his pocket." Ada mimes pulling out a pocket watch and flipping it open.

"Fancy. I better go in, then. No time to waste!"

"This is why I like to spend my days with flowers. They only want the simple things: water and sun. A little talking to. Time is not a worry."

I add another rose to the bouquet. Ada tucks the rose in a bit more. She steps back and admires our work. I join her. The guest who receives this bouquet will surely be happy with such a beautiful display.

"Flowers are pretty great but so is adventure," I say. *"Hasta luego!"*

I hesitate before Walter's door. The decision really boils down to this: Do you knock on the door, alerting those in the room to compose themselves, or do you barge right in, giving them no time to collect themselves? Sometimes a facial expression can tell an entire story. I like the element of surprise. Walt regularly says, "My door is always open," but I think he's saying it to the guests, not me. But if there is a guest in need behind this door, I should be right beside him. Sometimes Walter really needs my help.

I grab the knob of the door and swing it wide open.

"Sorry I'm late, Walt. Just finished the case of the missing ring. I'm here now and I'm ready."

At that very moment, Walt knocks over a glass of water located on his desk. Walt is forever flustered and clumsy, which is an interesting quality for a detective. He's good at his job. There's no doubt about that. Walt has taught me everything there is to know about being a detective. The importance of active listening. The importance of note taking. How to question people without seeming too nosy. Not only that, he's a great friend. He's always more than willing to help me work things out, even if I can be a little bit of a handful. I know he appreciates me.

"Goldie," Walt says with a sigh. He digs out a handkerchief from his back pocket and blots out the spill. This gives me more than enough time to study Mr. *Muy Importante*, who sits across from him.

"Aren't you the girl who parked my car?" Mr. *Muy Importante* says. In his hand he holds his watch. He opens and closes the pocket watch as if he marks the time by doing so. His lit cigar rests on a glass ashtray.

"I park cars and I *also* assist Mr. Tooey here with his house-detective duties. As you can see, this is a rather large property, and it's all hands on deck. Right, Walt?"

Walter continues to clean up the mess on the table.

"House detective? You?" the man chuckles.

Oh.

Mr. Very Important is *that* type of guy. Never underestimate a girl with a pad and pen at the ready. I pull out mine and jot down the inscription on his watch. I can barely make out the letters *C* and *J*. The man has got a bit of a squat build and a long, pointy nose, sort of like the actor from the film *Casablanca*, Humphrey Bogart, minus the quick one-liners that would endear movie audiences.

"Goldie, this is Mr. Davenport from the studios. Goldie was just about—"

"I'm Walter's apprentice. Goldie Vance, at your service." I reach out to shake Mr. Davenport's hand. Walt was about to kick me out of his office, but there is no way I'm going to miss the opportunity to get to know more about this peculiar man.

Mr. Davenport hesitates but eventually shakes my hand. This is before he places his watch back in the vest of his fancy, expensive suit. His handshake is brief and strong. A handshake that says he's a man of conviction. I walk over to Walt's side of the desk.

"Like I said, I expect delivery to happen tomorrow. Nine AM sharp," Mr. Davenport says. "We will have our own men securing the products, of course."

"Of course, we will provide secondary backup using only our top men," Walt says.

"Absolutely no one is to touch, stare, or make any comments about the products whatsoever. You do understand? They are very delicate."

"Delicate?" I say. "What exactly are we talking about?"

Mr. Davenport ignores my question. Probably because Mr. Davenport is used to always having his way. I've seen the type. They like to bark orders to the hotel staff. Make people jump around. I realize quickly that I asked my question too soon. Mr. Davenport and I haven't developed a trust yet. When you are a detective, you encounter a lot of different personalities. In order to get information, you must find a bridge that connects you to the client. Right now Mr. Davenport only sees me as a nuisance. I've got to change that real quick.

"The staff is well aware of your stipulations," Walt says. "Arrangements will be at the ready for the arrival."

"The entire production of this movie hinges on the well-being and maintenance of this delivery. No exceptions," Mr. Davenport says, slamming his hand on the desk for dramatic effect.

It works. Walt jumps from the noise.

"Crossed Palms wasn't my first choice. No, I wanted to continue filming in California, my backyard. But here we are. In Florida." Mr. Davenport starts to pace the office, pointing at Walter. Then it hits me. Mr. Davenport is no Humphrey Bogart. No. He's a great white shark, gliding at the bottom of the ocean, steady and menacing.

"I promise you, Mr. Davenport. Our staff has accepted many high-end deliveries," Walt reassures him. "From the jewels of the Taj Mahal to the rarest cockatoo from a little-known Caribbean island, discretion is of the utmost importance to us."

"It's true. One time a hotel guest—the famous French violinist George Blanc—misplaced his Stradivarius violin.

He was pretty old by then and never left home without it. Unfortunately, someone had the nerve to take it from his room. Well, we jumped to the scene. Uncovered exactly who took it and why." I lean in toward Mr. Davenport and whisper, "It was a former student of his. Green with envy. We apprehended the culprit and delivered the priceless violin to its rightful owner. Right, Walt?"

Mr. Davenport stares at me for a few seconds. I stare back with a smile. A reassuring grin. I want Mr. Davenport to feel secure I will take care of him. Sadly, Mr. Davenport does not return my smile. Oh well. Whatever is arriving tomorrow, I will keep it safe. This is my mission, and if it means always having Mr. Davenport scowl at me, so be it. He can't overlook a job well done, and that's exactly what I intend to do.

"Mr. Davenport. The Crossed Palms will dedicate their blood, sweat, and tears to ensure your products are guarded and well taken care of," I say. "We're really good at what we do."

"You better be." He grabs his cigar and places it between his lips. "There will be no movie if the products are not a hundred percent immaculate. Do I make myself clear?"

Mr. Davenport's not speaking to me. He directs his words only to Walter, who accidentally knocks the glass over again. Poor Walt.

"Yes, Mr. Davenport. Absolutely, Mr. Davenport. Yes. Yes, Mr. Davenport, yes..."

Oh boy. Walt can't stop repeating the word *yes*. I elbow him hard and he finally stops. Mr. Davenport puffs a big cloud of smoke into the air and walks out the door.

Walt collapses into his chair, his hands shaking in his lap. I grab the glass, pour some more water, and hand it to him.

"Take it easy, Walt. You need to relax. It's a good thing I arrived when I did."

He gulps down the water and I pour another. Soon his face loses its redness and he's back to being the Walter I've always known.

"Goldie. You've met Mr. Davenport. There's no fooling around. He means business. Mr. Maple, our boss, called me last night at two in the morning notifying me Mr. Davenport was coming in."

"Two in the morning!" I'm almost sure I was in my third dream at two in the morning. I usually have the same dream: me capturing the world's largest diamond thief. The funny thing is that as soon as I'm about to take off the diamond thief's mask, I always wake up. Dreams sure can be teases.

Walt pulls out a calendar and counts the days. The movie studio will be filming exterior shots in front of the hotel today and tomorrow morning. Later tomorrow, the studio moves production over to the Mermaid Club. Honestly, I can't wait. Mom promised I can hang out at the club all night if need be. It pays to know the right people.

"Don't worry, Walt. I'm on it," I say. "Mr. Davenport won't have time to bark any orders. He'll be too busy smoking his cigar and driving his silver Corvette."

Walt continues to grimace.

"Goldie. Do not be mistaken. Mr. Davenport has a reputation of getting people fired at every hotel he stays at. I know. I've spoken to said people."

I scrunch my nose. Why would anyone want to get people fired? Power-crazed men are so silly. I shake my head.

"Well, I won't give him any reason to do so. I promise."

"We don't have enough manpower to work as security while also making sure the actors and crew are well fed and getting what they want as well as tending to our own hotel guests...."

Walt begins to mutter to himself. He's spiraling again.

After high school, Walt worked at a tiny bookstore in Michigan, where he's from. He loved reading all kind of books, researching all kinds of topics, and helping customers locate their literary wishes. He had quite the knack for it. It's funny how Walt ended up at Crossed Palms. It was a total lark. His best friend, who was a great musician, applied to work the summer playing piano and convinced Walter to join him in Florida with a guarantee of sunshine. Walt ended up trying out a bunch of different hotel jobs, but it was house detective that ultimately fit his superb research skills. He always says if it weren't for the ivories, he probably would've dedicated his life to working at the tiny bookstore. His musician friend eventually joined a jazz band and now travels the world. One of their tour stops was at Crossed Palms last summer. They can bop!

"Walt, I've got one question for you: What exactly is arriving tomorrow? I want to map out the route and make a list of the people who will be engaging with it. From what Mr. Davenport says, he doesn't want just anyone accepting delivery. The less handling, the less chances of mishandling. Wouldn't you agree?"

"It's not a *what* I'm afraid," he says. "But a *who*."

"Huh? You've lost me. *Who* is one of the products?"

Walter slowly points his finger to the cover of the *Life* magazine on his desk. I can't believe it. He can't be serious.

"Holy Temptress of the Ocean!"

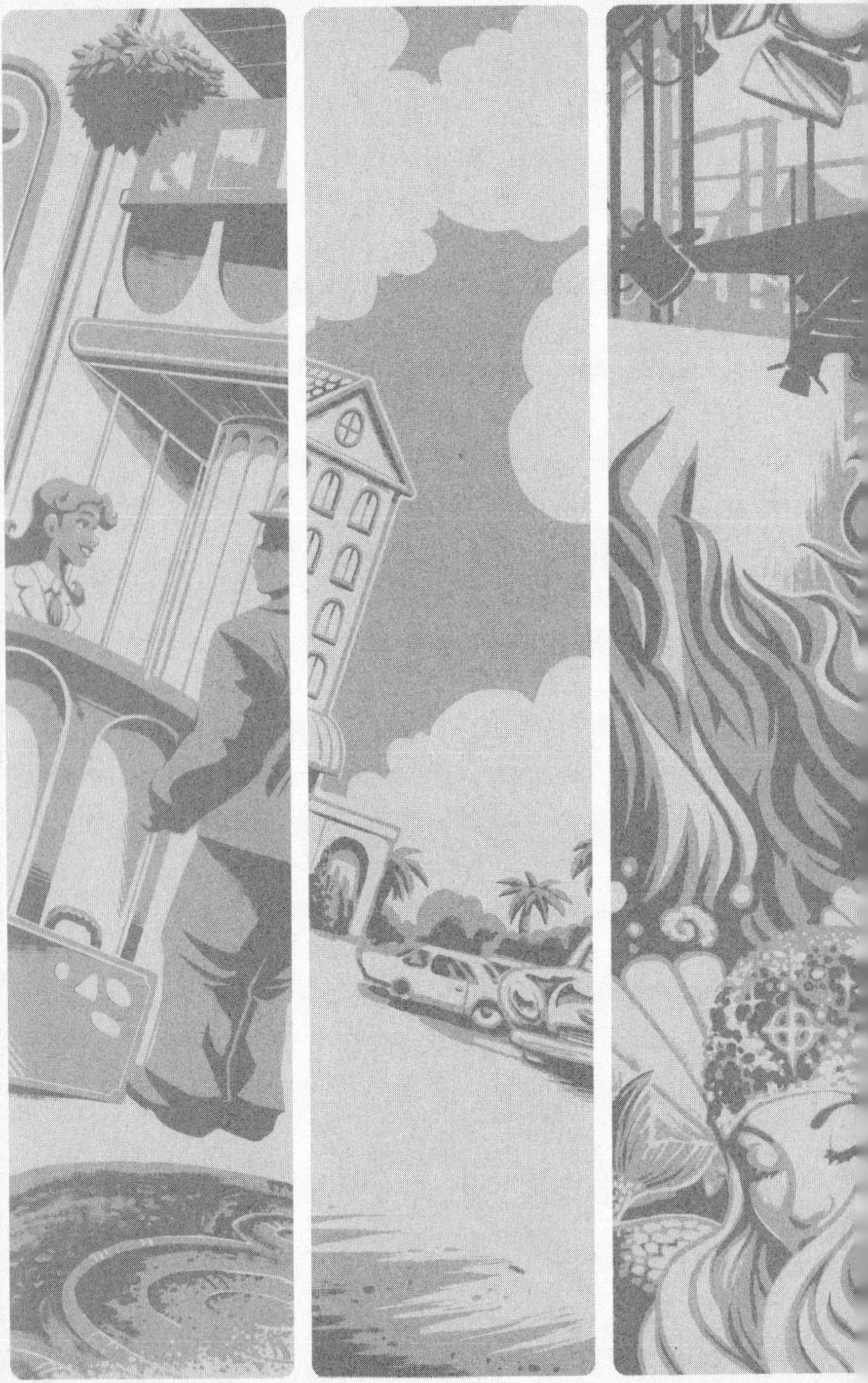

Chapter Three

HER REAL NAME IS JOSEPHINE WALTERS, BUT EVERYONE knows her by Delphine "the Temptress of the Ocean" Lucerne. Delphine packs a quadruple threat. Not only can she act, sing, and dance, but she's a professional swimmer. *Glamorous* can't even begin to describe her beauty. What's really great about her is that she has long dark hair, which is really rare for Hollywood starlets. Big studios always want their leading ladies to be blondes. Delphine changed that when she entered the movie studio system. Rumor has it she was a regular girl at a small five-and-dime store owned by her grandparents. Her parents died in a terrible car accident, and the only solace she could find was when she swam at the nearby public pool in her home of Youngstown, Ohio.

One day, a talent scout walked into the five-and-dime to pick up a pack of cigs and left declaring he'd found the next big star. Soon enough, the young, innocent Josephine Walters transformed into the glorious Delphine Lucerne.

"Wowza. Who would have thought the Temptress of the Ocean would be staying right here at Crossed Palms? She may be our biggest hotel guest yet," I say. Then it dawns on me. "Wait a minute. Mr. Davenport is calling her a product. I don't like that at all. She's a human as far as I know. Why is Mr. Davenport doing that?"

The more I think of it the angrier I get. Walt gets up, pours a glass of water, and hands *me* the cup this time.

"That's not very nice," I say.

"You met him. Mr. Davenport is very particular. No one knows about Delphine starring in the film," Walt says. "They've kept any mention of her name out of the papers in the hope of making the big reveal closer to the movie release. Since Baldwin Studios practically stole her from Powerhouse Productions, the whole studio is riding on this movie being their biggest seller. Or something like that. I don't know a thing about Hollywood."

I scratch my forehead.

"Is Mr. Davenport calling her a product because he wants to keep the mystery intact, or does he really think she's an inanimate object? Because if he does, Mr. Davenport has got a lot to learn, and I intend to educate him every chance I get."

I write down on my pad:

Examples of Products

* Yo-yos
* Cars
* The nifty watch in your pocket
* The stinky cigar you smoke

What Are Not Products

* Women
* Girls
* Humans
* And anyone whose name is Delphine Lucerne

"Now, wait a minute, Goldie. You are *not* to start any trouble. Mr. Davenport is a powerful man and it's important we keep the mystery intact."

Sometimes I wonder if Walt knows me. *Discreet* is

my middle name. Well, actually, I don't have a middle name.

"Walt, tomorrow is the big game. Will you have me watching the big game on the sidelines, or are you going to use your best-equipped player to strike the winning goal?"

I'm not sure if I'm using the right sports metaphors, but Walt has never been the type who likes sports. He's a books guy. I think he gets what I'm saying.

"Delphine will arrive tomorrow with a cloak covering her face. She will be staying at the Alcove Suite. Only two hotel staff members will be allowed to tend to her personally. No other contact. That includes you, Goldie. No contact with Delphine."

There's no way I will miss out on the biggest news hitting St. Pascal. It's not possible. Since I don't want to add to Walt's reluctance, I change the subject.

"If Delphine is the first product, what's the second?"

Walt starts to sweat. I pray he doesn't give me the name of Rock Hudson or Harry Belafonte or Dean Martin. Keeping Delphine under wraps will be hard enough, but add another Hollywood star to the mix and there's bound to be chaos. I was here when the legendary rock band the Tigers stayed here at

Crossed Palms, en route to their sold-out concert at the Coconut Grove Club. I spent most of my time wrangling their fans out from hiding in laundry baskets or janitor closets. It was a bit of a drag. I mean, I'm all for being a fan but it was a lot. I couldn't bear to watch the Tigers constantly being bombarded. Of course, I also couldn't help arranging an impromptu concert for the waitstaff. The Tigers loved it, though. They got to eat a home-cooked meal, courtesy of our incredibly talented chefs, in exchange for three songs. A win-win, if you ask me. Unfortunately, the fans got wind of the concert and infiltrated. Soon the kitchen was overrun with screaming young Tigerettes. Dad grounded me a week for that one.

"C'mon, Walter. I promise to leave Delphine alone and help in any way I can. You said it yourself: Crossed Palms doesn't have enough manpower. Consider me the extra woman-power you've been dreaming about."

Walt hesitates. He squints his eyes, rubs the sweat on the back of his neck. He then opens his desk drawer and pulls out an oversize yellow folder.

"The contents in this folder are never to be uttered, mentioned, speculated, or dreamt about. Agree?"

I fully commit by crossing my heart and hoping

to die. Slowly but surely Walt opens the envelope and pulls out one photograph.

I whistle.

My eyes are practically blinded by the image: hundreds upon hundreds of diamonds assembled on what appears to be a cap of some sort. It's the most brilliant, eye-catching thing I've ever seen. A crown that can be found only in fairy tales about mermaids who live in vast underwater worlds.

"What is it?" I say. I press my fingers to the photo as if the diamonds will materialize onto Walt's desk.

"The Bejeweled Aqua Chapeau. The crown jewel of the movie. A swim cap only befitting of the Temptress of the Ocean," Walt says. "Dreamt up by *the* famous costume designer to the stars, Edna Blanchett. From what Mr. Davenport said, Edna Blanchett not only designed the cap but she oversaw that every individual diamond was secured in place using special tools, exactly to her and the studio's liking. Days and days of work to create such a masterpiece. There are hundreds of individual diamonds on this cap worth more than a million dollars."

I've never seen anything quite like this. A swim cap covered in sparkling jewels. It's fantastical and so over-the-top, exactly what movie magic is all about. How can one person envision such a thing and find a way of creating it? Whoever this Edna Blanchett is, she must be a genius. Now I understand why Mr. Davenport is so worried. One sneak peek at this cap and the Crossed Palms will swarm with potential sticky fingers. It's one thing to take care of a Hollywood superstar; it's quite another to secure a priceless piece of art.

"Where will the Bejeweled Aqua Chapeau reside while they are filming? In the vault?" I ask. The vault is Crossed Palms's very own secured room where guests can store their valuables. I've never seen the inside of the vault, but I hope this changes very soon.

Walt closes the folder and shakes his head.

"Any good house detective will tell you that the less people who are aware of information, the less the risk becomes of the news leaking to the public. You've seen the picture of the cap. You know more than most."

I can't believe Walt is about to hold out on me, on his only assistant! How am I supposed to do my job if he insists on taking this path of not sharing information with me? It's not fair. Besides, how will I learn to be a house detective?

"I think it's way past your break time," he says as

he places the folder back inside his desk drawer. "Now I've got to do my rounds. C'mon."

"You can't be serious?"

He leads me toward the door.

"I'm sorry, Goldie. I can't let you get involved. Mr. Davenport will be eager to place blame if something goes wrong and I won't have him do so with you."

"What if I am as quiet and still as a mouse? I can be a stealthy house detective, sneaking in and out of the shadows with no trace." I lean my body up against the wall and act nonchalant while a couple of hotel guests walk past. Walt greets them and they nod hello.

"See?" I say. "They didn't even notice me!"

Walt keeps walking.

"They did notice you. They decided not to pay any mind to the strange girl pressed against the wall."

Sometimes Walt fails to use his imagination. I'm sure he had one back in Michigan somewhere.

"Please, please, please, Walt. You need me. There's no way you'll be able to handle this *and* Mr. Davenport *and* the delivery of the products. Help me help you."

"You're not going to stop asking, are you?" Walt wrings his hands a bit. He knows he needs me; he just doesn't quite see it as clearly as I do. Crossed Palms is my life. I've also learned a lot from watching my dad, and I want to make sure we keep it running as smoothly as possible. "*Persistent*, that's my middle name," I say.

"I thought you didn't have a middle name? Oh, never mind. I'm probably going to regret this. Be here no later than five in the morning."

"Yes! I'm on the case. You will not regret this. I swear to you and all the jewels found on that—"

Before I can say the word *cap* Walt presses his finger against my lips. Oops.

"Cap," I whisper. "I promise. I will be here. Quiet as a mouse, cunning as a fox."

Walt shakes his head. And with that, he walks off to begin his rounds, making sure the hotel is free of any drama. While he does that, I head to the parking lot to finish up my shift.

I can't wait to share the news with Mom and Cheryl. They won't believe it. The Temptress of the Ocean will be here! This is major. And wait until they hear about the Bejeweled Aqua Chapeau. Mom is simply going to flip. She loves everything Hollywood and sparkly.

Oh. Wait a minute. I'm not supposed to tell anyone about Delphine Lucerne or the lavish cap. This is going to be tricky. The biggest news that has ever landed right on my lap, and I'm forced to keep my lips sealed.

Well, the key to being a good house detective is to know when to divulge information and to whom. As my grandmother used to say, intelligence is better than money but you have to spend it wisely. The smart thing in this situation would be to keep this stuff to myself. This is going to be a true test of my willpower. Walt expects me to keep his secret. Mr. Davenport is ready to blow a gasket at the first sign of failure. I can't let Walt down. Quiet as a mouse. If you really think about it, mice are not that quiet. We used to have a mouse in my mom's apartment, and I couldn't sleep with the constant scratching and pitter-patter of its little feet. Not quiet. And where there's one mouse there are usually more. An army of mice! How squeaky and cute it would be! But I digress.

"Welcome to the Crossed Palms Resort, where your every wish is at your fingertips," I say to the man dressed in a nice linen suit. He calmly waits for his guest to step out of the car. She, too, is wearing linen, a pretty dress perfectly suited for Florida.

"Thank you so much," she says to me.

"You're welcome."

The man in the linen suit hands me the keys to his car while the bellhop pulls out the couple's luggage. Then Mr. Linen offers his hand to Miss Linen, and they walk together toward the entrance of the Crossed Palms. On their way in, they run into a couple of swamp monsters with seaweed dripping from their necks and hair. Miss Linen giggles at the sight.

I drive the car to the parking lot, this time holding off revving the engine too much. I wonder what life is like for Delphine Lucerne. She went from working the register of a store to gracing the cover of *Life* magazine. Whenever she steps outside, hundreds of reporters document her every move, while fans crave every little piece of her. To a fan, Delphine's life seems glamorous, but I've seen what fame can do to a person. Take the Tigers. The boys in the band just wanted to eat home-cooked chicken noodle soup with a grilled cheese sandwich, the type of meal their parents made when they were feeling under the weather. But a simple ask became a whole production.

Does Delphine feel the same way? Does she think about her hometown? Does she wish to be like the woman in the linen suit, freely laughing at scary costumes without having a cloak covering her smile? Delphine's life must feel like being in a bowl of water, like a goldfish. Everyone staring at you, tapping on the glass, when the only thing you want to do is swim.

Regardless of her circumstances, I will make sure to treat Delphine with the utmost respect. Just because she's on the cover of every magazine out there doesn't mean she doesn't want hot soup and a grilled cheese sandwich, just like everyone else. Tomorrow, Delphine Lucerne will get the Crossed Palms Resort treatment. We treat every guest like family.

I continue parking cars and thinking about the Bejeweled Aqua Chapeau, Delphine, and tomorrow until it's time to punch out.

Chapter Four

I CLOCK OUT OF WORK AND HOP ON MY TRUSTY BIKE, Big Blue. The first St. Pascal landmark I pass is the Deep End. Cheryl and I have shared many a burger and shake at the Deep End. She's probably there right now eating with Rob. Rob works with me as a valet and we're basically a trio. Cheryl, Rob, and me. Although our thing is usually to meet there after work to go over the highs and lows of our days, I won't go in today. I've got too much to prepare for tomorrow's main event. Besides, Mom is expecting me. I navigate Big Blue toward Lime Street. If I ride straight along Lime Street, I'll eventually hit the Mermaid Club, where Mom should be just about finishing her shift.

"Hi, Goldie!"

"Hi, Jim!"

I wave to Jim of Jim's Emporium. Jim's Emporium is a massive department store where people can basically shop for whatever they need. If you're looking for a television, you can buy one there. A nifty state-of-the-art fridge? Yup, they've got an entire row of 'em. In this month's catalog you'll find Mom posing in front of a new living room set. Mom does modeling for Jim from time to time. Unfortunately, we did not get the fancy living room set as payment.

As I pedal down Lime Street, I say hi to so many people. That's the great thing about living in St. Pascal—everyone knows everyone. I learned how to ride my bike on these streets, and now the shop and restaurant owners see me almost every day riding back and forth, from the resort to the club or nearby to where Mom lives. Although my preferred mode of transportation would be a racy Alfa Romeo, my trusty bike has gotten me into places most cars can't.

In the distance I see the one store in town that stands out more than any of the others on Lime Street. My feet automatically slow as I approach it. Wax Lips. It's the only record shop in St. Pascal, and for such a small shop, Wax Lips has an incredible selection of music, from hard-to-find jazz albums to the latest rock 'n' roll. Impromptu dance parties erupt at any time. But the best thing about Wax Lips isn't the albums or dance parties. No. What truly makes the store unique is the person working the cash register.

Diane.

Diane is by far the coolest person on Lime Street. Correction, Diane is by far the coolest person in all of St. Pascal, and she works at Wax Lips.

Before I realize it, my face is pressed against the glass window of the record shop, searching for Diane. She has short black hair and the coolest demeanor. She knows all there is to know about music, and she lines her eyes with dark eyeliner. She's taller than me but I don't care. Did I mention how cool she is? Very. Cool.

The record store is jam-packed with people wanting to buy music. Right in the midst of the commotion stands Diane, reigning supreme like a modern-day Joan of Arc, guiding the customers to their melodic choices. Even in all the craziness, Diane still manages to stop for a second and wave hello to me.

Like a fool I take a look around to make sure Diane is waving at little ol' *me* and not someone else. I wave back. She gestures for me to enter with a quick nod, but I say no by rubbing my belly to note that I'm hungry. I wonder if my gesture is kind of ridiculous. Then I start to get a little flustered and begin to question everything. Is my wave a little goofy? Does she understand that I promised my mom I would meet her at the Mermaid Club? Does Diane think I'm a weirdo standing in front of the store communicating with my hands?

While all this processes in my head, a customer asks Diane a question and she heads toward the stack of albums. Before she goes, Diane gives me a warm smile.

Sigh.

I pride myself on being able to talk to just about everyone. I've never been the type of person to get nervous. Never. Diane is different. I get tongue-tied whenever I'm around her. Cheryl thinks it's funny to see how I act around her. She says I should get the nerve and finally ask her out. I don't know what's stopping me. I am fearless. Brave in the face of adversity. There is no obstacle I am not willing to overcome. But asking Diane out on a date? I'm going to have to find real courage for that one. Besides, a girl as cool as Diane probably has her calendar *full* of dates.

I pedal away and continue down Lime Street.

IT'S NEARLY IMPOSSIBLE TO MISS THE MERMAID CLUB. Just drive straight down Lime Street until you see the gigantic mermaid lounging across a building with a bright neon MERMAID CLUB sign pulsating on and off above her head.

I climb off my bike and walk toward the back of the club to avoid the small crowd lining up to enter.

In order for a club to stand out, sometimes you need a gimmick. The gimmick of the Mermaid Club is that the club is filled with actual mermaids living their lives in a large tank. People can sit down and have a meal while watching mermaids swimming around their underwater homes. Mermaids combing their long, luxurious hair. Mermaids exercising. Mermaids dancing their elaborate water ballets. I love everything about the club. It's magical and wondrous and beautiful.

Like every kid, I, too, believed mermaids existed. I thought there must surely be scores of mermaid families living in the deep blue sea, dropping off their mermaid kids at their mermaid schools before heading to their mermaid jobs. But I can't truly recall when I discovered mermaids didn't exist. I do remember that soon after Mom started working at the club, I realized that the true magic doesn't exist solely when the mermaids synchronize swim, but can also be found behind the scenes: the workers maintaining the tank so that it's not too cold or too hot, or the hidden oxygen tanks where the mermaids swim to inhale and then float back out. I love illusions like this. We all need a break from reality sometimes.

I also remember seeing Mom's mermaid fin at home one day and thinking, *So that's what Mom's been doing*. Mermaids no longer were these mythical creatures; they became amazing alchemists creating wondrous feats in the water and making audiences *believe*. They are up there with Santa Claus and the Easter Bunny.

TABLES AND BOOTHS FAN OUT IN A SEMICIRCLE, FACING the large tank of water. In the tank, breathtaking mermaids swim about in choreographed underwater movements. At the far left of the tank I spot Mom. She twirls in the water with such grace. Her movements enrapture the entire audience. I sit at my booth off to the side, marked with a RESERVED sign, and wait, thinking of Diane, Delphine, and beauty.

"What's with the long face?" Mike is the bartender/co-owner of the Mermaid Club. He's like a mountain with big broad shoulders and large hands. Mike told me he used to be the Strong Man in a traveling circus. When people first meet Mike, they usually think he's menacing, but not that many people know that Mike is a poet. Like me, he always travels with a tiny pad in his back pocket, ready to jot down a new verse or two.

"Hey, Mike. I'm okay—just got a lot on my mind," I say. "Are the words flowing today?"

Mike pulls out the pad.

"The ocean reminds me of your eyes, endless and..." he says in his deep baritone. "Still trying to figure out what goes after *endless*."

The pencil in his hand looks like a toothpick.

"I'm sure the word is right at the tip of your tongue," I say. "Are you thinking of reciting at the coffee shop on Friday?"

Mike tucks the pencil behind his ear. "I think it needs a little more cooking before I debut my new poetry in front of a crowd. Besides, this week I'm working overtime." He points to the crowd of men offstage unloading equipment.

"Business must be booming."

Mike nods. "It's been nonstop."

"Mike, I'll need a couple of root beers for table four." A woman dressed in blue, matching the interior of the club, approaches the table. It's Angie, Mike's girlfriend. Angie used to be a dancer on Broadway but an ankle injury ended her chorus line days. She's now in charge of the mermaid choreography. "Goldie, I didn't see you there."

She gives me a hug. The club is about to pick up. A lot of workers come to the Mermaid Club to unwind.

"Tomorrow is going to be a nightmare," Angie says. Mike nods in agreement.

"What do you mean? I can't wait for tomorrow," I say. "This is the best thing to happen in St. Pascal. Movie madness!"

One of the film guys knocks into an oversize seashell that shatters to pieces.

"You nailed it, all right. Movie madness." Mike heads over to the workers and hands one of them a broom. The man doesn't even question Mike. He immediately starts picking up after himself. Mike soon returns with a tray of drinks for Angie. She trots off to serve them to the table.

"The only reason I said yes to the movie was because Mr. Maple said it would be great for both of our businesses, but I'm not too sure," Mike says. "It's hard for me to let random strangers take over. Set designers. Cameras. Lights. Don't get dazzled by Hollywood. It's just a lot of smoke and mirrors."

"I won't, Mike. I've got a strong head on my shoulders."

For a few seconds we watch Mom as she finishes up her dance. She attaches herself to what we like to call "the Spinner." It's a contraption that looks like a pole and it spins the mermaids rapidly when they connect themselves to it. How you can go around so much without getting dizzy is beyond me, but Mom is a pro.

"I like the new act," Mike says before going back to man the bar. "Every girl gets their own signature move and your mom has one of the best."

The audience loves it, too. I wait a bit longer before heading toward the dressing room. I knock three times. Three is the secret code between Mom and me.

"C'mon in, Goldie." Mom's colorful fins hang up to dry while she sits in front of the vanity table, slowly taking off the waterproof makeup.

"Hey, babe," she says. "Are you hungry?"

"Yup. Today has been a day full of surprises."

"Really? Tell me about it while I get into my clothes." She goes behind a wooden panel to change into her regular capri pants and matching top.

"Walt is letting me help out tomorrow! He wants me at the hotel super early when a special delivery is, *ummm*, being delivered," I say. "This may be the break I've been waiting for. If I can show Walt and Mr. Maple how good an assistant I am, maybe they'll promote me."

"Now, Goldie. I wouldn't place all of my bets on Mr. Maple paying attention to you tomorrow. There's so much going on. He might be busy."

"Okay. You're probably right. I'm just so excited I can barely stand it."

Mom laughs. "Well, if you're excited, I'm excited for you. Hand me my cardigan, will you, babe?"

"Besides, we get to work together tomorrow," I say.

Mom hugs me. "Yes, we do," she says. Mom places her reddish-brown hair up in a ponytail. I get my thick bangs from her. "Me and you against the world. So, how's your father doing?"

"He's good. He wants to make sure everything goes smoothly tomorrow. Mr. Maple is apparently on edge but what else is new."

"Same thing at the Mermaid Club. Mike had to post a long list of Dos and Don'ts for the workers tomorrow. This is one job that I'm almost regretting taking. So much fuss over who you can and cannot talk to. Who knows if I will even make the cut on the big screen? Baldwin Studios is really going all out on this movie. Poor Mike has to work through the night making sure the workers transform the Mermaid Club into a dazzling movie set."

She grabs her things and we both head out through the secret hallway to avoid anyone seeing her out of costume. This door leads out to the back of the club. Only the workers know about it. No one else. We walk over to my bike and I place it in the trunk of Mom's car. We drive toward her apartment, only a few blocks away.

Mom's place is located on the top floor in an apartment complex. Some might consider it small, but it's perfect for the two of us. I put my overnight bag in the bedroom off the living room while Mom places her bright-yellow mermaid fins and matching bikini top in the bathroom. In the living room Mom has framed pictures of us together. Mom, Dad, and me. There's the picture of us on vacation in Niagara Falls. It was sure cold that day. It's safe to say that I might not be made for cold weather. There are a few pictures of me on my first day of school. And there are plenty of pictures of me in front of our Christmas tree. My *favorite* picture is of all three of us in front of the Crossed Palms Resort. Mom had just dropped me off for my first *real* day of work with Dad, and the resort photographer was testing out her new camera. I love it because Mom and Dad are both holding me so tight it looks like I'm about to burst with love.

Mom pulls the casserole she made the other day from the fridge and turns the oven on to heat it up for us. Even without all the sequins and over-the-top makeup she has to wear as a mermaid, Mom is still the most beautiful woman in a room. I really wish I could tell her about Delphine and the Bejeweled Aqua Chapeau. I'm never one to keep things from Mom, especially news of this magnitude. How to tell her without telling her? Now, that's the key.

"Mom, what do you know about filming tomorrow? Did they tell you who will be on set?"

"Oh no. They are keeping everything under wraps. Hush-hush. I'm sure it's some big movie star. I just hope she's not too much of a diva. The Mermaid Club is already filled with divas. One more and the tank might shatter."

"You don't have any idea who it might be? No guesses at all?"

"*Hmmm.* Well, who do *you* think it is?"

"Who me? Oh, I don't know," I say with the goofiest grin plastered on my face. "It could be anyone. I mean, let's deduce the possibilities. The actress must be a pretty strong swimmer and not be too afraid to spend hours in the water. There aren't that many actresses out there who would be willing to do that, to be a queen of the ocean, so to speak."

Mom raises her eyebrows and serves us both a generous amount.

"A queen, huh?"

I nod.

"Well, whoever it is, she will be well taken care of by you," she says. "You are the best at making people feel at home in St. Pascal. You're our very own welcoming committee."

"Thanks." I let her words wash over me, but I can't seem to shake this tiny thing nagging at me. I try to forget about it while eating Mom's delicious casserole, but it's not working.

"Mom, what do you do when you are so nervous you know you'll be unable to sleep?"

She takes my empty plate, places it in the sink, and leans against the kitchen counter. With the sun setting behind her, the light creates such a radiant glow around her.

"What are you so nervous about? I thought working with Walter is what you wanted."

"Oh, it is. Definitely. But what if I make a mistake or something?"

She opens the fridge and takes out a bottle of milk. In a saucepan she heats the milk up and sprinkles just a pinch of cinnamon on it.

"First, warm milk is known to cure insomnia. Drink this up. Now, the only thing you can do to ensure tomorrow works in your favor is simply show up. Your dad and I raised you to be a strong, hard worker. A person who loves to help. Just show up tomorrow ready to be of service. If you do your best, you can't go wrong. Being afraid is good, but letting fear stop you from doing what you love, that's *not* good."

"Okay, I'll try to remember that," I say.

"Now, don't stay up late. What time are you meant to be at the resort tomorrow?"

"Five in the morning."

"Five in the morning! Drink this milk and head straight to bed. Tomorrow is going to be a long day for both of us."

"I promise I won't stay up," I say.

Mom heads to her bedroom, where she will place her hair in tiny braids to maintain the curl. She'll then wrap her hair up in what I like to call her sleeping scarf.

I sip the warm milk and pull out my pad. I make a list of the things I want to remember to bring with me tomorrow. At the top of the list is my magnifying glass. Mom gave it to me when I was seven years old. Back then, I was obsessed with the ants that suddenly invaded our kitchen. I wanted to investigate everything. When she gave me the magnifying glass, I patiently followed the line of ants to the tiny hole that led outside and finally located their home. Some of the neighborhood kids wanted to use my magnifying glass to do evil things to the ants. Not me. The magnifying glass showed me how hard the ants worked together. If you take your time and look closely, you can find the truth about things.

I'll listen to Mom. Tomorrow I'm going to show up to work ready to do my best.

Chapter Five

ALTHOUGH MOM'S CALL TIME ISN'T UNTIL TEN AM, SHE still wakes me up at four in the morning to make me a little breakfast—scrambled eggs and roasted asparagus—before I head out. I appreciate it so much. The butterflies stirring in my stomach are working overtime, but this home-cooked meal from Mom helps calm them down.

It's rare to see St. Pascal so quiet. The sky is still dark, but it is slowly breaking. The birds are already chirping, and in the distance, I can hear a rooster or two. I won't be the only one coming into work so early. The kitchen staff will already be at the hotel baking their scrumptious breads and muffins for the breakfast crowd. The hotel staff will still be checking people in. And down below, loads of laundry will be washed by the cleaning staff.

After placing my bike behind the valet tent, I pull out my white gloves from my back pocket and put them on. I adjust my vest and make sure my hair is not too windswept. It's time to make my appearance.

"Let's do this," I say to myself.

Walt stands in front of the entrance of the Crossed Palms. There are security staff lined up behind him with the most serious of faces. Pacing in front of everyone is Mr. Davenport. He holds tight to his unlit cigar.

"Good morning, everyone!" I say. "It's a beautiful and perfect day. Can you feel it?"

Mr. Davenport gives me quite the scowl. I guess he's not a morning person. Walt shakes his head. I stand by him.

"Where is she?" I ask.

"En route but there must have been a delay at the airport," Walt says.

Mr. Davenport pulls out his pocket watch, snaps it open, and then places it back in his vest. He does this a couple of times. He might be just as nervous as I am, maybe even more.

"Good morning, Mr. Davenport. Anything I can do to help? I can get you a cup of coffee, or perhaps breakfast might help ease your nerves."

Mr. Davenport tucks his watch back in his vest. He continues to pace and I join him.

"There is nothing you can do unless you have the ability to teleport," he says.

This subject is much more up Cheryl's alley than mine. "*Hmmm.* Nope, I definitely don't think I have the power to do that, but who knows. Maybe if I concentrate really hard."

Mr. Davenport stops pacing and just stares at me.

"What did you say your name was again?" he asks. His voice is all gruff.

"Goldie Vance! My full name is Marigold Vance, but everyone who knows me calls me Goldie."

He points at me with the hand holding his cigar. "Well, Goldie Vance. I don't like to chitchat in the morning, so if you can…" He points to where I should line up.

"The St. Pascal airport is exactly ten point three miles from here. That's roughly thirty minutes," I say. "There will be no traffic to hit unless they get caught behind a produce truck. The chances of that happening are really fifty-fifty. It's a small airport."

Mr. Davenport responds with a "harrumph." Then he says, "Thirty minutes. They should be here by now."

We both stare at the empty driveway. Mr. Davenport begins to pace again.

"On bike it would take me sixty minutes to get to the airport. I timed myself once. Watching the planes fly in and out is a favorite pastime of mine. You probably travel all the time. Do you like the window seat or the aisle seat? I have a theory about that. If you like the window seat, you want to enjoy the view. If you like the aisle seat, you prefer doing work. Where do you land on this theory, Mr. Davenport?"

I'm pretty certain I already know the answer to where Mr. Davenport prefers to sit. But I figure if I distract him, he won't be so overwhelmed with anxiety. It works for me sometimes. He is literally missing the hummingbird flying right above him because he is staring so intensely, waiting for Delphine Lucerne and the diamond cap to arrive.

"Has anyone ever told you that you are unrelenting?" he asks.

"Nope, not a soul," I say. "So, you're an aisle person, am I right?"

Before he can respond, a fleet of cars makes its way up the resort driveway. One car after another, driving up at a steady pace as if this were a presidential caravan.

Walt pats me on the shoulder and directs me to stand alongside the other workers. But Mr. Davenport doesn't seem to be distracted by my presence, so I stay put. I've got the best view.

The first three cars park farther down the driveway. The drivers step out and bellhops immediately start to unload the trunk. There are so many pieces of luggage. It is endless. I can't imagine traveling with so much baggage. My favorite pieces of clothing are my capri pants and worn-out loafers. Lucky for me, the hotel has a uniform that I have to wear. I don't really have to think about it. But if it were up to me I would live in my capri pants all day long. They have deep pockets, perfect to stash my pad, my magnifying glass, other knickknacks, and any evidence I might uncover. My uniform isn't ideal but it does the trick, too.

"What are you waiting for?" Mr. Davenport barks. "Get those into the suite immediately!"

Walt, in turn, quietly directs the bellhops to be careful with the suitcases. If Mr. Davenport would just politely ask for things, I'm sure he would get better service. Thankfully, the staff at Crossed Palms is extra professional. They work in unison, taking the luggage out of sight and to where it needs to be. By the time

Delphine Lucerne enters her suite, the clothes will already be hanging in the closet and tucked in the drawers.

Another car rolls up to the driveway, and by the way Mr. Davenport increases his screaming, I just know Delphine Lucerne is in it.

"Everyone, turn away!" he yells, and I am at once reminded how ridiculous men with loud voices can be. There's really no point. If he had truly paid attention to his surroundings, he would have noticed that the remaining staff was already facing away from the car. The only two people looking straight ahead are Walter and Mr. Davenport. Oh yeah, and me.

The car slows down right in front of Mr. Davenport. He tosses his ever-present cigar onto the ground. One of our workers rushes to clean it up but Walt stops him from moving. No one is to move from their spot. Mr. Davenport looks around one more time before opening the door of the car. Everyone at Crossed Palms holds their breaths in anticipation. This is it.

"Goldie, turn away," Walt urges me to comply. How am I supposed to get a glimpse of Delphine Lucerne if I'm facing the hotel? No way.

"Goldie!"

To appease Walt, I finally do as he says. Fortunately, I have a nifty compact mirror Mom gave me a while back. It's super handy whenever I'm trying to spy while still remaining casual. I pull it out and position it so that I can see exactly when Mr. Davenport opens the door.

Delphine's hand is the first thing to appear from the car. Against Mr. Davenport's large hands, hers look so tiny and fragile. The next thing I see is her strappy heels in bright red. Mr. Davenport helps her step out of the car. Oversize sunglasses practically conceal her whole face. Delphine also wears a scarf tied around her head that shields her profile. She is dressed in a simple black dress. There is no doubt that she is a star of the highest magnitude. It's true what they say—some people just have got "it," a magnetism that shines bright. Delphine simply glows.

She doesn't say a word. No one does. We wait for her to take the lead.

Suddenly, there is a commotion near the bushes located by the far end of the entrance. A rustling of sorts. Oh no.

"Walt! Over by the bushes! Ten o'clock!"

Walt immediately sees it: a photographer angling

to take a picture of Delphine Lucerne exiting the car. Walter runs over to the photographer. Mr. Davenport notices him, too.

"Hey, you!" Mr. Davenport barrels toward the man, leaving Delphine on her own. He looks like he's about to pulverize the photographer. Delphine, appearing a bit lost, takes a step in the direction of the entrance. But the first step ends up being a doozy. She seems to trip over something. Instead of a gracious walk, Delphine Lucerne is about to fall. I rush to her side, helping her before she completely hits the ground.

"Oh my goodness!" she exclaims.

"Don't worry; I've got you," I say.

"Well, thank goodness for quick recoveries," she says.

I'm surprised by Delphine's accent. There's a bit of a twang in her voice, one rarely heard when she appears on-screen. She has the biggest smile with the whitest teeth ever.

"It's my job," I say. "To be quick, that is."

"You just saved me from a heap a trouble. My legs are my most prized possessions."

Although I could have sworn she would be ten

feet tall, Delphine is very petite, not much taller than me. She bends down and picks up the cigar. The one Mr. Davenport so callously dropped.

"It looks like this may have been the culprit," says Delphine.

"It sure does. Cigars are pretty gross, don't you think?" I ask.

"It's a nasty habit some people can't seem to quit," she says. "Don't ever pick it up."

"Hey, you, get away from her!" Mr. Davenport now directs his anger at me. He rushes to Delphine's side, placing himself between us as if I'm the photographer or an annoying fan asking her for an autograph. "You've got to be more careful. Can you just imagine how much money it would cost if anything were to happen to them?"

Mr. Davenport points to Delphine's legs as if he's pointing to a priceless work of art, which I guess in a way he is. He goes on reprimanding her as if she had tripped on purpose.

"Oh, Cecil, please stop this nonsense. Can't you see… Excuse me, what is your name?"

"I'm Goldie Vance."

"Can't you see Miss Vance is only trying to help?" She hands the cigar to Mr. Davenport. "And if anything were to have happened, it would have been your fault. You are being quite silly."

Did she just call Mr. Davenport "Cecil" and tell him he's being silly? I must have heard wrong. That can't possibly be his name.

"Now, Delphine, we need to keep you and your assets unblemished. They are insured for a reason," he says. For the first time, Mr. Davenport's voice is sweet and not the gruff bark he always uses to communicate. It's funny to see how much he changes in front of Delphine. "Let's get you out of here. There are probably more photographers."

She pulls away from him.

"Miss Vance, can you show me to my room? Let the boys handle the pesky intruders while we girls settle in."

For once, Mr. Davenport is tongue-tied. I shrug at Walter. This isn't exactly what I expected to happen but who am I to question it? I'm about to escort *the* Delphine Lucerne to her room. I just go with the flow.

"You two follow close behind," Walt alerts the security guards.

Delphine holds out her arm for me to interlace with mine.

"Shall we?" she asks.

"This way!"

Behind us, Mr. Davenport—or Cecil—continues to yell at the photographer. I wonder if he will ever get tired of hearing his own voice. I know I already am. Eventually the shouting is drowned out by the chirping of birds and Delphine's heels on the pathway. I concentrate on making sure I lead Delphine to the right suite while also taking into account everything around me. Like how she isn't wearing gloves and her hands are free of rings. How there is a delicate gold necklace with a pendant around her neck. I can't really make out what the pendant says, but it's very pretty and understated. This close, I can smell Delphine's perfume. It is a mixture of lavender and rose, and I think I can smell hints of patchouli. Scents are really important when you are a detective.

"So, Cecil, huh?" I say. "Mr. Davenport's first name is Cecil. I never would have guessed that."

I can't help giggling, which leads to more laughing, and then soon I can't stop. Delphine joins me.

"Yes, that's his name," she says. "Sometimes it's nice to remind him."

We stroll across the gardens. The workers steer away from our path. They've all been alerted to keep clear. The security guards walk a few paces behind us. "How was your flight, Ms. Lucerne?" I ask.

"I've been on so many planes. You go up; you go down," she says. "You know what I like to do when I'm on a plane? Stare at the clouds."

I smile. It's obvious Delphine Lucerne loves the window seat, just like me.

"Do you ever get tired of the photographers?" I ask.

"It's all part of the game. Photographers, interviews, glamour shots," she says. "I can't be tired of this life. I asked for it."

The way she says this makes me think that she's not being completely honest. Being one of Hollywood's biggest stars is probably a dream every little girl has at one point or another, but no one ever talks about what you might have to give up for it. I mean, arriving incognito just so you can check in to your hotel; there is no way that is easy or fun.

"I hope you will enjoy your stay at Crossed Palms Resort," I say. "We have many activities. You can learn how to Hula-Hoop, take a painting class, or learn how to surf. Cheryl, our concierge, will help you if you have any questions."

"Thank you for the suggestions," she says. "I probably won't have much time. Cecil has me on a very tight schedule. You know how movie people are."

"Yeah, movie people," I say, although this is by far the closest I've been to Hollywood.

A security guard is already positioned in front of the door of her suite. I give him a nod and he opens the door. The suite is filled with tons of flowers, and not just any flower—daises. Practically every inch of the suite bursts with daisies. Ada the florist really went all out making sure Delphine is greeted with the most amazing floral explosion. The actress takes off her scarf and her heels, which brings a smile to my face. It's something Mom would totally do: take off her shoes as soon as she walks into her apartment to make herself comfortable.

"What a sweet thing to do! Who knew daisies are my favorite?" she asks. "Everyone loves roses but I prefer my daisies. Daisies always remind me of home. I used to get up early in the mornings and pick a bunch of them to enjoy while we ate breakfast. I always thought they brightened up the table."

I try to picture Delphine as a little girl, running around barefoot. She must have been fun.

"If there's anything else you need, just let me know," I say. "Anything at all."

"Thank you so much for escorting me, Miss Vance," she says.

"Oh, you can call me Goldie. Everyone does," I respond. "Well, I should be heading out. I don't want to be in your way."

"You? Not possible. What do you do here, Goldie, besides saving actresses from bad falls?" she asks with a laugh, and grabs a seat, her bare feet dangling.

"I'm assistant to Walter Tooey, the Crossed Palms Resort house detective. It's my job to make sure everything goes smoothly for your appearance," I say. "I also work as a valet. 'Driver extraordinaire' should really be my job title, if I'm being honest."

"Goldie, you are such a gas! A girl of many talents. That's really the key to life," she says. "When I was your age I used to be just as confident. If you can't toot your own horn, how will those around you see you?"

Without her large sunglasses and scarf, I can see she has a sprinkle of freckles across her nose. I would have never guessed it. I guess Hollywood doesn't want their starlets with freckles, but I think it just adds to her charm. Why hide something that's part of you?

Mr. Davenport barges into the suite, huffing and puffing. I swear, he's going to give himself a heart attack. He glares at me.

"You can go now," he says and points to the door. I guess my time is up.

"I'm really glad I got to meet you," I say. Delphine stands up.

"Cecil, I've been thinking. Since Goldie seems so well versed about things here, I would like for her to personally escort me to the set today," she says. "Goldie, would you mind if we steal you away a bit from your valet duties?"

"Me mind? Of course not," I say. "There will always be more cars to park tomorrow."

Mr. Davenport opens his mouth to say no but stops himself.

"Of course she can escort you," he says. "Meet us here at exactly twelve o'clock. Don't be late."

"Sure thing, Cecil. I'm sorry, I mean…Mr. Davenport!" His grumpy-looking face is worth every single mistake I've ever made in this life and the next. "Bye!"

Delphine Lucerne just asked me to be her escort. Never in a million trillion years did I expect to be so lucky. Although she's a big movie star, there's also something so normal about her. It must be the slight country accent and her freckles. Who would have predicted Delphine would be so approachable?

Now that Delphine is secured safely in her suite, it's time to find out what's happening with Mr. Davenport's second "product." Where is the famous Bejeweled Aqua Chapeau?

Chapter Six

WALT DIRECTS THE CROWD OF GUARDS AS IF HE'S conducting a grand symphony. The guards form a circular human barrier. At the center of the circle are two men holding up a large hatbox labeled FRAGILE.

"Is that it?" I ask.

Walt nods.

"Are you sure? Did you open the box and peek inside?" I ask. "What if it's missing, and what we're holding is only an empty box?"

Walt turns to me with a nervous look. I have to ask the tough questions. Someone has to! The guards wait for him to give them the word.

"Let's get this to the vault," he says.

I follow them through the lobby and past the concierge desk. The vault is located behind the concierge booth and down steps. Whenever guests want to store their valuables, they can do so by asking for access to the vaults. Similar to a bank, the vault has a super-heavy door that's impossible to penetrate. There are only a handful of people who have access to it. I am not one of those people, so I'm excited for this rare moment to see inside.

Walt draws out a large weighted key from inside his pocket and sends the majority of the guards to wait outside. Lucky for me, he hasn't kicked me out yet. Walt inserts the key, which needs a few jiggles, and opens the heavy door.

The vault has one long table in the center of the room. Against the walls are lockers, each with an individual lock and a number pertaining to a hotel room. There are no windows, and yet the room is way cooler than any of the other rooms in the hotel. Unlike upstairs, where each hotel nook has colorful decorations, this room is completely bare of such things. The walls have no art whatsoever. Not a thing. It almost feels as if I'm entering an operating room in a hospital. Paging Dr. Tooey!

Walt takes the box and places it in the center of the table.

"This feels like Christmas and a birthday wrapped up in one day," I say.

Walt wipes the sweat from his brow. "I hate to admit it. This is going to be quite the sight to see. Are you ready?"

"Ready as I'll ever be."

Using gloves to avoid any fingerprints, Walt slowly unties the hatbox. A layer of delicate tissue paper covers the top. He meticulously extracts each sheet and gently places them to the side. He grabs hold of both sides of the box—we each hold our breaths—and pulls them down gently, laying them flat against the surface of the table. There's just a little more tissue paper to excavate.

"Wowza," I say.

"Wow, indeed," Walt says.

Resting atop a mannequin's head is the Bejeweled Aqua Chapeau in all its splendor. The diamonds sparkle so intensely that the brilliance shines off the walls of the vault. The picture Walter had doesn't do justice to the real swimming cap. It is unlike anything I've ever seen. I reach to touch one of the diamonds, when Walter immediately swats my hand away.

"No touching," he says.

"But I have my gloves on!"

I wish I could try it on. When Delphine places this on her head, she will shine like the most dazzling star in the galaxy.

"Do you know what's really amazing about all of this?" I ask. "Just knowing that so many talented people created it! What's the name of the designer?"

"Edna Blanchett."

"Right. From Edna Blanchett designing the cap to sewing each diamond, hard work pays off," I say. "And here we are, helping bring this masterpiece to the big ol' screen. What a day!"

"Well, I'll be happy when the hat is filmed and taken back. In the meantime, we will be on super alert. The Bejeweled Aqua Chapeau will stay in the vault for only a few hours," Walt says. "Then it will be transported to the set over by the Mermaid Club. Mr. Davenport doesn't want anything to mess this schedule up."

"Not a problem. When will the transfer be done?"

"At exactly twelve fifteen PM today," he says.

"You don't know this yet, but I'm escorting Delphine Lucerne to the Mermaid Club," I say. "She wants me to accompany her to the set."

"Wait a sec. Why?" Walt says.

"Because I'm adorable?"

Walter frowns. One thing he doesn't like is a change in plans, but in my opinion, all good detectives have to be flexible.

"Don't worry, Walt. I'll make sure she arrives punctually. You just make sure this priceless gem gets there first."

Walt nods. "It is quite beautiful."

"Don't you feel as if it's just calling you to try it on?" My hands once again try reaching for the hat. This time Walt gently pushes them away. When he does, I do the right thing and help him put the chapeau back in its place. Every tissue exactly where it belongs.

"See you later, Bejeweled Aqua Chapeau," I say. "Get ready for your spotlight!"

The hotel clock rings. It's nine AM and the Crossed Palms will be in full swing. At least the arrival of our two most precious guests landed without much of a hitch. Well, except for the photographer. And speaking of…

"Hey, Walt. Who was the guy in the bushes?"

"A tabloid photographer. He said he had a hunch someone important was arriving today. Luckily, with your keen senses and hawk eyes, we nailed him before

79

he was able to take any pictures or see a thing. I'm sure we're going to see an uptick in these types of incidents."

Walt is right. Where there is one tabloid reporter, there are more. It will be a challenge transporting Delphine to the closed set without anyone noticing. This is going to take some thinking. A disguise will definitely be needed, but of what? *Hmmm.*

Walt closes the box and places it inside one of the vaults. He locks the door, puts his hands at his sides, and checks one more time to make sure it's locked. Then he carefully puts the key in his pocket.

"Keep your eyes peeled for anything strange or off. You take the lobby," he says. "I'm going to do my rounds."

"Got it," I say.

We break and I am alert, paying close attention for any lurking journalists or photographers. The hotel is still a sea of swamp monsters, mermaids, and scaly sea creatures. Honestly, any one of these people could be a newspaper guy in hiding, which makes me observe even more intensely. I also keep thinking about disguises and figuring out how to get Delphine to the Mermaid Club. There must be a way of distracting any pesky tabloid photographers and getting them off our tail.

"Goldie! Over here!" Cheryl waves me over.

"Everyone can't stop talking about all the commotion," she says. "Were you here for it?"

"Cheryl, a true detective doesn't divulge," I say. "But I will say that it's been quite the doozy of a morning, and the day is just beginning. I need your advice."

"What do you mean you can't tell me? I'm your best friend. Spill the beans or I won't help."

Cheryl *is* my best friend, but I can't just tell her about Delphine Lucerne and break my promise to Walt. She would understand. I think. I'm definitely in a pickle. We both wait until two mermaids walk past us before continuing.

"Honestly, if I could tell you what happened, I would, but my detective hat is officially on," I say. "Let's just say there's a very important guest and I have to figure out how to move the very important guest without anyone noticing. Any ideas?"

"What on earth are you doing, Goldie?" Cheryl laughs. "Transporting people?"

"From point A to point B without alerting the press. It's not easy when the person is a living, breathing, well-known person."

Cheryl leans in. "A famous person?" she whispers.

I look around, too, making sure no one is listening in on our conversation, before giving an affirmative head nod.

"*Hmmm.* Okay, I get you can't tell me, but pinky swear right here and now that you will when you can."

We lock pinkies and seal the deal.

"So what do you think?" I ask.

"What you'll need to do is figure out a way of hiding the person's face. Now, if they were an astronaut, they could easily be concealed in a space suit, although they might faint from the heat."

"Hey, Goldie." Rob joins us at the concierge booth. He hasn't changed into his valet uniform yet. He slaps my back as a greeting but gives a shy wave to Cheryl. Rob and I both started working as valets around the same time. He's been pining for Cheryl ever since we parked our first cars. I think Cheryl likes him, too, but she also gets annoyed by him sometimes. "Hi, Cheryl."

"Rob, what do you think about concealing a person's face?"

Rob rubs his cheek. "I say, don't do it, Goldie. Your face is what God gave you, and it's not a bad face. I mean, it's not Cheryl's, but still…"

"Not her, silly," Cheryl says. "A hotel guest who doesn't want to be seen."

"Oh." There's a long pause as we each rack our brains for ideas.

"I got it!" Rob says. "Beekeepers."

"Huh?" Cheryl and I both say.

"Beekeepers. Mr. Santiago is the Crossed Palms Resort's beekeeper. Have you ever seen him suit up in order to tend to the beehives over at the south end of the Crossed Palms? He wears this elaborate mask that practically covers his body."

"Rob's right! Mr. Santiago has an amazing suit. The hat alone would be enough to hide whoever you are trying to hide."

"Who *are* we trying to hide?" Rob asks.

"Don't ask. This one isn't naming names yet," Cheryl says. "Or maybe you can get it out of her."

"Me?" Rob replies. "No way. When Goldie sets her mind to things she's like an impenetrable safe."

"A beekeeper. Huh?" I say. "You might be onto something, Rob."

The phone rings. Cheryl picks it up and uses her most professional voice.

"Yes, Mr. Maple. Right away, Mr. Maple."

"Mr. Maple wants us both in his office." Cheryl matches her grimace with mine. I pray I didn't do anything wrong. It's not my fault Delphine Lucerne wants me around. What if Mr. Davenport refuses her request to have me escort her? I'll have to state my case, which means I need to think of one on the way.

"Did he say why?"

Cheryl shakes her head.

"Yikes. I better go. Don't want to give Mr. Maple any reason to call me in," Rob says. "I'll see you guys later. Dinner at the Deep End?"

"Today's the first day of the big movie scene being filmed at the Mermaid Club," I say. "I doubt I'll have time for the Deep End."

Rob shrugs. "What about you, Cheryl? There are fries and a chocolate milk shake with your name on it."

"Maybe. I feel like today is going to be really intense," Cheryl says. "I mean, take a look around."

A boy buries his head against his mother after a swamp thing walks past him. Seconds later, the little boy starts to cry.

"Here, make sure the little one gets this." Cheryl hands Rob a yo-yo from her drawer. "We better go. Shouldn't keep the big boss waiting."

"Good luck!" Rob says as he walks toward the crying boy.

"Who knows? Mr. Maple might be calling me in because I'm being promoted for all my great work this morning. What do you think, Cheryl?"

"I don't even know what you did this morning, but I'll tell you what," Cheryl says. "He didn't seem all that happy."

Similar to Mr. Davenport, Mr. Maple can be very intimidating. I guess you have to be when you're running such a grand hotel. Mr. Maple also has very strong opinions. He likes what he likes. The Crossed Palms Resort has been in his family for a long time.

Mr. Maple's office is located on the second floor of the hotel. The door has no signage whatsoever. If you are called to his office you have to figure out where it is. I've only been to Mr. Maple's office once. I guess I must have been around six years old. I got as many kids together as I could for some go-kart racing. The final race had me competing against Sugar Maple. That's right, Mr. Maple has a daughter my age. We were actually friends until I beat her fair and square. Sugar didn't like it, so she squealed about the whole thing. I got a big talking-to, and from that day, Sugar and I became sworn enemies. Needless to say, I'm not feeling all that great being called in again. At least Cheryl is with me this time.

"What's this thing about you and Delphine Lucerne?" he says before the door has a chance to close behind us. Mr. Maple is a short man, and his shortness is made even more obvious by the *giant* chair he insists on sitting in. He has a pencil-thin mustache with slight twirls at the ends. His suit is tailor-made for him, and yet it still overwhelms his small frame. None of this matters. Mr. Maple is an imposing figure, whatever his height. "I thought Walter Tooey told the staff they are not to approach or talk to Delphine Lucerne."

"Delphine Lucerne is here?" Cheryl gasps. Mr. Maple huffs a bit, and Cheryl composes herself.

"I didn't approach her," I say. "See, a photographer tried to get her picture, and Mr. Davenport threw away his cigar, and she practically tripped over it."

Mr. Maple presses the palms of his hands flat on his desk like he's the commander of a strategic war room.

"Delphine Lucerne specifically asked for you, and because of this, you are to represent Crossed Palms Resort. Do you know what that means?"

I nod.

"There will be no fooling around," Mr. Maple continues. "Cheryl, I want you to be in constant communication with Goldie. Anything Ms. Lucerne wants, you are to make sure it arrives before she even finishes her sentence. Do I make myself clear?"

"Yes, Mr. Maple."

"And another thing. Goldie, you are not to make Ms. Lucerne think of anything stressful or involve her in any of your schemes. Absolutely no detour from the schedule. She needs to be on that set ready to work. You have the tendency to get distracted."

Distracted? Boy, is Mr. Maple wrong about me. I'm enthusiastic, aware, alert, smart, organized, and outgoing. Sure, my curiosity gets me into sticky situations, but it's all for the betterment of the Crossed Palms Resort.

"I will do my job, Mr. Maple. I promise to escort Delphine Lucerne to the set without any hiccups or drama or funny business."

He stares at me for a full minute. I stare back. I feel like if I blink, I will fail. So I don't.

"I'm going to keep my eye on you," he finally says. "One screwup and you are out of here."

Wow, this meeting really took a turn. I don't want to get fired.

"Okay, back to your positions."

And with that, Mr. Maple dismisses us from his office.

Outside, Cheryl lets out a long breath. "I thought for sure I was going to faint."

"You and me both. And did you notice? There were pictures of Sugar *everywhere.*"

"Goldie! Why are you focusing on Sugar when we have way more important things to think about?"

"I know, I know!" I point to my eyes. "I can't help that I've got hawk eyes. Besides, I'm nervous. He said the *f* word. Fired. Talk about pressure."

"True. So Delphine Lucerne. What is she like?" Cheryl whispers as we walk past a sea creature heading toward the valet.

"She's a regular girl, like you and me, with freckles and a love for daisies," I say.

"A regular girl? That's not possible when you are on the big screen and everyone knows your name."

"I'm serious, Cheryl. Wait until you meet her. You'll see what I mean."

"Not if Mr. Maple or Mr. Davenport has anything to do with it. They'll keep her caged up in her suite and on the set," she says. "She won't even be able to enjoy herself."

Cheryl is right.

"Well, Mr. Maple did say we are to take care of her. It's on us to help her see a little bit of St. Pascal."

"I don't know, Goldie."

"I'm not asking you to do anything yet. Just be prepared. You never know what Delphine Lucerne will want to see during her stay at the Crossed Palms. While you think of the possibilities, I've got a date with a Mr. Santiago and some bees!"

I head off toward the south side of the hotel, wishing a good morning to the sea creatures I meet along the way.

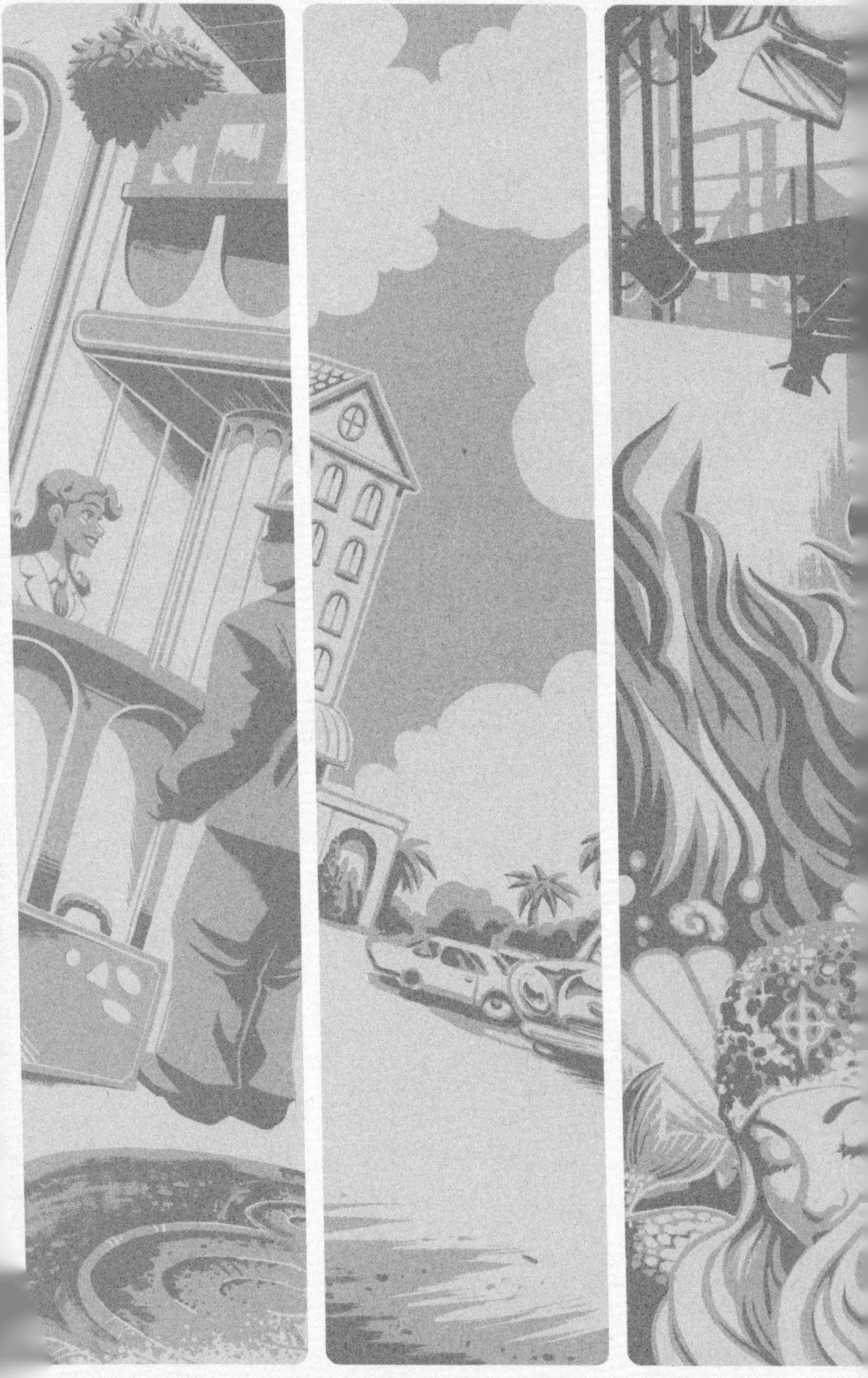

Chapter Seven

"HOW DO YOU FEEL ABOUT BEES?"

Delphine is dressed in yet another glamorous outfit. This time, she's not wearing black, but a beautiful blue dress with a matching scarf tied around her neck. She has a really tiny waist, made all the tinier with a cinched belt.

"Excuse me?" Delphine laughs. "Bees?"

It's eleven thirty AM and it's time to take Delphine to the Mermaid Club, and I've got a plan. All I need is her approval. I hope she's game.

"Yes, those flying bugs that pollinate flowers," I say.

"I don't think I like it when they sting if that's what you're getting at," she says.

"Because of our unwelcome guest this morning, it's important we get you to the Mermaid Club without anyone seeing you," I say. "Not an easy task. It took a bit of planning, but I think I've figured out how. I've got an idea."

Delphine listens intensely. I'm so glad Mr. Davenport is with Walter, huffing and puffing over the swimming cap, and not here. I can only imagine what he would think of my proposal.

I grab the oversize bag I've brought with me and dump the contents onto Delphine's bed. Delphine stares at the clothing. I lift the beekeeper's hat and show it to her.

"This is from Mr. Santiago. He's the hotel's beekeeper in charge of tending to the beehive on the property," I say. "He was generous enough to let me borrow these two suits for the day. I'll have to bring them back in one piece, of course. One for me. And one for you."

At first Delphine starts to giggle; then the giggle turns into a hearty laugh. Maybe I'm asking too much. She's a movie star for goodness' sake. She doesn't want to shove herself into a beekeeper's uniform just to avoid roving journalists. Does she?

"Now, I'm not too sure how I feel about placing that thing on my head," she says. "What will the bees think? I would hate to confuse them."

To demonstrate, I place the hat over mine. "See? Not a problem." I yell this because with the beekeeper hat on, it feels as if I'm in a submarine. Communication is going to be a problem. We'll have to come up with signs.

"We will put these on. Walk across the hotel and into the waiting car with the driver who will drive us over to the Mermaid Club," I say. "The good thing is no one will notice us. They will think we are simply beekeepers on our way to collect honey."

Delphine takes hold of the suit. "What will you think of next?" she says. "Okay, Goldie, I'm game."

"Great! We should probably come up with a couple of hand gestures. Thumbs-up for everything is okay. Thumbs-down if it isn't," I say, scratching my head. "What else?"

"You know what my favorite thing to do was when I was your age? Besides swimming?" Delphine asks. "Dressing up for Halloween. I think it's why I love acting so much. It's all pretending."

"Being a house detective is kind of the same. I sure love disguises. Shall we?"

We both put on our suits. Thank goodness Mr. Santiago is a small man. When Delphine's ready, I give her

a thumbs-up, and she in turn does the same. The security guards were alerted to my plan beforehand. They
are to case the surrounding areas and make sure there
are no surprises hiding in the bushes or anywhere else
for that matter.

I suddenly start to giggle, which in turn makes
Delphine laugh. I love how laughter is contagious,
but I'm at work, so I try to contain it. I try my best to
keep a straight face, but we both look ridiculous. And,
boy, it sure is hot in this thing. How do beekeepers do
this? Delphine steps out of the hotel first. She honestly
looks as if she were taking her first steps on Mars. She
stops in front of the roses and leans in as though she
is smelling their fragrance. Then she does a little turn.
Funny how even in a beekeeper suit Delphine exudes
movie magic and grace. She takes an elaborate bow.
I point her toward the path that leads to the hotel
entrance.

We are almost by the lobby. Most of the guests,
including the mermaid and sea creature having a chat
by the fountain, don't pay us any mind. I guess with
all the swamp things and mermaids walking around,
what's weird about a couple of beekeepers? We're basically boring hotel workers to them.

The driver is right where he said he would be. I can feel the pool of sweat dripping down my back, and I can't wait to take this thing off. I didn't really have to wear the suit, but I figured I would keep Delphine company. Solidarity. Our driver was smart and covered the windows with these cute little curtains to conceal us. As soon as we enter the car, I tear off the hat. My face is slick with sweat.

"Oh my, that was something!" Delphine exclaims as she pulls off her hat, too. "Who would have thought walking around in a beekeeper's outfit would be such work?"

"It was fun, but, boy, am I sweaty," I say.

"A while back, I had to play Marie Antoinette for a theater production on Broadway. I almost never do theater but I did this show," she says. "Anyway, the corset and the dress were so heavy. It was like carrying milk crates. It reminded me of my days working at the five-and-dime, stocking the shelves. So many heavy boxes. I used to do it by myself. Costumes are so tricky. You just have to learn how to manage them and not let them manage you."

I can totally picture Delphine working at the five-and-dime. To be such a great swimmer and dancer, you must have strength. Her arms may be concealed in her beekeeper's uniform, but Delphine has muscles.

"Do you ever miss working at the store?" I ask.

Delphine touches up her hair. "I do sometimes. I think I miss home more than the store. I miss the luxury of time. Time to fish. Time to take a dip in the pool," she says. "Time for adventures. It seems my time is spent on the set pretending, instead of enjoying it. I mean, don't get me wrong, I love the work I do. Like I said, who doesn't like to pretend?"

The drive is very short. Not long enough to really get into an in-depth conversation with Delphine, but long enough to learn a few things: She loves disguises, she misses her home, and she has a great laugh.

As the driver reaches the Mermaid Club, we can see a large crowd has formed outside. Movie madness is hitting St. Pascal and everyone wants in on the action. The driver knows well enough to drive past the crowd and head to the rear of the club.

"We're here," I say. "We should place the hats back even though we are going through the Mermaid Club's private entrance. Ready?"

"Ready!" she says.

Delphine follows me. We take the same entrance

Mom and her coworkers use to avoid anyone seeing them out of their mermaid costumes. Thankfully, there are no surprises. Once inside, we take off the hats and uniforms. With a flick of her hair, Delphine is back to being a glamorous movie star, and I'm back to being Goldie. I store the uniforms in a safe place.

"This way," I say. Delphine follows me until we reach the door marked ENTRANCE and I push it open.

Wow! I take it all in. The Mermaid Club is no longer the Mermaid Club. It has been transformed into an aquatic underwater world fit for a queen. The tables and booths have been taken away, and in their place are grand rock formations. Walls have been draped with moss and bright coral-like plants. Everything is in an oceanic blue hue. Two majestic thrones in turquoise are in front of the water tank.

As soon as we appear, movie people immediately rush to Delphine.

"Ms. Lucerne, are you okay? Do you need anything? Are you thirsty?"

The questions are never ending. They don't really wait for her to answer, they just ask and ask, primping her hair and offering her things. A glass of water with a straw in it. A tiny bite of a sandwich.

"Please, everyone, no need to fuss," she says. "Goldie here has been doing a fine job taking care of me. Now, where am I needed?"

A very fashionable woman with super-short bangs, a pin cushion on her wrist, and a measuring tape around her neck approaches Delphine.

"We must dress you," she says with a heavy French accent. "Yes?"

"Goldie, this is Edna Blanchett. She is in charge of all the glamorous costumes."

"Nice to meet you. I—"

Before I can tell her how much I love the Bejeweled Aqua Chapeau, Ms. Blanchett takes Delphine by the hand. I follow them to the dressing room, which has been cleared of the usual Mermaid Club costumes and accessories. Delphine's countless outfits hang up on a wooden pole. The vanity table is overrun with makeup and a long line of different types of wigs. Long hair wigs. Short hair wigs. Multicolored wigs. What a field day I would have with these wigs.

Soon Edna Blanchett and a couple of her assistants bring different fabrics and lay them against Delphine's frame. Delphine slips off her dress and starts trying on the different costumes, each one more elaborate than the next. So much gold and sequins and metallics. The women pin things and cut materials. Ms. Blanchett never cracks a smile, not once.

"Ouch!" Delphine exclaims. "Please be careful with those pins."

"Impossible. Working in this small room with such little light is a hazard," Edna says. "There's not enough time."

"You always seem to make it work," Delphine says. "I believe in you."

Ms. Blanchett continues to complain while sewing the dress right onto Delphine's body. I get nervous every time she wields the large steel scissors and snips off the bottom of the dress without so much as a warning to Delphine.

"At Powerhouse Productions they allowed me my freedom."

"We're part of the Baldwin Studios now," Delphine says, trying to calm Edna down.

"Yes, and therein lies the problem," Edna says. She continues to work, muttering French words to herself that I can't make out. Delphine tries to soothe Edna's worries to no avail.

"*Voilà.* You are ready."

The dress is perfect.

Next up, the makeup artists are excited to transform Delphine's face with vibrant green eye shadow and bold red lips.

"Wow!" I say when they finish.

"These artists know what they're doing," Delphine says. "Thank you, ladies."

There's a loud knock on the door. "Stand by for the chapeau."

With Delphine's hair trapped underneath a net, her hairstylist selects a flowing black wig for her to wear. Minutes later, two men enter the dressing room holding the Bejeweled Aqua Chapeau. It's my second time seeing it, and I'm still blown away. Edna takes the diamond swimming cap and places it on Delphine's head.

"So much drama for this," Edna says.

"Too much," they say in unison. The women both roll their eyes.

"Shall we?" Delphine asks. Edna nods a reluctant approval.

And with a snap of a finger, Delphine is no longer the freckled young woman who giggled while twirling in a beekeeper's outfit just this morning. She is the Queen of the Mermaids, regal and stunning.

"Clear for Delphine Lucerne!" one of the workers screams, alerting the crew. The movie magic is about to begin, and I've got a front-row seat. Unfortunately, so does Mr. Davenport.

"Make sure you get a tight shot of the crown. No pulling back," Mr. Davenport yells at the director, who is seated beside him. With cigar in hand, he keeps pointing toward Delphine while she gets situated on the set. "Hey, you, off the set!"

Oh boy. Mr. Davenport has spotted me.

"Good afternoon, Mr. Davenport," I say. "It's great to see you, too!"

"Get her out of there," he says.

Trying to find the best place to stand and not get noticed is going to be a challenge. Every inch of the set is being overrun by the crew or camera operators, costume designers, and makeup people.

"The extras are getting ready over there." One of the crew members addresses me and points backstage.

I don't bother correcting him that I'm not an extra. And as much as I would love to stay on set and watch Delphine in all her splendor, I'm on the job. It's important to keep my eyes and ears open. The Bejeweled Aqua Chapeau is out in the open and so is Delphine.

I need to make sure they both remain safe. So I head backstage.

The backstage is an assembly line of monster-and-mermaid makeup mayhem. Men and women are in line waiting to sit down in three chairs. The makeup crew works overtime to get each of them prepped and ready. In another corner, the costume designers suit up the monsters in sea creature outfits. Mermaids try on different fins. It's a kaleidoscopic swirl of color and disorder.

"I don't remember there being a kid on the set list today." A woman taps a pencil on a clipboard.

"Oh no, I'm not part of the movie. I'm security."

She looks me up and down. "Clever," she says.

I walk away and keep inspecting the backstage, taking inventory of everyone. Observation is key when it comes to being a detective. It's important to pay attention to what is said, and who is saying it. I notice how one of the extras insists on wearing the most glamorous fins available, ones that are meant for Delphine.

"These match my eyes," she says. "Obviously I'm meant to wear them."

Edna Blanchett shakes her head and hands her a brown fin instead. The actress is not happy.

"I heard Delphine refuses to speak to anyone unless

they address her by her character's name. She never breaks character on set," another mermaid says. "Can you just imagine?"

"That isn't true," one of Edna's assistant costume designers speaks up. He has blond hair, and, like Edna, a measuring tape dangles around his neck. I detect a bit of an accent on him. It might be Spanish or French.

"What makes you so sure?" the mermaid asks.

"Because I've worked on *every* film with her."

"Oh, la-di-da." The mermaid moves on.

"What is she like?" I ask him.

"She's a professional. Always. A *perfectionniste*. A star in the truest sense," he says. "Sadly, this role is beneath her. She should be doing a real film. I can play a sea creature, but Delphine? She deserves so much more."

Boy, someone really has an opinion. Grumpy Costume Guy continues to talk about how monster movies aren't award winning or artistic. He has a lot of opinions about the matter.

"Maybe she likes making movies that make people happy or scared," I say. "There's nothing wrong with that."

"She deserves to act in the greatest films, not a

movie like this one," he says. "Back at Powerhouse, Delphine was set to play her first dramatic role. It would have been a nod to her small-town roots. I was going to be cast alongside her as her brother, but then—"

"*Faire taire!*" says Edna Blanchett. The assistant quickly pipes down and gets working on another costume. I guess Edna doesn't tolerate talkative costumers. It's odd that he seems so sure of what Delphine should do with her life. He kind of reminds me of Mr. Davenport, thinking about what's best for Delphine when she can do that herself.

"Darling! Isn't this quite the scene?" I detect a familiar whisper talk.

"Miss Dupart, so good to see you!" Miss Dupart is up next to be transformed into a mermaid, although she already looks like one with her majestic jewelry. "What's your role today?"

Miss Dupart leans in and makes sure those around her are not listening. "I'm meant to play a sort of mother figure to the mermaids. Only makes sense since I am the most regal person here."

She gestures to the crowd, sweeping her arm across for illustration. Miss Dupart is already in character as a Mermaid Mama. There's really no point in a costume. Miss Dupart is a real queen.

"I just saw your mother. She already looks like my mermaid sister," Miss Dupart says. "What will you be changing into?"

I look around. Everything is so gender specific. If you're a girl, you're a mermaid. If you're a boy, you're a sea creature. "If it were up to me, I would be both. A sea creature mermaid! But I'm on the job, so I don't get to participate."

A makeup assistant calls out, "Next!" and Miss Dupart takes her seat to be primped and prepped.

"My fans are waiting," Miss Dupart says.

"I'll see you on the set. Break a fin!"

The line is so long it continues outside the club. I walk along it, searching for Mom. It doesn't take long. She's already commanding a crowd. I can tell by her expression that she's regaling them with a story. Mom is a great storyteller. I'm almost certain her storytelling skills were passed down to me.

"Mom!"

"Hey, babe. Everyone, this is Goldie, my daughter."

The crowd greets me with hearty hellos and more:

"What a gem!" "You are truly blessed." "Is she a mermaid, too?"

Mom beams with pride. "No, no, no. Goldie is here on official hotel business. Right, Goldie?"

"I sure am," I say. "Just doing my rounds."

Those in the line nod.

"Isn't she something?" Mom gives me a really tight hug. It's nice working alongside her. I can't wait for Mom to meet Delphine. I think they would really hit it off. They both have a lot in common. They are both actresses, they both love the water, and they both think I'm swell.

In mid-hug, I spot him. The guy from the bushes, the photographer who tried to take Delphine's picture. He's in line pretending to be an extra. There's no way he's going to get away with this.

"Hey, I know you," I say.

"Don't know you. I'm just one of the sea creatures," he says, pulling down his baseball cap to cover his face. He can't fool me.

"No way, mister. You're the photographer." I can see his camera bulging from underneath his jacket.

"I don't know what you're talking about, kid. I'm

here to get my first movie break just like everyone else."

The crowd slowly turns to him. They're not buying what he's selling, either. St. Pascal is a small town, and like I said, everyone pretty much knows everyone. Besides, I'm really good at remembering faces.

"Sorry, you're out of luck. I'm going to have to ask you to come with me."

The photographer frowns. He's caught and he knows it.

"Let's go, sir."

Mike, the Mermaid Club owner, pops up from backstage. "Need help, Goldie?" he asks, giving the photographer the evil eye.

"Nope. I got it all under control," I say. "But thanks, Mike."

"Okay, okay, I'm leaving. No problem." The photographer lifts his hands up and reluctantly follows me. "Listen, kid. What are they paying you? Interested in a side job? Tell me what's going on inside, and I'll compensate you. What do you say?"

He talks *really* fast. I guess when you are in his line of business, you must be born with a rapid-fire tongue.

"There's nothing to see," I say. "Just a bunch of mermaids."

"Yeah right. I heard there's a big-time movie actress in the club right now. What do you say you just look away and allow me to do my job?"

I shake my head.

"Sorry, sir."

"You can call me Scoops Malone."

"Well, Scoops Malone, it's my job to keep the likes of you off this set. My advice to you is to find another movie to bother."

"I can see you won't be changing your mind soon. Don't worry. I've got my ways."

It looks as if Scoops is going to make my job a litter harder. That's okay. I'm ready.

He walks off and I stand alert by the entrance. He won't get past me. That's for sure.

Chapter Eight

ALTHOUGH THE EXTRAS HAVE BEEN TOLD TIME AND again not to address Delphine or look at her, she does not do the same. In fact, she does the exact opposite. Delphine greets every one of the extras warmly, smiling and asking them how they are doing. She jokes with the crew and the cameramen. When Miss Dupart is placed farther back in the crowd, Delphine somehow notices the oversight and corrects it by making sure Miss Dupart stands right beside her. Miss Dupart, like everyone else on the set, instantly falls in love with her.

Really can't say the same thing for Mr. Davenport.

"Hey, you, the one with the big head. Move far to the left," Mr. Davenport says, as his cigar smoke swirls above the entire set, which reeks of the awful stench.

It's hard to make out who is the director of this film when Mr. Davenport seems to be dictating every single shot.

Apparently, shooting just one scene can take hours and hours. It is by far the most tedious thing I've ever had to witness. The director yells action, the actors do their thing, the director yells cut, and then Mr. Davenport complains about what is wrong with the scene. They shoot again and the cycle begins anew. I don't know how Delphine and the rest of the actors on the set can stay in character. As Dad always says, I'm way too antsy to be kept in one spot.

"Quiet on the set!"

Delphine descends from the backstage wearing the Bejeweled Aqua Chapeau. Her Technicolor costume practically exudes its own spotlight. She radiates.

"There needs to be better lighting on her," barks Mr. Davenport. "No one is going to see the diamonds."

I don't understand what Mr. Davenport is talking about. Martians on Mars will be able to see the Aqua Chapeau. Its brightness takes over the entire set. The first time Delphine appeared, everyone—and I do mean everyone—completely gasped. The sight was pure magic. Mr. Davenport should have his eyes examined.

While all that's going on, I step outside of the club to make sure Scoops doesn't decide to make a return visit. The sun is setting in St. Pascal with the sky transforming into rich colors of orange and red. Today has been a pretty long day, and it doesn't look like it will be ending any time soon. Detective life can't always be full of excitement. For the most part it's just this: walking around and waiting for something to happen. At least I get the chance to see the sun slowly dip into the horizon. What a view.

"Ahhhhhhhh!"

Oh no! I hear a scream from inside the club. I run in to find the place is completely dark. Who turned off the lights? Suddenly, there's a sound of someone crashing into something. Another scream. This is not good.

"Stop moving, people! Not one step," a voice says. "Not a one."

The Mermaid Club lost all its lights. Lucky for me, I always carry my flashlight around for such occasions. I switch it on and try to shine a light on the chaos.

"Too much power," another voice says.

"Well, turn it back on!" shouts Mr. Davenport, the only obvious voice in the darkness. I carefully locate Delphine and Mom and Miss Dupart. They are doing okay.

"Well, isn't this something?" Delphine says. "Perhaps we should change the movie to something way more mysterious like *The Invisible Woman*. What do you think, Goldie?"

"This is a fairly old building. It can't possibly sustain all that electrical juice being generated by so many cameras and lights," I say. "They'll have to unplug."

Unless of course someone turned the lights off on purpose! We may be in the dark, but I concentrate extra hard to listen to any unusual noises. The only good thing is that both Delphine and the diamond cap are right beside me.

"They should start with the dressing rooms." Even in the pitch dark I can recognize Mom's sweet voice. "Ms. Lucerne, if you take two steps back you can sit down on your throne. That swimming cap can't possibly be comfortable on your head."

I flash my light so Delphine can see what Mom means. She slowly takes one step, then two.

"Thank you. I feel like my head is about to roll off with this thing," she says. "It's true what they say: Beauty is pain."

"Whoever came up with that should be forced to wear a crown and Mom's mermaid fins and—" I say.

"My girdle," Miss Dupart says.

Delphine and Mom laugh, as do most of those waiting around us.

"Quiet on the set!" someone yells. And just when my eyes have adjusted to the dark room, the lights turn on.

"Goodness! And here I thought we were going to live in the dark forever," Delphine says. She turns to Mom. "This thing…"

"Let me help you there." Mom reaches out to the Bejeweled Aqua Chapeau. To alleviate the weight, she lifts it slightly off Delphine's head.

"I didn't realize how heavy this thing is," Delphine says.

"It's quite beautiful," Mom says. "What with all those diamonds, it must weigh a ton."

"It actually weighs ten pounds with over thousands of diamonds." The assistant costume designer from earlier speaks up. "It is the most expensive swimming cap ever made. It took hours and hours to produce. Nothing has ever been created with such precision and beauty."

The extras around us "*ooooooh*" in unison.

"I second that. It is quite beautiful," Delphine says. "Edna did amazing work."

I make a note to myself: The assistant knows a lot about the diamond cap. I wonder if *he* was in charge of setting and sewing all those diamonds. It would explain his air of confidence and the chip on his shoulder. It looks like a lot of hard work!

Mr. Davenport storms over to Delphine, pushing everyone, including the assistant, out of the way.

"What do you think you are doing?" he asks Mom.

"Cecil, stop fussing," Delphine says and rolls her eyes. "She's simply offering me some relief." Mom gently places the swimming cap back on Delphine's head and returns to her mermaid position. Mr. Davenport shoots her a glare. "I don't understand why they couldn't have used the prototype to film. No one would have been the wiser."

"Let's continue!" Mr. Davenport shouts, ignoring Delphine's quip about the prototype.

They shoot one more shot of Delphine on her throne, addressing the court, but everyone can see she's tired. Unfortunately, it doesn't matter; it's time to film the underwater scenes. Mom and two of her coworkers are to dance around Delphine as a sort of homage to the queen of the ocean. While everyone else takes their places, the actress goes off to change into another elaborate costume.

"Poor Delphine," I say to Mom. "I know the saying is 'the show must go on,' but maybe sometimes it shouldn't."

"She's a pro just like us all," Mom says. "I better go. The choreographer wants to go over the routine one more time."

When Delphine arrives she's in a majestic green sequin swimsuit with matching makeup. The cap is once again secure on her head. The choreographer walks over and takes Mom, Delphine, and the other dancer to the side. She starts counting and clapping her hands while the three rehearse their dance moves. I notice how the Bejeweled Aqua Chapeau seems to slip from Delphine's head every time she does any elaborate motion.

"Don't worry. It should hold up in the water," the choreographer says. "Why don't we go over the dance routine one more time?"

I keep an eye on them while also paying attention to everything else on set. With so many people, it's challenging. The lights turning off could easily have been caused by a blown fuse, but I'm going to investigate that further as soon as I can.

"I don't know about this," Delphine says. She hesitates at the edge of the tank. The choreographer, Katherine Robbins, urges Delphine to enter the water.

"It's important you count to five, then flip," she says. "Always remember to lift your face toward the camera."

Mr. Davenport yells to begin. I'd like to see him try to learn this much choreography as quickly as these women *and* wear such a heavy cap. It does not look easy.

"It's going to be great," Mr. Davenport says.

Delphine enters the water and is quickly surrounded by the dancers. They start their choreographed moves.

It's a pretty simple setup. Mom has been doing dances like this for years at the Mermaid Club. They look beautiful with Delphine right in the center of it, like oceanic royalty. But every time she tries to do a somersault in the tank of water, the Bejeweled Aqua Chapeau finds a way of slipping off her head. To avoid it floating to the bottom of the tank, Mom must help secure it. They swim up to the surface before trying again.

"No touching Delphine or the chapeau," Mr. Davenport says to Mom. Mom opens her mouth to defend herself, but she thinks twice.

"Delphine. It's a one-two count, flip, and look at the camera," Katherine says. "Try to ignore the cap and do it like we've been practicing."

They try again but the same thing happens. The cap slips off, and Mom is forced to help Delphine. They do it once. Then twice. Same thing. Mom rushes to make sure the cap doesn't fall off Delphine's head.

"Don't touch the chapeau!" Mr. Davenport roars again. Delphine is getting upset and so is Mom. Instead of explaining what's happening, Katherine just gives Delphine silly pointers on how to keep dancing. I can't take it anymore. Mr. Davenport and the choreographer must see this is not working. Mom is only trying to help. I can't just stand here silently.

"Mr. Davenport! It's obvious the swimming cap is too much for Delphine to dance in," I say. "And my mom is only trying to help. You should figure out another angle to shoot from or give Delphine a break."

Everyone is stunned into silence. I might have said all this a little too loudly. I guess Mr. Davenport is not the only one screaming on the set today.

"You, out of here. Right now."

Mr. Davenport signals at two of the security guards to escort me off the set. I can't believe this is happening. My first big detective break and I'm managing to royally mess it up.

"Cecil, she's just a child," Delphine says.

"Exactly. No kids on the set," he says. "Let's go."

"But, Mr. Davenport, I'm here to help."

"Your services are no longer needed," he says.

Although Delphine pleads for me, Mr. Davenport refuses to budge. There's nothing I can do. I have to leave. Before I head out the door, Mom gives me a quick wink. I'm so bummed out. I should have kept my mouth shut. I couldn't help it. Mr. Davenport is too quick to yell at people, overlooking how everyone only wants the best for Delphine and the movie.

The security guards, who are very polite, walk me to the entrance of the Mermaid Club. I'm not going to beat myself up for speaking out, so I continue working. I don't have a choice. Mr. Davenport might think I'm off the clock, but a detective's work is never done. I might as well use this time to figure out what really happened with the blackout.

Outside, the crowd that was here earlier trying to catch a glimpse of the movie making has gone home. I start to look around for anything weird. I'm sure the fuse box is out in the back somewhere. Better take a look. I take a stroll around to the rear of the club, making sure to keep my eyes peeled for anything that might stand out.

The fuse box is open. There are a couple of footprints, signs of it having been worked on by several people. Nothing unusual. But wait, what's this? Lying on the ground is a small white piece of paper. No, it's not a paper. It's half of a matchbook with a couple of matches still attached. It's barely decipherable, but the matchbook is definitely one of ours. I can tell by the drawing of the palm tree and the exterior of the Crossed Palms Resort. On the back of the cardstock is some scribbling I can't make out. Strange.

"Ahhhhh!" I scream as someone places a hand on my shoulder.

"Sorry. Didn't mean to scare you. It's just me."

Walt bends down to join me.

"Next time give me a sign. I almost had a heart attack."

"What you got there?" he asks.

"Not sure yet. Probably nothing. Just one of our matchbooks," I say and pocket it.

"So, how's it going in there?"

"Well, it was great until I got kicked out," I say. "Apparently, Mr. Davenport is not a fan of anyone speaking their mind."

Walt smacks his forehead. "Weren't you in my office with him? The only thing that man understands is his way. What made you think you can do differently?"

"I don't know. Hope?" I say. "There's a time to be

quiet and a time to speak up. I might have mistaken which time it was."

Walt pats my shoulder. "We've both been working hard on this one. It's been a challenge managing detective duties over at the hotel while coordinating with Mike and the Mermaid Club to make sure everything is still running smoothly," he says. "I came over as soon as I heard about the blackout. Mr. Maple wanted me to make sure our good friend from Baldwin Studios, aka Mr. Davenport, was okay. I guess the answer is no."

"He's still barking at people, so I'd say he's more than fine."

"You're doing a great job, Goldie," Walt says. "Don't let this one hiccup get you down."

He's right. "Thanks, Walt! I was planning to go around the club, make sure the blackout was a blown fuse and not some other strange coincidence."

"Sounds like a plan," he says. "Exactly what a true detective would do in such circumstances."

Walt and I both walk toward the front entrance of the club. At least Walt appreciates the work I'm doing. It means a lot to me. Mr. Davenport may not appreciate me, but Walt does, and Mom *and* Delphine!

All of a sudden, I hear a rustling sound. I stop and hold Walt's arm to stop him from continuing.

"Did you hear that?" I ask. Walt shakes his head.

There is definitely something going on. Walt doesn't hear it, but I can, and it's as clear as day. It's not a sound of an animal, or at least I don't think it is.

I hear the rustling noise again, but this time it's joined with a banging sound. Is Scoops back trying to get inside the club? He'd better not be! This time Walt hears it, too.

"It sounds like it's coming from where we just left," he says. I follow him as we walk quietly toward the back.

With Mom by her side, Delphine Lucerne storms out of the back entrance of the Mermaid Club. They both wear robes and both seem determined to make it out of there. We can hear Mr. Davenport screaming somewhere behind them.

"I'm done. Let's go," Delphine says. "Your mother mentioned there are still leftovers from her casserole. I'm hungry. Aren't you?"

Walt looks petrified. This isn't exactly what he had

in mind. I think he would have preferred to find Scoops or another tabloid photographer. I didn't expect this, either. I offer him a shrug.

"My car is just around the corner," Mom says.

Instead of following us, Walt heads inside the club. "I better take care of the volcano that's about to erupt. I'll check in with you later," he says. Then he leans forward to whisper: "And, Goldie, make sure she returns to the set in one hour or less. Preferably less. I guess I'll go deal with this and make sure the diamond swimming cap is safe."

And just like that, I'm on the job! What a day. I can't wait to see what else is in store for me. Delphine sits in the back of Mom's car while I take the front seat. I can't believe my eyes. Delphine is about to come to our house, and I don't know what to think.

"What will happen to Mr. Davenport and the film?" I say. "Won't he be angry?"

"There is no movie without the star," she says. "Besides, I think we all deserve a break, don't you?"

"Well, you are more than welcome to take a break over by us," Mom says. "We don't have much, but what we do have we freely offer."

"The adventure continues," I declare.

As we drive up Lime Street, I point to the various stores and the owners. I make sure to add priceless tidbits of information about each thing or person we pass. I'm Delphine's very own tour guide.

"This is the spot where Miss Dupart says she was serenaded by Nat King Cole," I say. "And this is where I was able to locate a missing bike. It was taken by a ten-year-old neighborhood boy who wanted to impress a girl. Unfortunately, he didn't impress the girl when he tried to do a bike trick and kissed the dirt instead, destroying the bike in the process."

"I remember that," Mom says. "He ended up getting a job at Crossed Palms to pay off the debt. Didn't he?"

"Yup. I got him the job. And now he's a bellhop."

"You must be so proud of your daughter," Delphine says. "She always seems to be leading with her heart, helping those around her. You've raised her right."

"Goldie has always been that way," Mom says. "She loves to be in the center of the action, and she loves a good mystery. Even as a baby, she would never sit still for long. Always trying to see what was happening in the rooms next door. And when they moved to Crossed Palms, her inventiveness just flourished."

"They? Crossed Palms? Do you mean Goldie lives in the Crossed Palms?"

"Oh yes! Crossed Palms is my home," I say. "I live part of the time with my dad. He's the manager of Crossed Palms. We have our own little cottage on the grounds. The other part I stay with Mom in her downtown apartment."

Delphine looks wistfully out the window. She seems deep in thought.

"I spend so much of my time in hotels all over the world," she says. She tugs her damp hair behind her ears. Her makeup is still intact even after being in the water. "I can't say it ever feels like home. There's just something so transitory and cold about hotels."

"Oh no. You shouldn't think of them that way at all," I say. "The best way to make any hotel feel like home is by bringing a little something with you. What's the one thing you miss the most? Whatever the item is, bring a little piece of it with you wherever you go."

"I'll remember that for the next time," she says.

I bet fans are always offering a big movie star like Delphine all types of gifts. Fancy new clothes and cars and the like. But sometimes the best gifts are the quieter ones. They may not be worth much, but they hold such special meaning.

After a short pause, I continue the tour.

"And that's Wax Lips, where the coolest girl in all of St. Pascal works." I can't help letting out a long sigh.

Mom smiles. She's heard this before.

"I thought for sure you were the coolest girl in St. Pascal," Delphine says.

I vehemently shake my head.

"No way. I can't compare. Diane not only works at the record shop, but she also is really tall and has a killer short haircut and—"

I'm rambling, but Delphine doesn't seem to mind. And yet, I'm feeling a little bit self-conscious about it. Maybe I've said too much.

"Anyway, she's great."

"Why don't we invite her over for dinner?" Mom says.

"Yes, why not?" Delphine says. "The more the merrier."

I know what Mom is doing. She's nudging me to do something I'm afraid to do: ask Diane out. I don't think I'm ready. Sure, I'll confront Mr. Davenport and his loud mouth any day, but asking Diane out? I can't do it. Not yet anyway.

"She's very busy," I say. "Maybe next time."

"I get nervous every time I step in front of the camera. Every single time," Delphine says. "Do you know what my trick is to overcome nerves? I remind myself no one is perfect. I can only give my very best. People will see that and appreciate it."

I chew a little on Delphine's words. She might be onto something.

"You shouldn't let fear stop you from doing what you want," Mom says. She's said that exact phrase many times before, but it never hurts to be reminded. One of these days I'll find the courage to ask Diane out. I will.

"Home, sweet home."

We finally arrive.

"I'll be right back," I say as I grab the phone and give Cheryl a ring at the hotel.

"Cheryl, code ocean blue."

"Code ocean blue? What's code ocean blue?" she asks, totally confused.

"Delphine left the set and is sitting at my kitchen table right now, and my mom is serving her a cup of coffee," I say. "Call me if we need to vacate the premises or something."

"On it," she says. Cheryl agrees to be my eyes and ears at the hotel. You just never know when or how your boss might get wind of the drama...and then what will he do? Knowing Cheryl is on watch, I head back to the kitchen and make sure our guest is enjoying herself.

Before Delphine made herself at home at our kitchen table, she walked around the small apartment picking up trinkets and such. Delphine picked up a picture of me taking a dip in the Crossed Palms hotel pool. I must have been seven years old. She holds it up and studies it while she sips her coffee.

"Goldie, you haven't changed a bit," she says.

"Of course I have. I no longer wear my hair like that," I say. "Do you ever get tired of the water, especially with Mr. Davenport screaming at you?"

"Oh, Cecil. Here's a little tidbit for you: I actually taught Mr. Davenport how to swim when we were both eight years old, about the same age as you are in this picture. He had a deathly fear of the water. One summer we spent hours in the nearby pool until he overcame his fear," she says. "We've known each other since we were little kids, running around barefoot in Youngstown, Ohio. Don't be fooled by him. He's mostly bark and not much bite."

No way. I can't even picture Mr. Davenport as a little kid. In my mind he was born in a suit with a cigar dangling from his mouth.

Mom serves us the casserole while I make sure to pour us each a glass of water. Delphine sits down, but still asks if she can help. Mom and I both immediately refuse. She's our guest after all. Finally, Mom and I sit, and we all share a meal.

"What about the whole story of you being discovered while working at a five-and-dime shop?" I ask.

"I was never really 'discovered' by a talent scout while working at the store," she says. "I left town to pursue my dreams of being an actress. Swimming came naturally to me, so I tried to combine both talents. When I left, Cecil soon followed. In Hollywood, rumors and speculation are way better than the actual facts."

I guess it's true what they say; everyone has a story to tell. I wonder what Mr. Davenport's story is.... Has he always been so angry?

We keep eating as Delphine shares stories of her early days in Hollywood. How she auditioned for any and every type of role. She even had to dress like an apple and sing the importance of an apple a day to keep the doctor away. She said the lyrics didn't make any sense but that she still sang it with gusto. Mom and I can't stop laughing.

The phone unexpectedly rings. Cheryl is on the other end.

"Code ocean blue," she says. "Mr. Maple just stormed across the lobby and I heard *your* name being mentioned. I think you'd better get Delphine back to the set."

"Thanks for the heads-up."

As much as I love having Delphine in my house and discovering the real deal with her and Mr. Davenport, I don't want to incur the wrath of my boss. "We better get you back to the Mermaid Club," I say. "The show must go on. Right?"

"It always does," Delphine says. "Thanks for the lovely detour. St. Pascal continues to delight."

"You are always welcome. You *and* Cecil," I say. "I mean, Mr. Davenport."

Delphine smiles. "I'll let him know, but I can't imagine Mr. Davenport ever taking a detour. He did at one time when he was young. Funny how people change, right?"

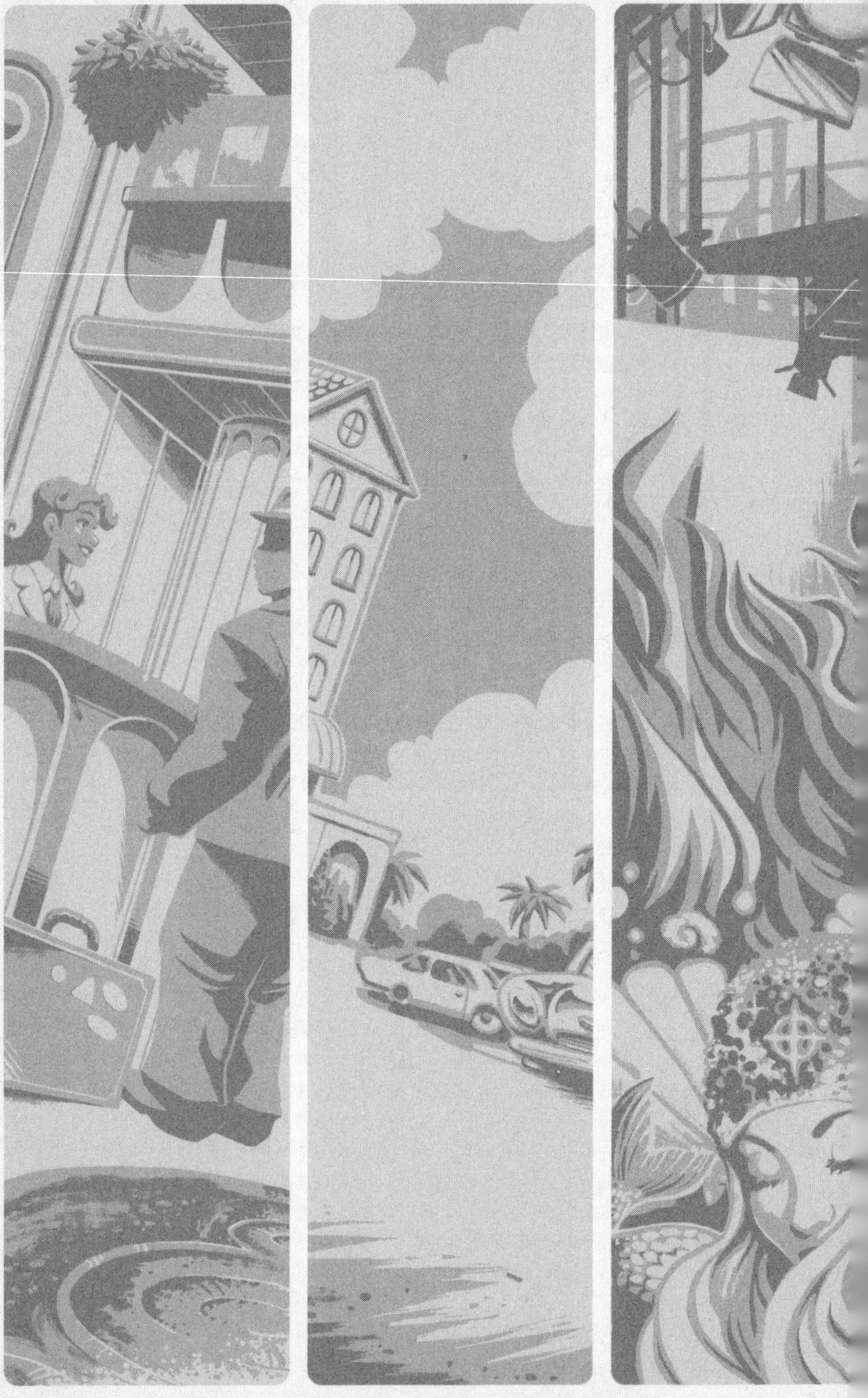

Chapter Nine

"THANK YOU BOTH FOR BEING SUCH GRACIOUS HOSTS,"
Delphine says. Within seconds, she is whisked away for
more makeup and a wardrobe change. Unfortunately, I
am not taken backstage. Instead, I am marched right
up to Mr. Davenport. Walt stands behind him with a
worried look on his face.

"Goldie, Mr. Davenport thinks it's best for everyone that you stick outside for the remainder of filming," Walt says. Uh-oh. Mr. Davenport must have been
so angry when Delphine left.

"What about Mom?"

"She can join the others." Mr. Davenport points to
the left side of the tank. Most of the extras have been
sent home, leaving only Miss Dupart and the one other

dancer. Mom walks over to them, and a makeup artist starts touching up her face.

Before I leave, I decide to try a different approach with Mr. Davenport.

"Mr. Davenport, do you prefer the butterfly stroke or do you like the front crawl?"

Mr. Davenport stares at me, looking extremely irritated by my question.

"What?" he says. He clutches his unlit cigar. I wonder if you can judge his mood by whether or not his cigar is lit.

"Butterfly stroke or front crawl? Ms. Lucerne said you were quite the swimmer back in Youngstown, Ohio," I say. His face transforms. He doesn't explode like a volcano. Instead he seems to disappear into his thoughts. Maybe he's remembering his life back then. Being a little boy, jumping into the pool with Delphine by his side. But his pensive reaction doesn't last very long. I do take note of what appears to be a softer side.

"Uh. Um. I don't know what you're talking about." He bristles.

"You better get going," Walt says.

Oh well, I tried. I guess Hollywood can do that to a person—make them deny or forget their past.

There's only one more scene to shoot at the club, and then the whole crew will move to the beach for an extravagant battle scene between the sea creatures and the mermaids. To be honest, I can't really follow the plot of the movie. I understand Delphine is some type of reluctant Queen of the Mermaids and the sea monsters are out to get them. But like in every movie, the queen falls in love with one of the sea creatures. Hence the struggle. Will she protect her mermaid people, or will she follow her heart?

It's the perfect popcorn-eating film to watch at the drive-in. I'll be waiting in line to see the film five hundred million times. Maybe even more. Action. A love story. Costumes. And Delphine right in the center of it all.

I lean against the streetlamp and listen to the night. St. Pascal is settling in. A few couples stroll by holding hands. Families round up their children to head inside. I wave to a few of my friends. I wonder what Cheryl and Rob are doing. Did Cheryl take Rob up on his offer to meet at the Deep End? That seems like ages ago. I patrol around the back of the club. Everything seems pretty calm.

A familiar face appears from in between two cars. Scoops Malone!

"Hey, kid—I think you better come over quick. I thought I heard someone over there," he says. "In fact, you should be thanking me. I'm practically doing your job."

Scoops thumbs to the direction of a type of shed, off to the side of the club. "I've been tailing this guy because he was acting pretty suspicious, and now I'm positive he is up to no good. I saw it with my own eyes. I saw him trying to climb up on a tree to peek into the club through the roof. When I saw him do that, I knew he was trouble and came straightaway looking for you."

"In there?" I say.

"That's right. You think I'm bad? Well, he's not even a reporter. He's just a random crazed fan. You don't want him to get inside the club. Do you?"

No way. I remember when the Tigers were out here. Fans practically ripped their clothes off. I don't want something like that happening to Delphine.

"I'll check it out," I say.

"Good thinking," Scoops says. "And if there's a

story to tell, I'll make sure you're the hero. How do you spell your name again, kid? Is it *Goldie* with an *i* or a *y*? I know how to spell *Vance*."

I spell my name for Scoops, and then I cautiously tiptoe toward the shed. It's hard to hear anything so I creep in closer. Scoops follows close behind. The door is slightly ajar. I look over to Scoops and give him a nod. I'm going in.

Using the element of surprise, I bust open the door, but there's absolutely no one in there. I quickly search up and down and side to side, but it's empty except for brooms and tools and a large tarp covering things. The normal items you would find in any old shed.

Wham!

Before I can scream *Harry Belafonte*, Scoops slams the door shut in my face. And that's when I realize I'm locked in! He's locked me in!

"Open this door!"

"Sorry, kid," Scoops says. "I've got a job to do and you're in my way."

Scoops may be a conniving liar, but he's no match for me. I pull out my flashlight and shine the beam inside the small shed.

I pull out my flashlight
and shine the beam
inside the small shed.

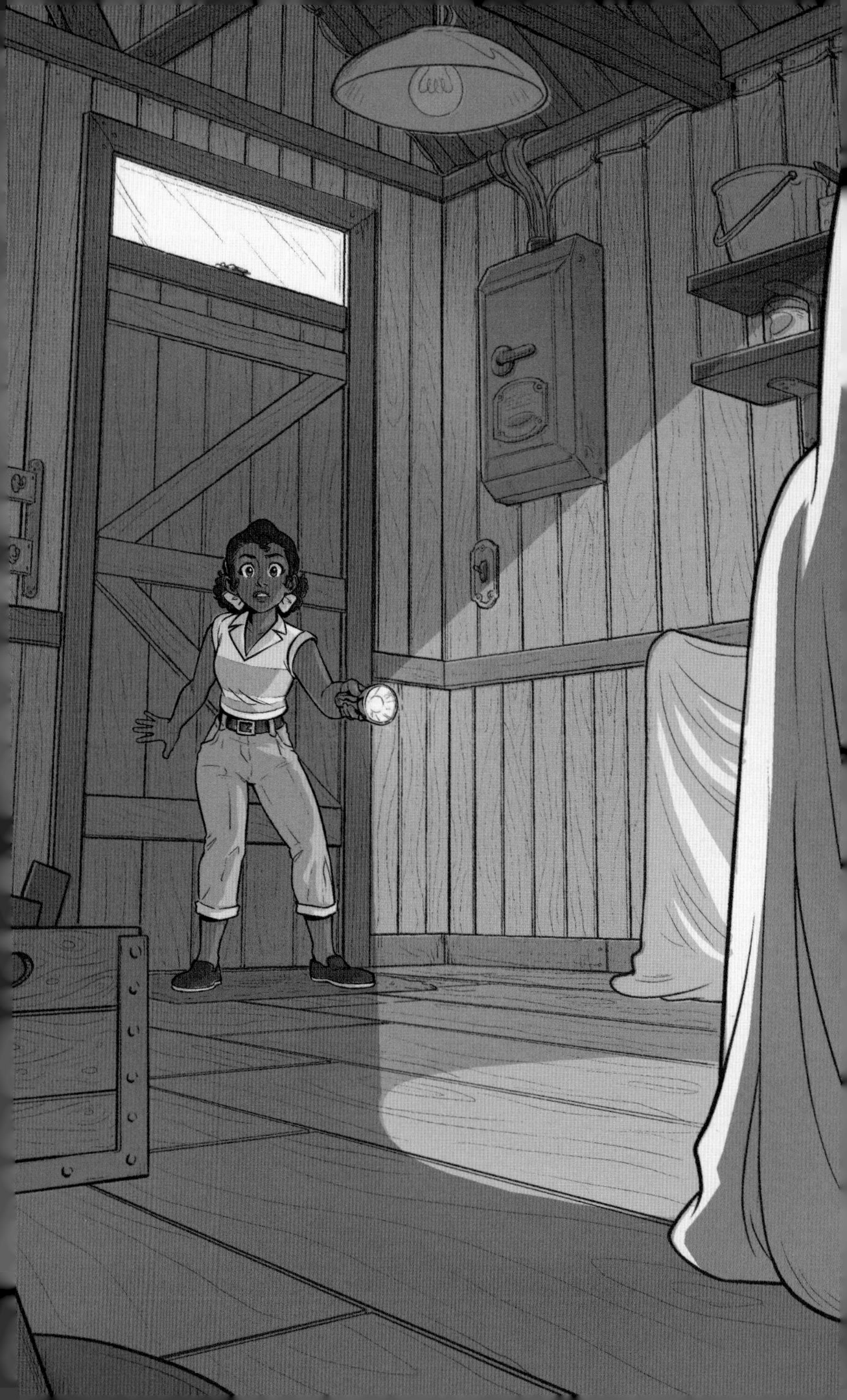

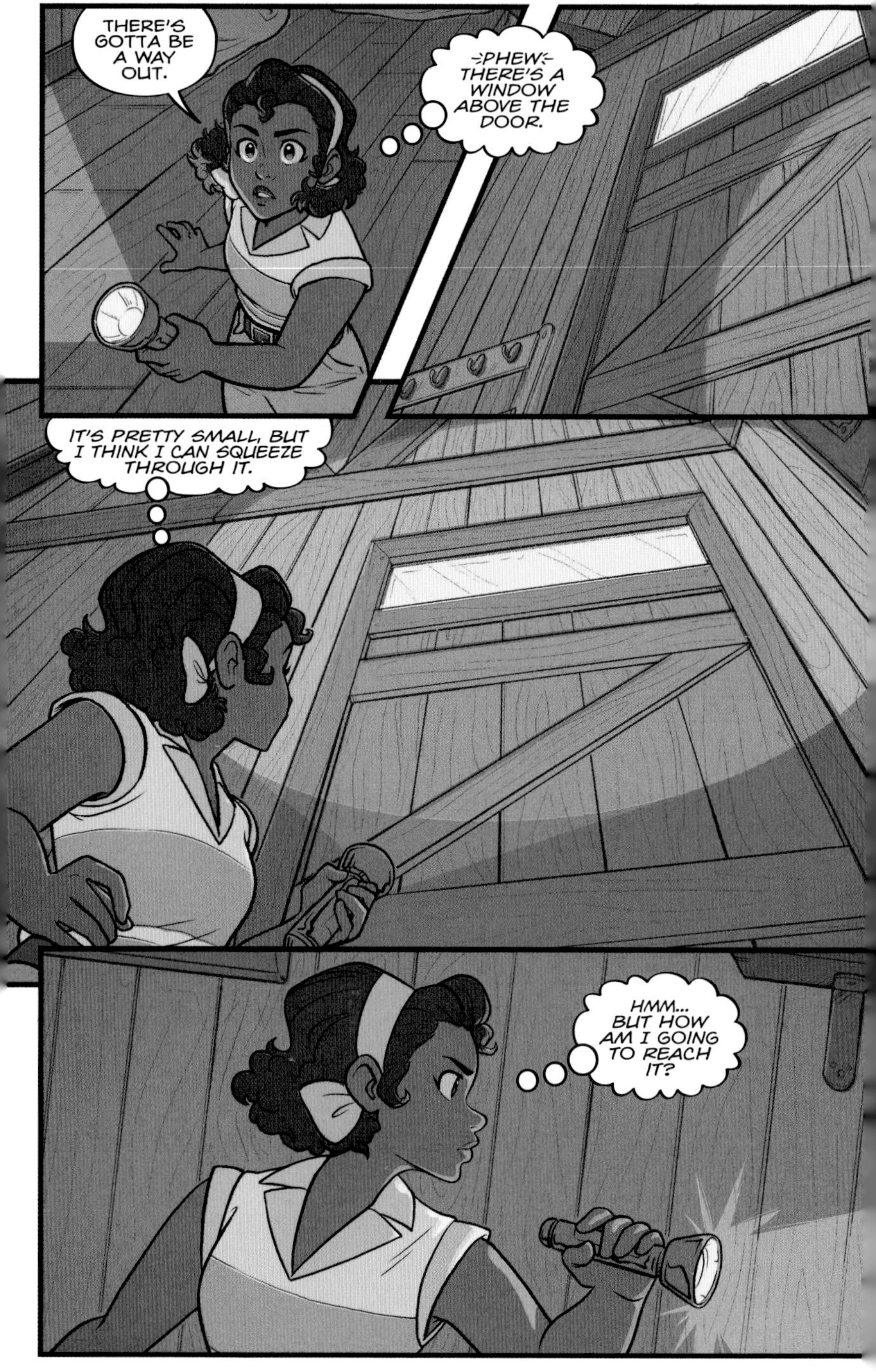
THERE'S GOTTA BE A WAY OUT.
PHEW THERE'S A WINDOW ABOVE THE DOOR.
IT'S PRETTY SMALL, BUT I THINK I CAN SQUEEZE THROUGH IT.
HMM... BUT HOW AM I GOING TO REACH IT?

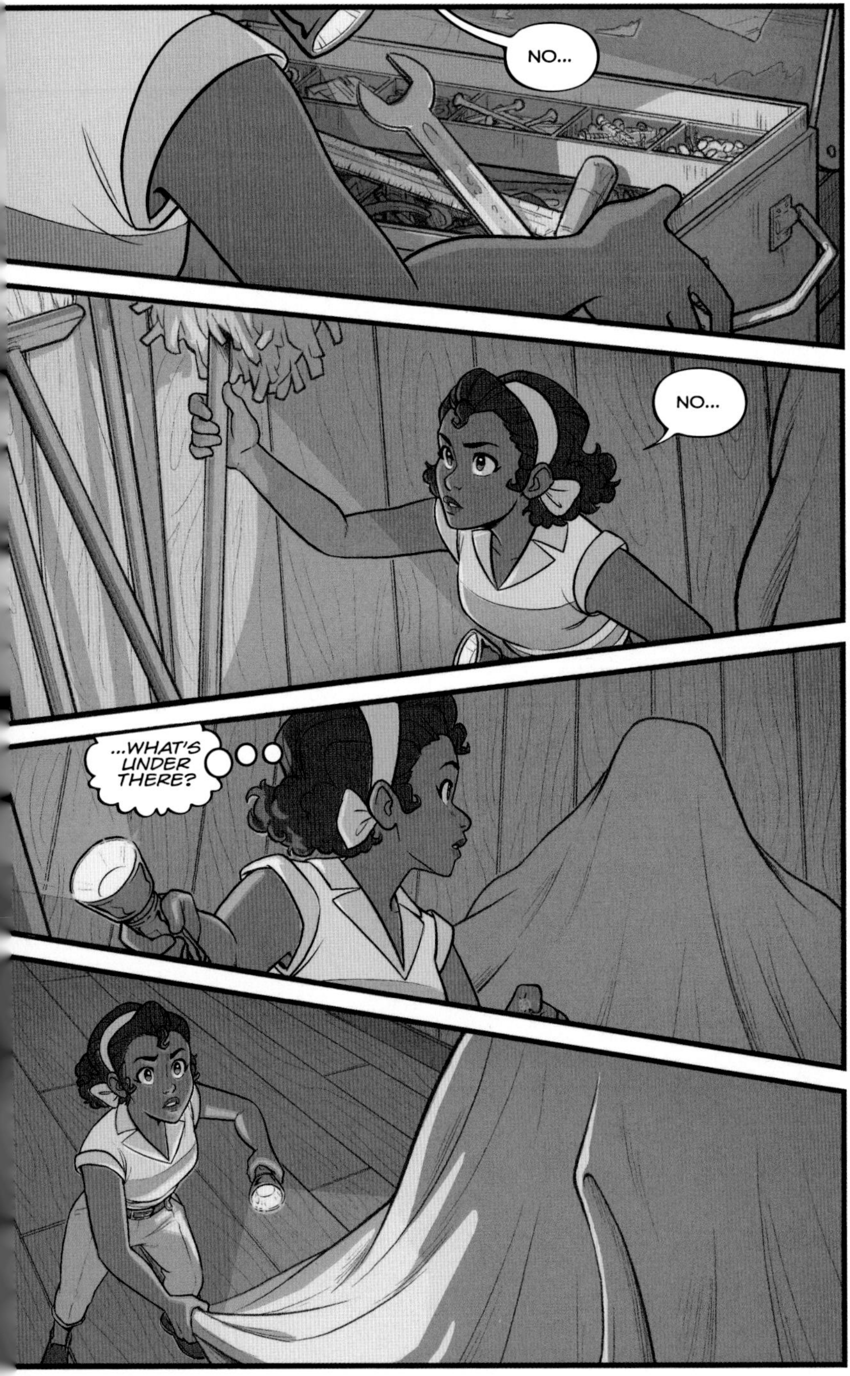
NO...
NO...
...WHAT'S UNDER THERE?

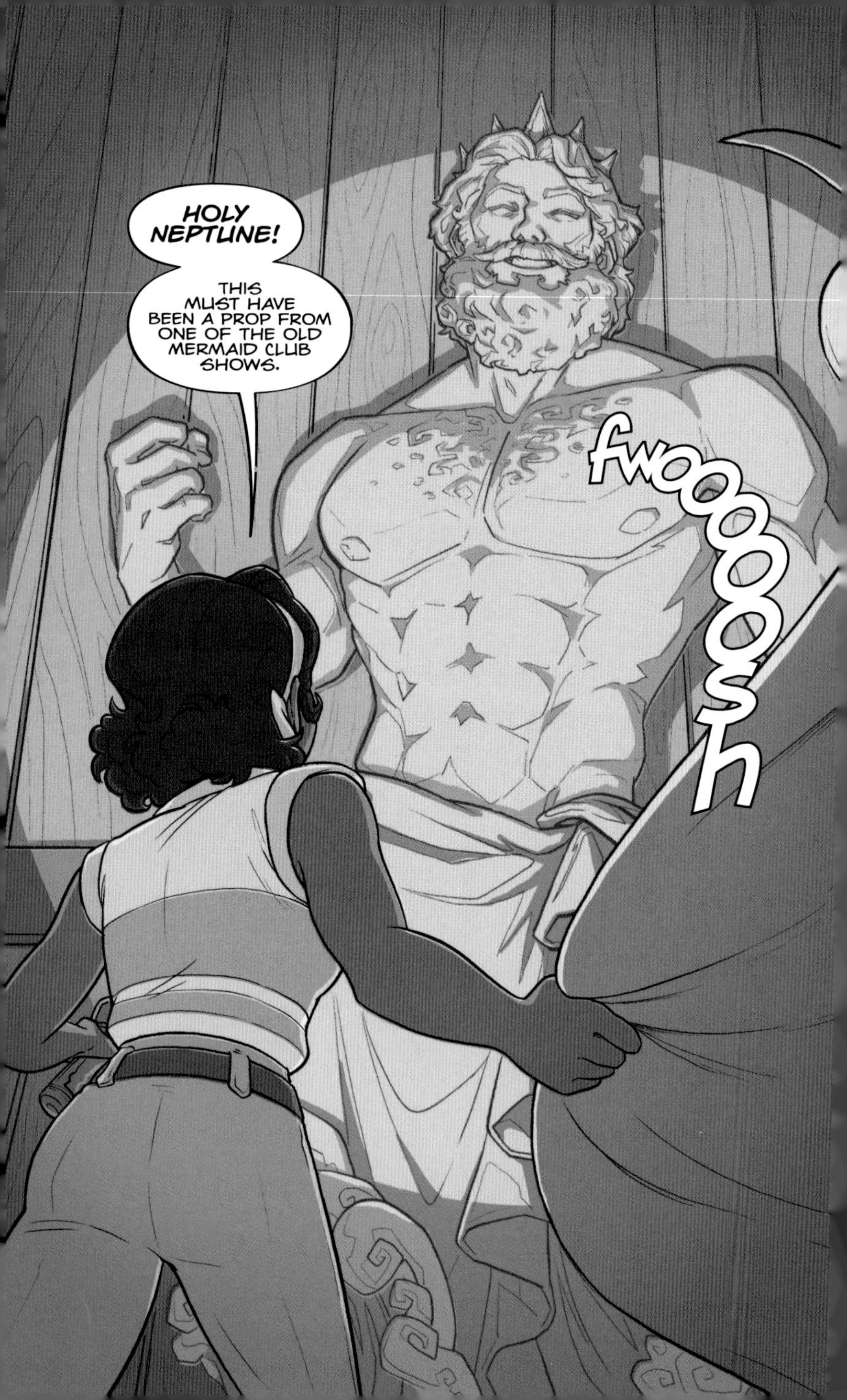
HOLY NEPTUNE!
THIS MUST HAVE BEEN A PROP FROM ONE OF THE OLD MERMAID CLUB SHOWS.
fwoooooosh

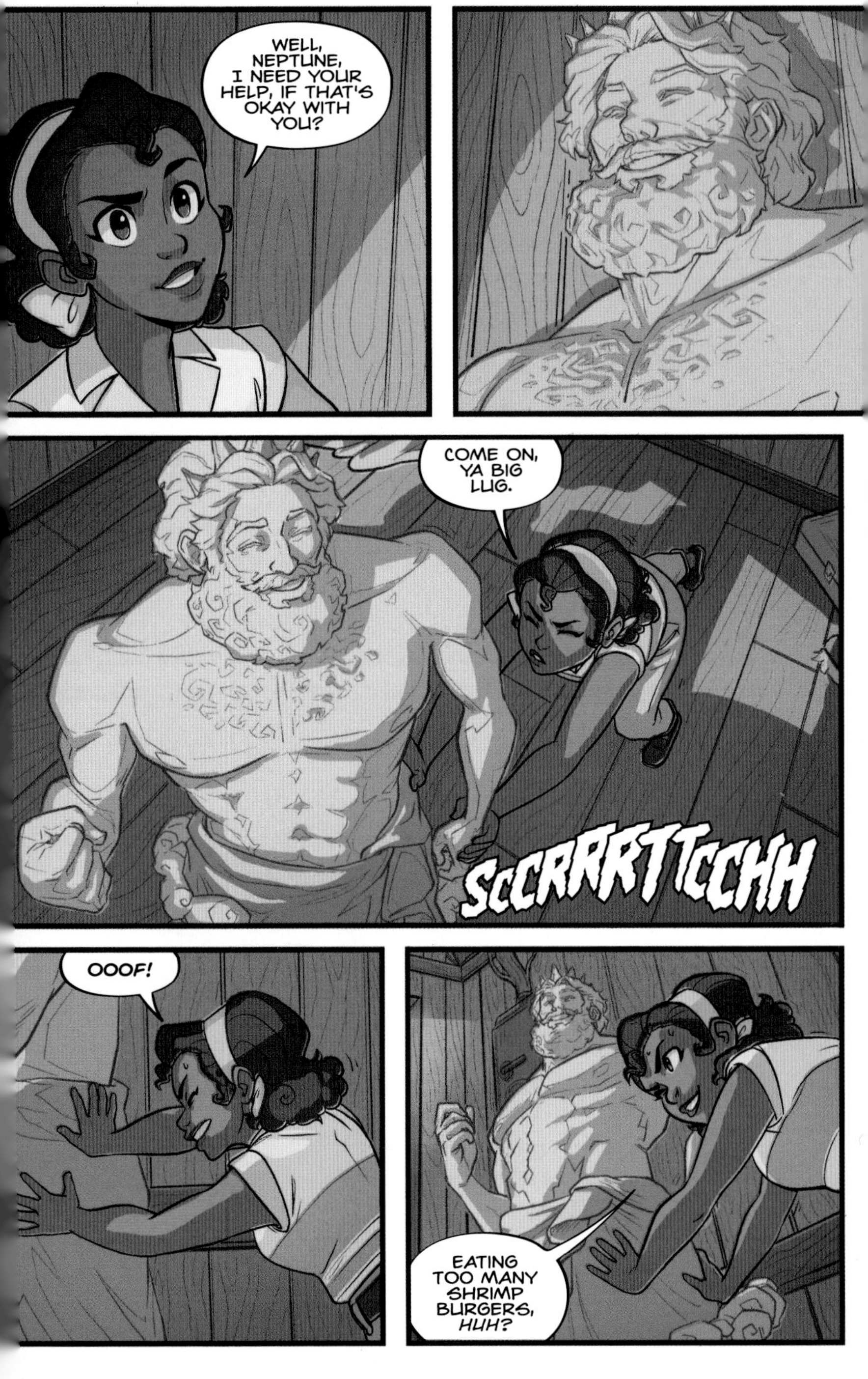
WELL, NEPTUNE, I NEED YOUR HELP, IF THAT'S OKAY WITH YOU?
COME ON, YA BIG LUG.
SCCRRRTTCCHH
OOOF!
EATING TOO MANY SHRIMP BURGERS, HUH?

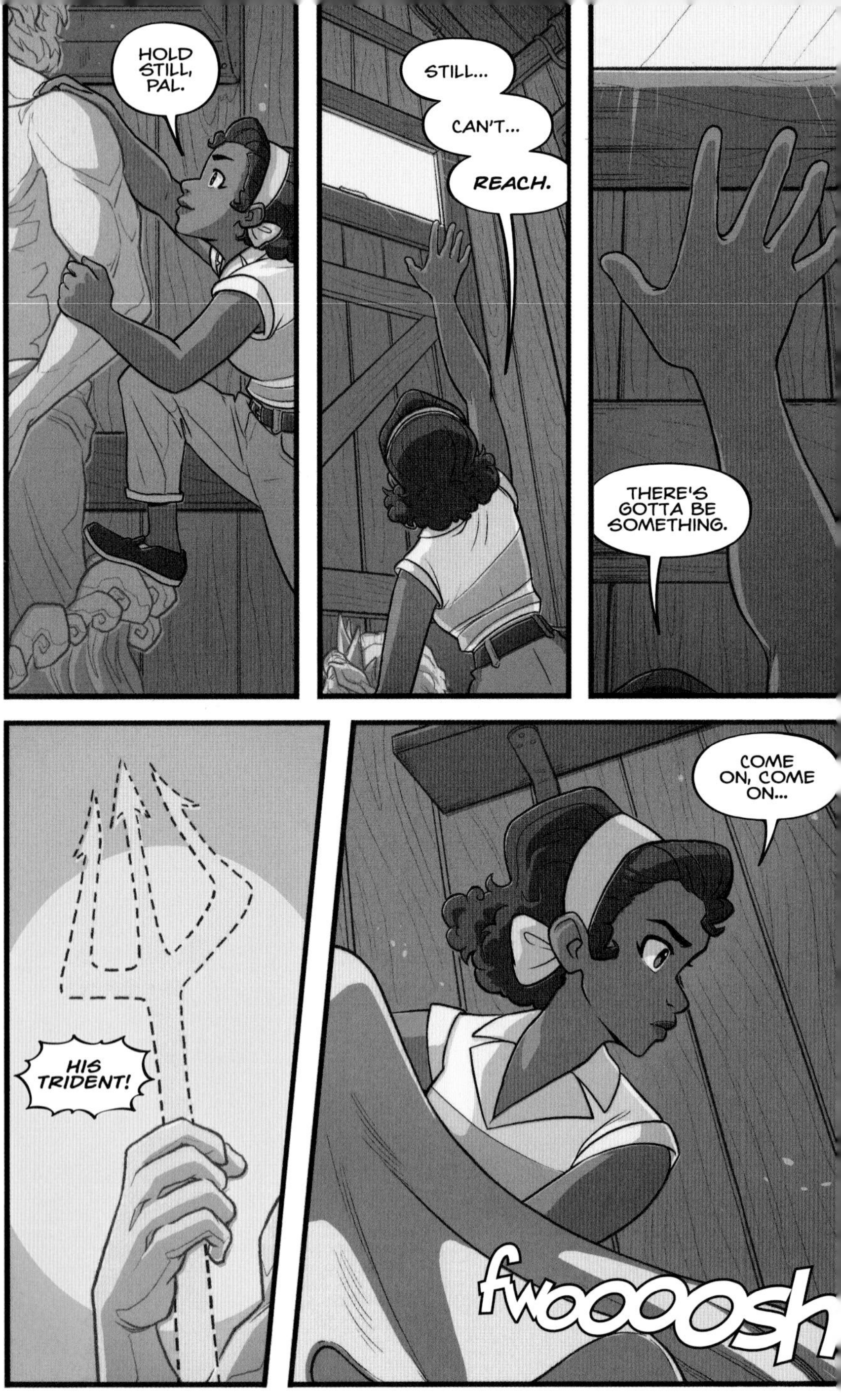

HOLD STILL, PAL.
STILL...
CAN'T...
REACH.
THERE'S GOTTA BE SOMETHING.
HIS TRIDENT!
COME ON, COME ON...
fwoooosh

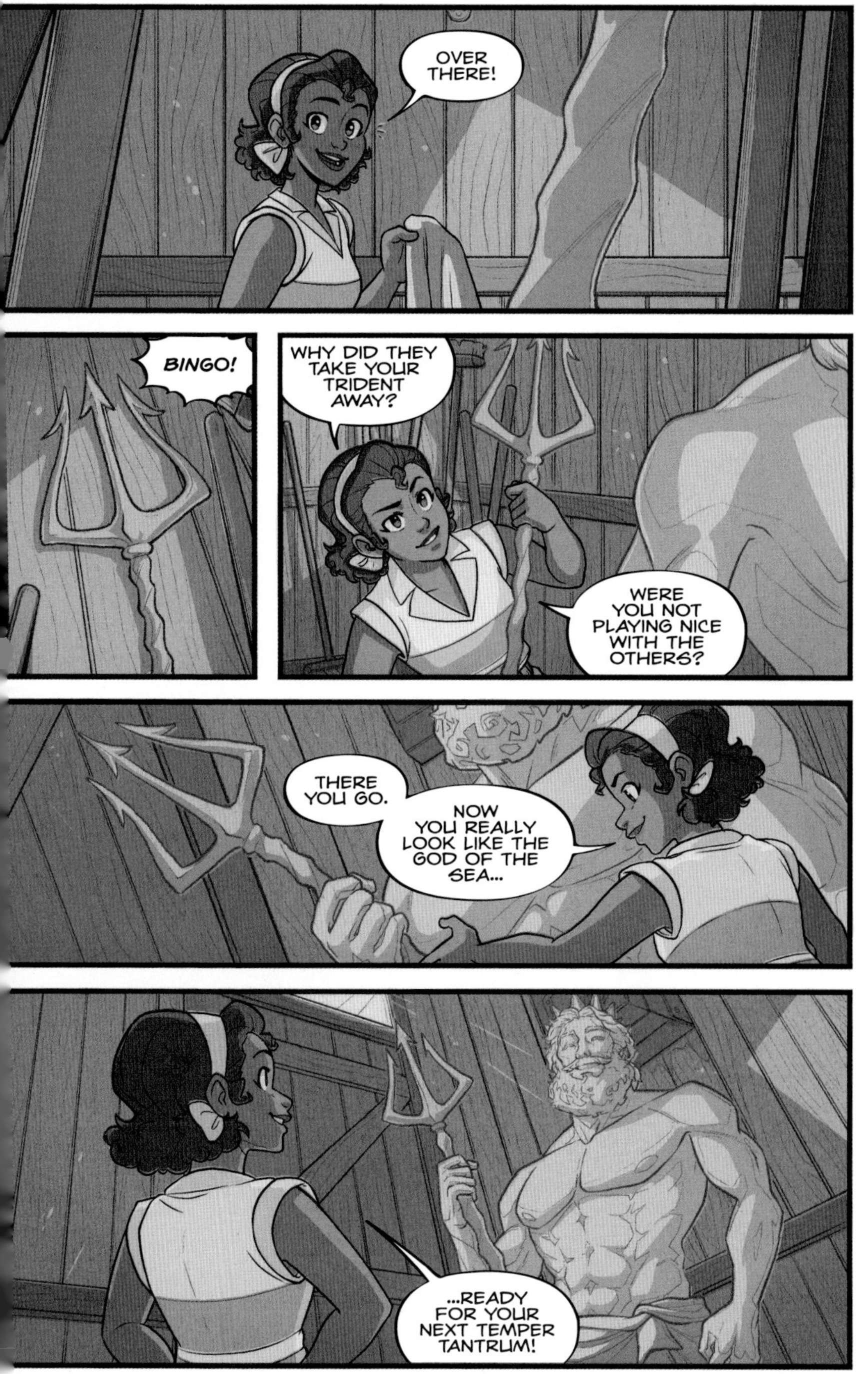
OVER THERE!
BINGO!
WHY DID THEY TAKE YOUR TRIDENT AWAY?
WERE YOU NOT PLAYING NICE WITH THE OTHERS?
THERE YOU GO.
NOW YOU REALLY LOOK LIKE THE GOD OF THE SEA...
...READY FOR YOUR NEXT TEMPER TANTRUM!

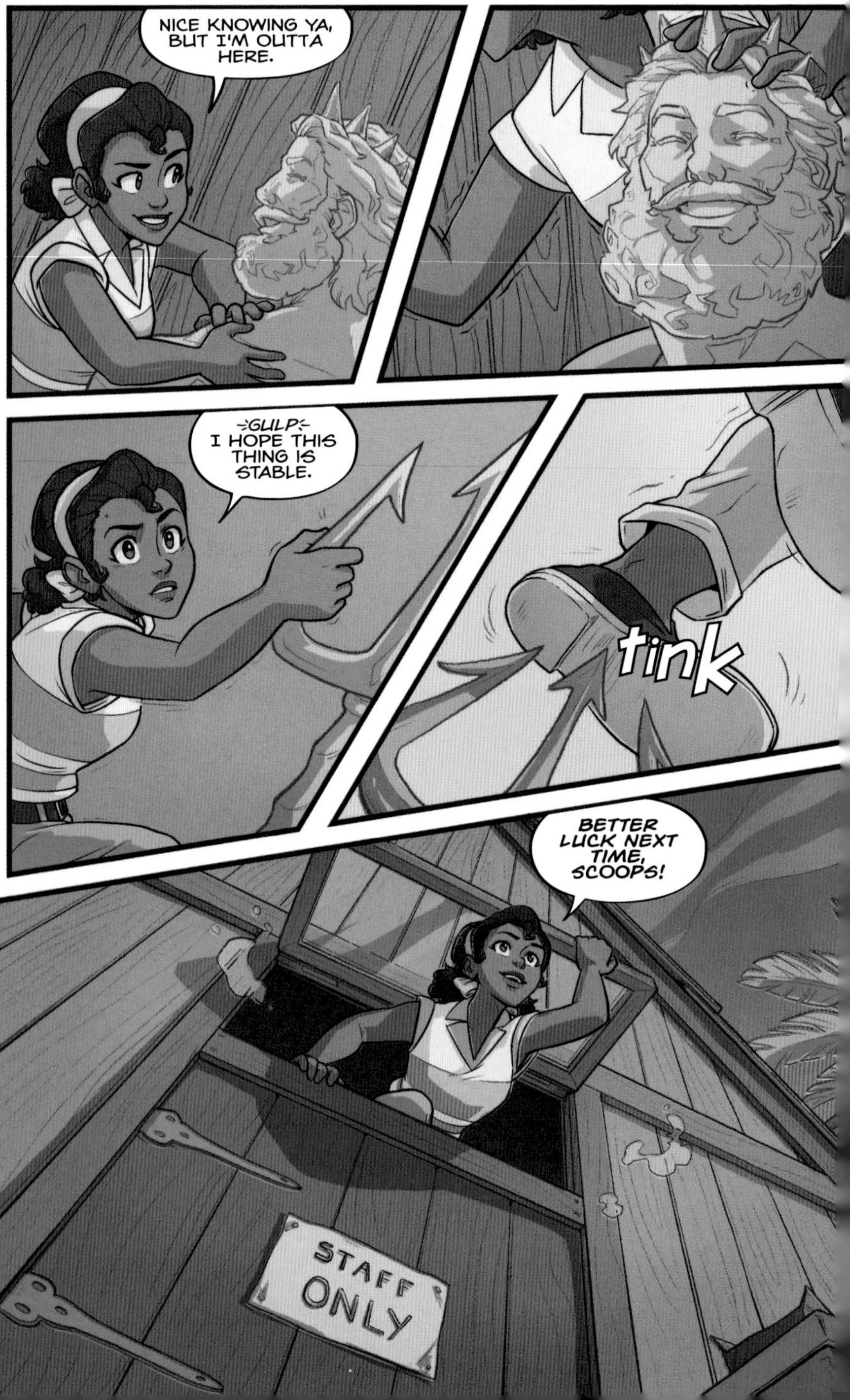
NICE KNOWING YA, BUT I'M OUTTA HERE.
GULP
I HOPE THIS THING IS STABLE.
tink
BETTER LUCK NEXT TIME, SCOOPS!
STAFF ONLY

A quick drop and I'm off. I've got to get to Scoops before he gets to Delphine or the movie set and starts causing trouble. I stumble into the entrance of the club and once again find myself in complete darkness. How and why are the lights out *again*? This time it feels doubly dark. At least no one is screaming. I follow the voices toward the set, using my flashlight as my guide.

"Turn the lights back on!" Mr. Davenport's booming voice fills the room. At least I can always count on Mr. Davenport to bestow his loud bark on the masses. I need to hurry up. I can't have Scoops roaming around. Too much at risk.

"Everyone!" I say. "There's a reporter on the loose somewhere inside. Scoops, show your face."

I realize, a second too late, that Scoops can't actually show his face because there are no lights. Oh well, I can't take back my words now. I just have to go with the flow.

There's a jostling. A crash. It's definitely the sound of shattering glass. It's hard to follow the action, but I keep moving my flashlight around, trying my best to pinpoint where the commotion is coming from.

"We got him," a voice says. I recognize the voice. It's Mike. I let out a sigh of relief. Thank goodness.

"He locked me in the shed in order to sneak in here," I say. Every flashlight shines on Scoops's face. He can't deny it.

"Okay, okay. I know this may look bad, but I have a very good explanation as to why I'm here," he says. Mike grabs Scoops's collar. He won't get away this time. "I got it from a reliable source that there's some shady business going on in relation to this very movie, Mr. Davenport, and that something big is going to happen as a result. Is it true, Mr. Davenport, that you stole a very precious gem from Powerhouse Productions and that the budget for *this* movie is so high that the bigwigs are itching to pull the plug? What do you have to say about that? Do you deny it?"

Mr. Davenport strolls over to Scoops and gets right in his face.

"Whoever you are talking to is feeding you baloney," he says.

"It's a good thing the lights turned off before he could see anything of importance," Walt chimes in. "Scoops, you might as well give it up. There's no story to tell."

"There's always a story," Scoops insists. "Right, Mr. Davenport?"

"Get him out of my sight. I better not see you anywhere near this set. Do you hear me? Or the person who will end up on the front page of your newspaper will be you."

"Hold on a minute. I'm telling you the truth. Someone is trying to—"

Scoops continues to yell out as they drag him off the set.

It takes a good fifteen minutes before the lights are turned back on, and when they are, I'm happy to see Delphine was shielded from any onlookers by an oversize hat concealing her face. Miss Dupart, Edna Blanchett, and the choreographer, Katherine Robbins, also stand in front of her, making sure Scoops couldn't see her.

"Everyone okay?" I ask.

"I'm ready to call it a night," Delphine says, taking off her robe. "But we need to make one last run at the scene. Come on, everyone. Let's do this. The end is near!"

"The movie business is always so full of surprises." Miss Dupart beams. She's probably having a way better time here than lounging by the pool at Crossed Palms. Miss Dupart adjusts her jangly bracelets and large rings while a worker places her on her mark, right in front of the tank.

Delphine is right. Now that Scoops is out of the way, there's only one more scene to film.

"We're already behind schedule, people. Let's shoot Delphine's close-up with the chapeau," Mr. Davenport says. "Let's go."

A crew member runs offstage to find the chapeau and place it back on Delphine. I notice Delphine begin to pace back and forth. She's reciting her long award-worthy speech meant to boost the morale of her mermaids before they go into battle with the sea creatures. Delphine asks for a run-through before the actual shoot. One more practice.

"My beautiful sisters. You are powerful and brave. Look not at this moment with dread," Delphine says, clutching her hand to her heart. "We have been here before, countless times. If there is anything I know, it is this: If you fight with the truth by your side, you can never lose."

The monologue continues on and on, and as it does, I notice a number of people around the set getting all misty-eyed. There's sniffling. Someone pulls out a handkerchief. And another. Soon there's not a dry eye in the room. Even I get caught up in her impassioned words. It's almost impossible not to. I, too, want to put some fins on and join her mermaid army!

"Wow. She really is amazing," I say.

Someone sniffles beside me. Even tough guy Mr. Davenport can't hide his emotions. But when I try to make eye contact with him and share this moment, he goes right back to being the Mr. Davenport I know. Tough and cold. But now I've confirmed his little secret. He has a soft spot.

"There's never a dull moment, huh, Mr. Davenport?" I say.

"Never a dull moment," he says, quickly wiping away a tear.

"That reporter's story was as full of holes as a block of Swiss cheese."

"I trust these sea creatures before I trust anything reported to me by someone named Scoops," he replies.

Now, if I'm not mistaken, I think Mr. Davenport just made a joke. How is that even possible? Who knew he had it in him?

"Well, you can't blame him for trying," I say. "Everyone in St. Pascal is excited about the movie. Maybe Scoops took his excitement to extreme levels, but at least we caught him before he could do any real harm."

"Here's a little advice: You can't trust a person with a pen and pad. They will always bend the truth."

Mr. Davenport has got it all wrong. Newspaper folks are like everyone else. They are doing their job. Sure, Scoops is crafty—the guy locked me in a shed, which I will never forgive him for—but he's desperate for gossip. Gossip is his job. He doesn't care about real news. I do respect his drive, though. It's exactly how I feel when I'm trying to crack a case; I'll do whatever it takes to uncover the truth.

"What's taking that kid so long?" Mr. Davenport asks.

The crew begins to get a little restless. Something is definitely amiss. Another person is sent back to check on the assistant getting the chapeau. Then another. Then one more.

Soon, Mr. Davenport gets fed up, and he storms away in their direction. I follow close by.

"What's the holdup?" he demands.

The workers are silent. They are afraid to say

anything. Mr. Davenport doesn't make it easy. You can feel he's about to blow any second.

"It's the Bejeweled Aqua Chapeau..." says an assistant, drenched in sweat. He steps forward.

"What about it?"

"We can't find it," he says. "We looked everywhere, Mr. Davenport. It's not here."

"Excuse me? What do you mean it's not here?" bellows Mr. Davenport.

This can't be happening. No way. There must be a mistake. It's not possible. How could anyone misplace the most valuable piece on set?

"The diamond-encrusted swimming cap has to be around here somewhere," I say. "Did you check the other room? Maybe someone hid it when Scoops got inside, as a safety precaution.".

"We've checked everywhere and with everyone. The Bejeweled Aqua Chapeau is nowhere to be found."

Mr. Davenport's face becomes fiery red. Oh no. This can't be.

"You better check again!" he shouts. The entire crew starts running amok.

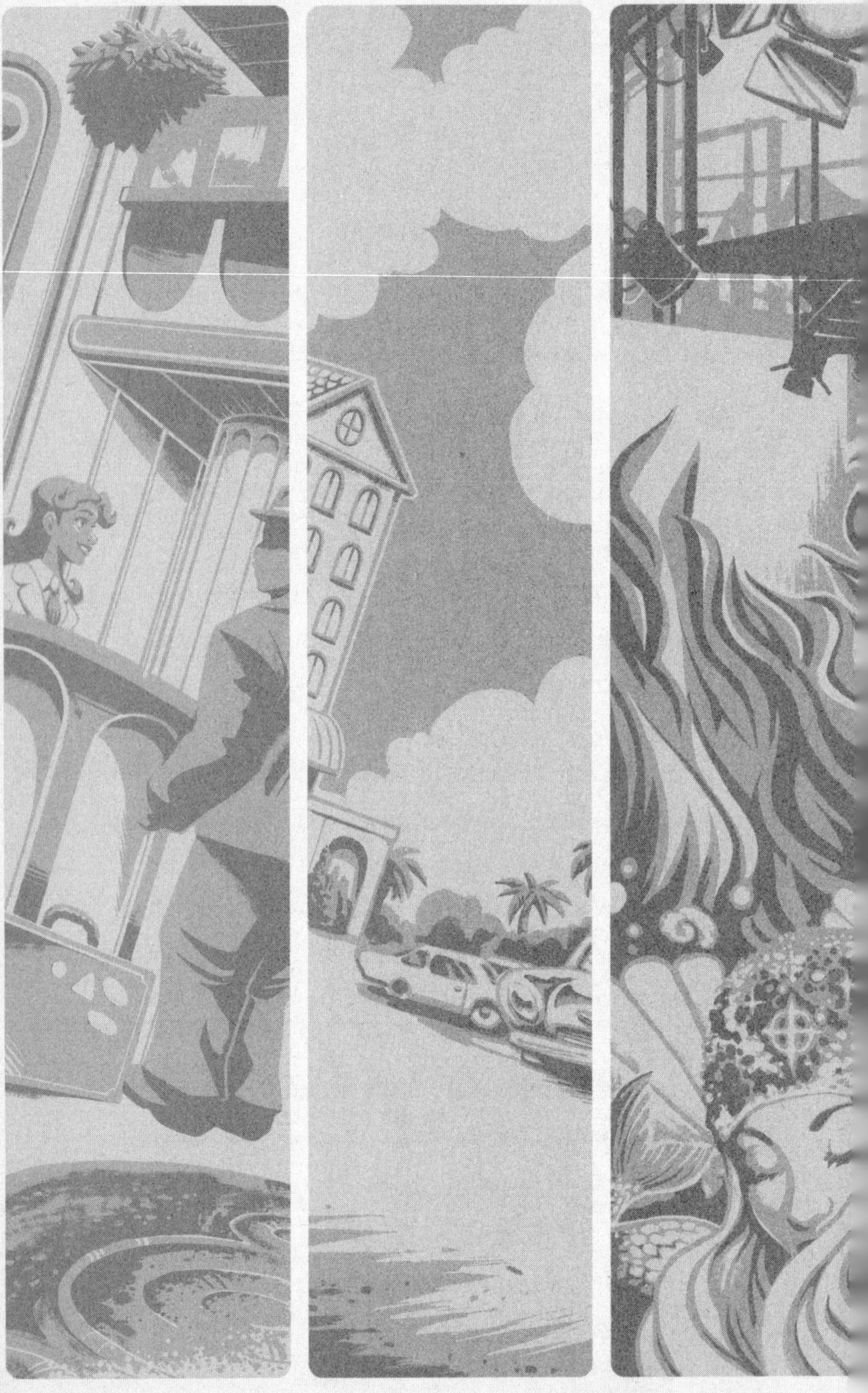

Chapter Ten

MR. DAVENPORT'S RAGE FORCES EVERYONE TO RUN around in circles trying to locate the bejeweled swimming cap. If there's anything I know, it's this: If the Bejeweled Aqua Chapeau is not where it was supposed to be, then it's certainly not "lost" somewhere in the club. It's abundantly clear that someone stole the Bejeweled Aqua Chapeau, but who?

"Keep looking!"

Walt hurries over and joins me in the already-crowded dressing room. Workers scramble to appease Mr. Davenport, who tosses items that look nothing like the chapeau all over the floor and off tables. Anger will never solve problems or get results. Sadly, Mr. Davenport is spiraling, and I don't see him calming down anytime soon.

"We've got to interview everyone who last saw or handled the diamond swimming cap," I say, pulling out my pad and pencil. "None of the workers should be allowed to leave. Don't you think, Walt?"

"Correct," Walt says. "Everyone! Let's form a line right here—"

"Have you two lost your minds?" Mr. Davenport yells. "Whoever took the diamond cap is probably outside right now making his getaway! And you two want to conduct a survey! This is your fault!"

Mr. Davenport points his finger, still knuckling his cigar, and jabs it at Walter's chest. Walt inhales every time Mr. Davenport punctuates his exclamations.

"Now, Mr. Davenport, we took every precaution to ensure the diamond swimming cap was safe," Walt defends himself. "No one could have predicted the blackouts. Now, if we can speak to the crew, we can create a timeline."

"Timeline! Timeline! It's pretty obvious what just happened," Mr. Davenport says. He continues to pick up items off tables and slam them back down, as if a powdered compact case would conceal a bejeweled swimming cap. Every time he does this, a crew member follows his movements, checking to see if

Mr. Davenport missed something while also cleaning up his messes. It's a bunch of hustle and bustle, causing more chaos than is warranted.

"You told me you've had experience with this type of product," Mr. Davenport continues. His face turns redder and redder. "You told me Crossed Palms has handled rare jewels before. Wasn't it your idea to film in the Mermaid Club? How did this come to pass? How?"

Walt starts to sweat. It's obvious this isn't his fault. I remember Walt saying Mr. Davenport is notorious for getting people fired. He's blown his top, and I can sense he's about to go down that very path. I can't allow this to happen. I have to distract Mr. Davenport and remind him we know what we are doing.

"Mr. Davenport, time is of the essence," I say. "Let's talk to the crew before they start forgetting what happened."

"Cecil, let them do their job," Delphine says, but Mr. Davenport continues shouting. He is in such a tantrum that he has forgotten about the star of the movie as well as the entire cast who are tired and waiting patiently. Delphine's hair drips wet, forming a puddle on the floor. She trembles a bit.

Mr. Davenport finally starts to calm down. Not entirely, but it's progress. He focuses away from Walt and yells at a crew member instead.

"Someone should take her back to the hotel," I say. "Don't you think, Mr. Davenport? The longer she stays here, the more likely Ms. Lucerne will catch a cold."

"Yeah, yeah. Someone get her out of here."

Mr. Davenport will not be satisfied until the chapeau falls from the ceiling and lands, *plop*, right on his head.

"I'll be leaving now, Cecil. Good luck," Delphine says. Edna hands Delphine an oversize robe. "What would I do without you?" Delphine says to Edna.

"This would never have happened at Powerhouse," Edna replies with a scowl.

Mr. Davenport doesn't bother looking her way. He's much too busy bossing people around. Although she wears large sunglasses, I bet underneath them Delphine is just as upset as Mr. Davenport, only she doesn't need to scream at people to express herself.

I walk out of the room with Delphine.

"Before you go," I say, "can I ask you a couple of questions?"

Unfortunately, everyone is a potential suspect right

now. The only way to eliminate suspects is by finding out where they were in the last thirty minutes. There's no clear-cut reason why Delphine would want to steal the Bejeweled Aqua Chapeau, but you just never know.

"Of course," Delphine says. "Let's go over here for a little bit of privacy."

Delphine and I find a quiet corner in front of the mermaid tank. The glow from the lights emanating from inside the tank gives an ominous feel.

I miss when the club was just a club. When I could swing by after work, chat with Mike about poetry, and see my mother swimming. When friends and visitors could sit at a table and enjoy the mermaid show. But currently, the club is in a state of disarray. Too many huge wires everywhere. The dressing room too crowded and messy. Oversize cameras abandoned for the time being. Lights. Costumes. Nothing is what it seems.

I clear out a chair filled with movie equipment and urge Delphine to take a seat.

"Can you tell me when the last time you saw the Bejeweled Aqua Chapeau was?"

Delphine tucks a long, wet strand of hair behind her ear. Her makeup is *still* intact, which is pretty amazing considering how long she's been underwater today.

"Well, let me think. After we returned from our break, Cecil was still so annoyed with me," she says. "We had one last shot with the diamond cap, wasn't it? It's hard to keep track."

Delphine is right. Before Mr. Davenport sent me to work outside, and before Scoops locked me in the shed, Delphine was about to film scenes in the tank.

"Do you remember who placed the Bejeweled Aqua Chapeau on your head?"

She frowns and stares down at her perfectly painted toenails. This is really key. There's a good chance whoever handed her the cap last would have seen or heard something suspicious. Every little detail can lead to a clue.

"I remember still being angry with Cecil. He can be so pigheaded sometimes. I remember thinking to myself, *This tank is much too cold.* I also kept thinking, how does your mother tolerate it?" she says. I can practically see her thoughts churning. "*Hmmm.* The swimming cap was definitely not cooperating in the water."

I, too, remember Mom spending most of her time helping Delphine keep the cap from coming off while they did their underwater flips. This was right before Mr. Davenport kicked me off the set.

"Yes. I stepped out of the tank after the cap once again slipped off my head," she says. "There really wasn't any point in continuing. He was being ridiculous."

I can't argue with Delphine on that.

She furrows her brows. "Edna placed the cap back on my head. I remember because she inserted a couple more bobby pins to help secure it in place."

"Were you in the water when the blackout happened?"

"No. We just finished getting the shot. It wasn't perfect, but I somehow managed," she says. "Your mother was gracious enough to help me take the cap off. It was so tight on my head that I could feel my temples pounding."

"So Mom had the cap. And then what?"

"The blackout! The whole place turned dark. No, wait a minute," she says. "That's not completely true. Just before the lights went out, your mother took the cap and walked back to the dressing room. I'm guessing to make sure it was placed in a safe spot."

"*Hmmm.*" This is interesting. If Mom was the last person to see the swimming cap, she might have seen some random person walking in. Who knows? Mom may hold the key to solving this case. This just might be a family affair!

"The lights went out. Do you recall seeing anyone? Anything out of the ordinary? Anything suspicious?"

"There was that one reporter. Besides him, everyone really was truly lovely today. Everyone. There wasn't one person who stood out as suspicious or conniving."

Of course, Scoops. He's on the top of my list for sure. Maybe he was some sort of red herring, a distraction. Maybe he's working in cahoots with an international diamond-stealing gang. I'll need to talk to Scoops. *Pronto.*

"Delphine. Think. Sometimes a person who treats you nicely can have ulterior motives," I say. I hate this about people, but it's true. Diamonds can make a person go slightly mad from their brilliance. They are a quick financial fix, too.

Delphine shakes her head.

"I can't think of a soul," she says. "If I do, I promise to let you know."

I thank Delphine for her time and walk her toward the secret exit. I locate the beekeeper's uniform, right where I left it last. I help Delphine into the outfit.

"I hope they find the Bejeweled Aqua Chapeau," she says before placing the beekeeper's hat on.

"Me too," I say, and give her a thumbs-up. One of the security guards gently takes her arm and leads her out to the car waiting to return her to Crossed Palms.

I jump back into the fray.

Walter interviews most of the camera crew. Because the extras were dismissed earlier, there aren't that many people left to speak to. The only other workers on the set right before the blackout—and Scoops's ill-timed appearance—were the costume designer, Edna Blanchett; the choreographer, Katherine Robbins; Miss Dupart; and one of the dancers who works with Mom. And Mom, of course. While Walt continues grilling the crew, I take the opportunity to speak to the choreographer.

"Ms. Robbins, do you have a moment? Just want to ask a couple of questions."

The choreographer has a ballerina's body. All lithe and long. While we are talking, she continues to move, tapping her leg or pointing a toe. It must be a nervous dancer habit, unless of course she's guilty. Then this is a guilty dancer habit.

"Where were you during the blackout?"

"I was standing by Delphine and the dancers.

Counting off." Katherine has a heavy New York accent. While she talks she places her hair in a bun and sticks a bobby pin in.

"The lights went out. Then what?"

"The lights went out, and I did what anyone would do; I waited for the lights to turn back on," she says. "I let the professionals handle it. This isn't my first time at the rodeo. You have to be flexible when shooting on location."

I pay attention to her fingers and her movements. Sometimes you can see if a person is telling the truth. They might appear nervous, start to sweat, or avoid eye contact. She doesn't do any of those things.

"When did you last see the Bejeweled Aqua Chapeau?" I ask.

"On Delphine as she finished shooting the dance routine. She had the cap on. I helped her step out of the tank and it took all three of us to get the cap off her head," she says, pointing and flexing her foot. "When we finally did, Ms. Bell took the cap backstage. Then—poof—the lights went out."

Her story totally lines up with Delphine's.

"You didn't go backstage?"

"No, I didn't. Just ask Edna. She was there right beside me," she says. "Is that all?"

I'll definitely want to speak to Edna next. "One more thing, Katherine. Did you see or hear anything?"

"The only thing I heard was Mr. Davenport screaming like a garbage truck in the early morning."

Interesting. I take it Katherine is not a big Cecil fan. Enemies can make some passionate decisions, like stealing a diamond cap to sabotage a movie. But how would she have done it? She was next to Delphine the entire time.

Edna does not want to be bothered. She is too busy packing away the costumes and the mermaid outfits. She keeps muttering to herself in French.

"*Excusez-moi*," I say. The look of disgust on Edna's face tells me she does not like me trying to speak French.

"I just have a couple of questions to ask you," I say, and show her my pad.

"There is no time," she says, trying to dismiss me with a flick of a wrist. I stand in front of the mermaid skirt she was just about to grab.

"This won't take long, I promise. Where were you when the lights went out?"

Edna Blanchett lets out a long sigh. "By Delphine, where I always am. Right by her side for more than ten years." The costume designer continues to pack her costumes.

"Did you hear or see anything? And what about the diamond cap?"

Edna places the mermaid skirt on the table before her. "I wish I had never made the Bejeweled Aqua Chapeau. They don't deserve it."

She didn't really answer my question. I ask again.

"I saw and heard nothing. The cap was taken backstage, then everything went dark. I was by Delphine. That is all."

She is not a very agreeable suspect. Then again, it's late and everyone is tired, including me. Walt and I exchange notes. One of my many great detective skills is my neat, legible handwriting. Walter, not so much, but that's fine because I've learned to read his chicken scratch. I start to read back what Delphine told me and wait for Walt to give input.

"Everyone pretty much has an alibi. The blackout lasted only a few minutes, not nearly long enough for a person to run back to the dressing room, in the dark, without falling," Walt says. "Whoever stole the cap knew exactly where it would be kept and was able to leave during the blackout without being detected."

"I doubt that it was an inside job. It must be Scoops Malone. No one else locked me in the shed while working on his or her 'story,'" I say. "He was desperate enough to do that; maybe he's desperate enough to steal the cap for a front-page headline."

Walt doesn't agree. "He left empty-handed. I saw to it myself. He also wasn't here long enough to venture anywhere but a few feet from the entrance before we nailed him. You've got to remember; the place was completely dark."

A blackout. Another blown fuse or did someone purposely cause the club to go dark?

"I'm going to look out back for more clues," I say. Walt continues with his interviews.

There are so many different ways to generate electricity into the club, but only one fuse box. It's not far from where Scoops locked me in the shed, so I walk gingerly over to it and use my magnifying glass to search for clues, from the obvious to the almost invisible. Evidence can come in all shapes and sizes, like a receipt, a tossed cigarette, or even hair. Anything at all. The dirt is dry enough that I can see a few shoe prints. So many workers dealt with the fuse box today, especially after the blackouts, so it will be hard to pinpoint any differences.

"Hold on. What is this?" I say.

I kneel down closer to the ground. I find several footprints, but these sets of footprints don't quite follow the same pattern as the others. For starters, the footprints show toes with tiny wings attached to them. Are they the footprints of an animal? Alligators, geckos, and birds all call St. Pascal home, but these prints are kind of strange. Whatever or whoever walked behind here earlier exhibited fabulous and unusual webbed toes. I follow the footprints and they lead right to the secret back entrance of the club. This is definitely a clue.

Strangely, the footprints show someone entering the club but not exiting the same way. Where did the culprit run to afterward? They surely didn't leave the same way they came in, but there would have been no way for them to exit through the main entrance. I would have run into them as I was entering the club, and I didn't see anyone.

Unless...

Unless, once inside, the thief was hiding in the dark somewhere, and when I came running through the front door, they could have easily exited. I go back to the front entrance of the club and search the area with my magnifying glass. The thief could have dropped an item while they rushed out of here.

I find something! More strange footprints similar to the ones near the back entrance. The suspect must have bided his or her time until the coast was clear to storm out of the entrance. My guess is they took advantage of both the blackout and the Scoops Malone distraction. This person knew what they were doing and had a plan to steal the cap. This wasn't random. I take a couple more steps, and I notice something white.

"What is this?" I shine my flashlight on it. A worn white leather glove. I search for the other one of the pair but come up with nothing.

Hmmm. Whoever dropped this glove surely must have its companion? And who wears leather gloves in June? In Florida? In this heat? Whoever wore these gloves wanted to avoid leaving any fingerprints. Suspicious. Very suspicious.

I tuck the glove into my pocket and write down in my pad my latest findings. I can't wait to share my discoveries with Walter. As I continue, I consider that the person who stole the Bejeweled Aqua Chapeau must have walked around shoeless at some point to avoid making any noise. But how would they have left the club without being detected? And does this all tie back to the Crossed Palms? So many questions and not enough time to answer them. I'm missing something. But what?

Inside, Mr. Davenport is just beginning his own interrogation. His approach involves accusing the person closest to him of failing to do their job and then yelling at the next person and the next. What a gentleman, right? (That's sarcasm.)

As soon as Mr. Davenport sees me, he makes a beeline in my direction.

"I'll have you know that *your* mother was the last one seen with the chapeau." Mr. Davenport points his cigar in my face, which I do *not* appreciate.

Walt rushes over to my side, shaking his head back and forth slightly, as if to say, *Turn around—you don't want to be here for this.* What is going on? Mr. Davenport continues to scream about my mother and the chapeau. Walt places a hand on my shoulder and that's when things start to click together. I totally get it. Mr. Davenport has really jumped in the deep end.

He cannot be serious. Mr. Davenport can't possibly think my mother has anything to do with the missing diamond cap.

"Is it not true that your mother was the last person to take the cap back to the dressing room? No one else saw her give the cap to anyone else. She said she secured it." Mr. Davenport is on a horrible roll. "I told her not to touch the cap, but for whatever reason, she couldn't keep her mitts off it. Why? Because she wanted the cap for herself."

I can't believe the words coming out of his mouth. He's a fool. I want to take his cigar and crush it so he can't use it to point in people's faces.

"Now, hold on a minute," Walt says. "Ms. Bell has been working at the Mermaid Club for years. She was vetted to work on this movie not only by the Crossed Palms Resort but by the very owners of this club. She has absolutely no reason to steal such a valuable piece of work, especially at the cost of her whole livelihood and her family."

Mr. Davenport won't stop. "It's precisely because of her family she would do it," he says. "Everyone always needs more money. I know people. Everyone is capable of corruption."

"You're wrong. She would never steal a thing," I say. "Mom would never jeopardize her job. Our life. *Me*."

He turns to Walt with a growl. "If you do not do

something to rectify this, it will be your head," he says. "You are a detective, aren't you? I insist you question her and her motives."

Mr. Davenport points to Mom, who has sat listening to this entire conversation, looking very worried. Walt is horrified. I'm horrified. This can't be happening.

"Do something," Mr. Davenport says.

Walt doesn't know where to turn or look.

"Walt, you can't be serious!" I say.

"I'm sorry, Goldie." Walt walks over to Mike. Seconds later, they call Mom for questioning.

My stomach is about to drop. This can't be happening. Walt can't possibly have it in him to convince the Mermaid Club owners, my mom's bosses for so many years, to not only get her fired but to also send her to the cops. What is this movie madness? I wish Mr. Davenport and this entire creature feature had never come to Crossed Palms. The longest movie shoot day ever has now turned into the most horrible day, all because of a diamond swimming cap and a man who can't see beyond his fury.

But I won't get angry. I need to think fast, act fast, and find the thief!

Chapter Eleven

MR. DAVENPORT HAS VEHEMENTLY DECIDED MOM IS guilty of stealing the bejeweled swimming cap. Yet Mom has absolutely no motive to take it. Even if Mom decided she needed the Bejeweled Aqua Chapeau in order to become the Queen of the Mermaids or to get rich quick, how would she unload such a thing without everyone finding out? St. Pascal is a small town. She couldn't just show up at Jim's Emporium with a diamond swimming cap and ask if he wanted to buy it. Mom wouldn't jeopardize the things she loves, especially her daughter and her job. Mom loves working at the Mermaid Club.

Mike places his hand on Mom's shoulder. She nods to him. I can't read their lips but I can imagine the exchange. Mom grabs her things and walks over to me.

"I'll be heading over to the precinct with Mike. I

want you to go straight to your dad's. Understand?" She places her hand under my chin. "Babe. No worries. This will all be sorted out soon. Promise me you will go to Crossed Palms."

"I promise, Mom," I say, and give her a hug. "I'm not worried. I'm determined."

Mr. Davenport has a smug look on his face. If I weren't just a sixteen-year-old girl, I would give him a piece of my mind. But that wouldn't help. Plus, it would probably only get Mom in more trouble. Mr. Davenport thinks he's got it all figured out, but I know in my gut that he is dead wrong, which means there is still a case to be solved. The sooner I find out who stole the diamond cap, the quicker my mom will be cleared.

"Walt, I need to go," I say. I don't wait for him to respond. Time is of the essence.

"Now, hold on there," Walt says. "I'm going to take you to your dad. It's what your mom wants."

"But, Walt! It's important I speak to Scoops Malone. And what about the weird footprints and—"

"It's been a long night," he says. "Yes, we have to process everything we've seen. Go over clues. Devise a plan for tomorrow. You also have to rest."

My engine is revving up, not slowing down, especially now with Mr. Davenport trying to place the blame on my innocent mom. I need to solve this case ASAP. Jobs are at stake. Entire careers. Reputations. Most important, my mom's reputation. She's spent all her life working hard, taking care of me, making sure I'm well fed, and buying me the right capris (ones that have tons of pockets and allow me to climb or run). She's my everything. And I've only known her to be honest and fair.

As Walt drives us slowly up Lime Street, I go over the events from the past two days, from the minute I met Mr. Davenport in Walt's office to Delphine almost tripping in front of Crossed Palms to the last blackout. Each of these moments must be connected in some way. They can't all be coincidences.

"What is going to happen to Mom?"

Walt keeps his eyes on the road, but I know he's also thinking really hard. He would never sugarcoat anything. Being a detective means uncovering the ugly, and sometimes hard, truth. I don't expect him to hold back now.

"What do we do when we are presented with evidence?" he asks.

"We log it down."

"Mr. Davenport has no proof of your mom taking the Bejeweled Aqua Chapeau," he says. "He only has his anger and a lot of hot air."

"And a stinky cigar," I say.

"Exactly. Your mom will be taken to the precinct. She'll share what she heard and saw, which she has already shared with me. They will let her go, and that will be the end of that for now. She'll probably be fired from the movie set."

"No movie! I can't believe it," I say. "Mom's Hollywood dreams crushed before they even make it on to the big screen."

"The important thing for us to do is to keep our heads up and our eyes wide open. The sooner we can find out the real culprit the better it will be for your mom, for me, and for everyone involved," he adds. "Now tell me what you found."

I tell Walt about the unusual footprints and the white leather glove. I also tell him about my theory. Walt slows down the car as we approach the entrance to the Crossed Palms. It's late. There's not the same level of commotion as earlier, with sea creatures and bejeweled swimming caps making their entrances. Instead, it's just a few guests taking a peaceful stroll on the grounds. I wonder if Delphine has settled in by now, and whether she knows anything about what has happened to my mom. I would like to think she would be upset.

"Scoops Malone must have known about this

incident, don't you think?" I ask. "He was so persistent in getting into the club. He must have something to do with the robbery."

"I wouldn't be so quick to judge. Think of motivation. Why would Scoops Malone want the swimming cap?"

"It doesn't pay to be a writer?"

Walt laughs at this.

"To steal something as extravagant as the bejeweled swimming cap, Scoops would have had to line up a buyer right away," he says. "Keeping the cap under wraps would be hard to do."

Hmmm. Walt might be right. Who would be motivated to steal the cap?

He parks the car. "It's time to let the evidence you've collected start percolating inside your head. Try to get some sleep and hopefully some answers will come to us by morning," Walt says. "Hey, your mother is beloved and we all believe her. Mr. Davenport's loudness will be shut down by the truth."

"Yes," I say. "You're right. Mom didn't do a thing, and Mr. Davenport is going to know soon enough. Tomorrow is the perfect day to solve this mystery."

"Get some rest, Goldie. I'll see you tomorrow."

I bypass the entrance of the hotel and head across the way to the cottage. The wail of a saxophone can be heard from our door. After a long day, Dad likes to listen to music from his large collection of jazz albums.

"Hey, Dad," I say. He places his glass down on the coffee table. His suit jacket hangs across the back of a dining room chair. His tie is slightly loosened.

"Just got off the phone with Mom," he says. Dad pats the sofa, urging me to sit beside him. "I think you deserve a big bowl of ice cream. What do you think?"

"Yeah." I slump beside him. "Vanilla ice cream would be amazing."

"One bowl of ice cream for my little girl," he says. Before he gets up, Dad gives me a long hug. I really needed it and I really need the ice cream. I take my time, enjoying every sweet spoonful.

"Mom says you are not to worry. She will be fine. The owners of the Mermaid Club reassured her that this is only a technicality until things are cleared up," he says. I take another large spoonful.

"Ouch ouch ouch!" Brain freeze.

Can today get any worse? I can't even enjoy my ice cream. I push the bowl aside. "Dad, what if I can't find the person who stole the diamond swimming cap? What if they blame Mom and she ends up going to jail?"

"There are way too many 'what-ifs' happening. Slow down your mind. It's the end of the workday and we should not bring our problems with us to the pillow. There is simply no room for them on there. Is there?"

I shake my head.

"Come. Lay your head right here." He points to his heart. "Listen to Charlie Parker play his tune. Do you follow the notes? Let the melody soothe you. Go on, close your eyes."

My head feels heavy against his chest. Before I can even stop myself, I let out a bit of a snore. Oops.

"Time for sleep," Dad says. Although he doesn't carry me to bed, he does the thing he always used to do when he tucked me in: Dad gives me a kiss on the forehead.

I RIDE MY BIKE DOWN LIME STREET, STRAIGHT TO THE office of the *Daily Gazette*, which is located in a plain, unimpressive storefront. Nothing about it screams *news* or that a reporter works there. You would only know from the small sign that says, GOT A TIP? CALL SCOOPS MALONE.

The door is slightly ajar and all I can hear is the clanking of a typewriter. I'm expecting to see a newsroom full of reporters on the phones, gathering tips and interviewing leads. Instead, the office consists of a small desk, a file drawer, and copies of newspapers haphazardly thrown up on the wall. A fan swirls mostly hot air. At the solitary desk sits Scoops Malone, hunched over the phone while simultaneously typing. It appears the *Daily Gazette* is a one-man job.

"I'll be with you in a sec," Scoops says, writing down a message on the back of an envelope. When Scoops finishes with his conversation, he turns around and is slightly startled to see me.

"Well, if it isn't Goldie Vance! You are up bright and early this morning. How are you doing?" Scoops turns the envelope over to the other side. "I heard a really important diamond cap went missing last night. Do you care to comment?"

The guy never stops. "No can do. In fact, I'm here to ask *you* questions," I say. "I figured you owe me, especially after the whole locking-me-up-in-a-shed bit. You do remember that, don't you?"

"Now, now. There are no hard feelings. Are there, Goldie?" Scoops places the palms of his hands together as in prayer. "You can't blame a guy for trying, right? I just wanted to capture the great Delphine Lucerne in action. She was filming there yesterday. Wasn't she?"

I have no idea if Scoops really knows Delphine was filming in the Mermaid Club or if he is just testing to see if I will answer. He probably has proof, but my job is to keep Delphine Lucerne's secret a secret. So I refuse to confirm or deny. Instead, I do what Scoops does. I smile widely until we are both just standing there, eyes wide and making funny faces, waiting for the other person to blink.

"When I was ten years old, I challenged a boy staying at the Crossed Palms Resort to a staring contest," I say. "He was from Lubbock, Texas, and he swore he was the state champion in staring. The trick to staring is to not think about how long or what the person is thinking of as they are staring. The trick is to think of nothing. *Zen* is what Mom called it one day while we were gardening. I'm almost sure the boy is still crying over losing. He finally blinked after five long minutes."

Scoops continues to grin. In fact, his grin might have grown even more. I go Zen until I notice the slight twitch from his bottom lip. He's about to break and I know it.

And as predicted, Scoops looks away.

"You are good, for a kid anyway," he says.

"I'm good, period."

Scoops reclines in his chair and places his hands on the back of his head.

"What do you know about what happened last night after the blackout?" I ask.

Scoops's grin turns into a glower. He rolls up his sleeves and shows me a black and blue with a few scratches.

"I became personally acquainted with the street after being kicked out of the club, if that's what you are talking about."

I'm sure that was Mike giving Scoops the ol' heave-ho. Walt doesn't believe in roughing up anyone, but sometimes Mike needs to take action with the men and women who come into the club and get aggressive. I get a tiny bit of pleasure knowing Scoops got a taste of his own medicine. He deserves it for being such a busybody and locking me up in the shed.

"Did you also forget this?" I pull out the white glove. Scoops gives me a quizzical look.

"Leather gloves are not my style, kid," he says.

"Oh yeah? Are you sure about that? Maybe they are your partner's."

Scoops shakes his head. "Partner? That's a big *NO*. I like to ride solo. Easier to get in and out of situations alone."

Scoops picks up the glove. "I bet you Jim's Emporium sells theses by the dozens. You should ask him about the gloves."

The phone rings and Scoops answers it. "What you got for me?" he says. He scribbles on the envelope. "Uh-huh... Yup... Are you sure about that?... Got it."

He slams down the phone.

"Can you confirm Delphine Lucerne is the one shooting at the Mermaid Club?" he asks. "We both know she's there. My only job is to take a picture of her for the *Gazette*. No picture and no one really cares. At least let me know she's there."

As much as I hate Mr. Davenport for accusing Mom of stealing the diamond cap and for treating Delphine so coldly, I know how to keep a secret, and I've never been the type who squeals. I took an oath and my word is as good as gold. But perhaps I can offer a little hint, enough for Scoops to give up some information.

"I will not confirm or deny the name Delphine Lucerne," I say. "I will say this: A big-time movie star is filming. My question to you is, how did you know about the stolen object, and do you know who stole it and why?"

Scoops ponders my question.

"Well, that's the million-dollar question, isn't it?"

he says, chuckling to himself. "My sources say the stolen movie prop may just be a decoy. There are other more nefarious impending threats," he says. "That's all I'm going to say. Gotta go! I've got a hot tip I've got to chase down."

"Threat? What do you mean? Who stole the Bejeweled Aqua Chapeau? Do you know?"

"Goldie, I like you. You've got chutzpah, and that will take you far in this business," he says, all the while gathering his camera and pad and pencils. "Can I offer you a piece of advice? You have to look beyond the normal suspects. For this case you are going to have to dive in the deep end to uncover the truth."

He turns off the fan and hides the typewriter underneath his desk.

"Do you know how to swim?" Scoops asks.

"Yeah."

"Then it'll be a cinch. Good luck."

And like that, he escorts me out of his office and heads to his car.

Swimming? Scoops has given me a clue. It's now on me to decipher his cryptic message into something that actually makes sense.

Chapter Twelve

THE BRAIN FOOD CAPABLE OF AIDING ME IN THIS MOST difficult time can only be found at the Deep End.

"I'll need pork sliders, french fries, and a root beer float," I say. "Did I mention french fries? Double up on the fries."

"Extra fries?" Cheryl says. "This is very serious."

Cheryl and Rob sit opposite from me in the booth. They're both wearing their Crossed Palms uniforms. I'm not technically working today. Dad said I could take the day off, but we both knew I would not be lounging by the pool or doing anything relaxing. I've been nonstop. I can't stop thinking of Mom and jail. That alone had me pedaling all over St. Pascal in the hopes of cracking the case. But this pit stop at the Deep End is necessary. I need to refuel, and I need huddle time with my friends.

"I called this emergency meeting because you are the only two people who can help clear my thoughts," I say.

"And your fries," Rob adds.

"That, too," I say. "Cheryl must have updated you on the whole 'Dolphin and Shark Face' thing. Correct?"

"I think so," Rob says. "Shark Face is bad, right?"

Cheryl smacks him softly on his back. "How many times do I have to explain it?"

"Dolphin is a big movie star, and she's been filming a big movie right here in St. Pascal," I whisper, making sure no one at the Deep End hears me. The diner is jam-packed. Tourists, movie extras, and the regulars mingle around, creating a kaleidoscope of orchestrated mayhem. I'm used to it, but with Mom being accused of stealing the diamond swimming cap, I can't help scrutinizing everyone and everything.

"But that's not what is important. What's really important is someone stole the, um, 'Fish Bait,' and Shark Face is blaming my mom for it," I say. "I need to find the real thief, clear my mother's name, and save the day. All in that order. And *pronto*."

Rob whistles. "Hence the fries."

"Exactly."

"I'm really sorry to hear about your mom," Cheryl says. "Walt spent most of this morning in Mr. Maple's office. You can guess the rest."

I sure can. Not only did Walt get chewed out by Mr. Davenport, but he got another chunk bitten off by our boss. When it rains, it pours.

"Before we move on, what in the world is the Fish Bait?" Rob asks. Walt was kind enough to slip me a picture of the dazzling cap before he went off to work, and I went out to question Scoops Malone. I show the diamond swimming cap to Rob and Cheryl.

"Yowza," Rob says. "Someone sporting Fish Bait at their next pool party will definitely get noticed. Don't you think?"

"If I had the Fish Bait, I would trade it for something truly valuable, like paying for college," Cheryl says. "Something of actual value."

Rob and Cheryl start to imagine what they would do with the swimming cap. Rob wants a really cool convertible in white with tail fins on the bumper, so when he starts the engine, tiny explosions go off. This is all very insightful, but not at all helpful, considering Mom is still up the creek and I can't stop stuffing my mouth with fries.

"Hey! Can we concentrate for a sec?" I say. "Who would take the Fish Bait and why?"

Cheryl leans over and grabs a french fry. "What do you got, Goldie?"

I pull out my notebook, open it up, and scan the pages.

"I've got this white leather glove. A bunch of strange footprints and mysterious blackouts," I say. "And no witnesses."

Rob and I dig into the fries.

C'mon, fries, do your magic!

"Doesn't seem like much to me," Rob says, stating the obvious.

"That's not true. What do you expect? A note with a picture of the person who took the Fish Bait?" Cheryl says, slightly annoyed.

"I also spoke to the reporter Scoops Malone. I thought he was at the top of my list of potential thieves, but after speaking to him I'm not too sure," I say. "He swears there's some sort of foul play afoot."

"See. You do have clues," Cheryl says.

I'm glad Cheryl is sticking up for me. I was starting to have doubts.

"Who would steal the Fish Bait? And why, aside from being desperate for money?" Rob asks.

"Jealousy," Cheryl says. "I remember at school when I was in fifth grade, my nemesis, Ginger Adams, was getting perfect scores on every single one of our science quizzes, just like me. I wished more than anything in the world that she would get just one question wrong. Okay, maybe two...or three. It never happened. Anyway, what I am trying to say is maybe there's someone who wanted to be Dolphin. A person who would have done anything."

I think hard about the people on set. When I spoke to Delphine last, she was so keen in thanking everyone. She couldn't think of a single person who stood out as being mean or suspicious. I can't think of anyone, either. And yet, why was it that her swimming cap kept coming off her head? Isn't that strange? The one important aspect of her costume couldn't stay put. What about all that Hollywood magic? I've seen crazier things stay on actors' and actresses' heads. *Hmmm.*

"There was this one strange thing. The Fish Bait kept falling off her head. It was as if it had a mind of its own," I say. "Of all the things on Dolphin, the Fish Bait was the most important."

"Who is in charge of that?" asks Rob.

"The costume designer!"

Could Edna Blanchett possibly have anything to do with this?

"Why would a costume designer want to sabotage Dolphin?" Rob asks. "Her entire job is making sure everyone looks great. Don't you think?"

"Envy is a green-eyed monster," says Cheryl.

Edna Blanchett. When I first met her, she wasn't too keen about her working environment. Perhaps she was hired away from her previous job, just like Delphine. I'll have to find out. The only person who would know this is Delphine herself.

I look down, and the large plate of french fries is practically empty. How did that happen?

"I guess we were all really hungry."

A girl walks past us holding the latest edition of *Life* magazine. On the cover is Delphine with the question IS DELPHINE HAPPY? A strange headline since the photo of Delphine shows her with the widest grin, her eyes sparkling. The press really loves to create drama. Case in point: Scoops Malone and his determination to out Delphine as the star of this new movie.

"Maybe the gloves belong to Edna Blanchett?" I say. "Dolphin might be protecting her."

"Why do you say that?" Rob asks, searching for the last bits of fries. I'm not judging; those are the best, the crispiest.

"I don't know. It's like a gut thing." I pat my full belly. "I need to speak to Dolphin."

"The crew spent most of this morning transferring their equipment over to the beach," Cheryl says. "I had to deal with directing at least fifty sea creatures over there, dressed in their sea creature–esque costumes. It was a thing."

That means Delphine will be shooting the highly anticipated battle scene on the beach. I heard someone say it was going to be *epic*, and that it's the scene in which Delphine leads an army of mermaids, and that there would be hundreds of extras charging the sands with her. Any other time and I would be so excited about watching such a grand movie-making experience. Right now all I can think about is Mom.

"Did either of you ever want to be a movie star?" I ask.

Rob shakes his head. "No way. I'm living my dream driving other people's cars."

"Don't be silly," Cheryl says. "Who doesn't want to be on the big screen? Remember when Alan Shepard was on the *Larry Laughs Variety Show*?"

Rob drops the tiny fry he was about to pop in his mouth. Every time Cheryl mentions her astronaut crush, Alan Shepard, he almost always fumbles. It's hard to compete for Cheryl's affection when her eyes are set on a man whose life mission involves traveling to the moon.

"I don't know. I mean, he didn't seem all that talented on the show," Rob mutters to himself.

"You can't be serious," Cheryl replies. "His hidden talent is playing the kazoo. The kazoo!"

Cheryl can't contain herself. After witnessing Alan exhibit his skills, she insisted we learn how to play the kazoo. Rob agreed to but I could tell he didn't love it.

"Hidden talents or not, being a performer is extremely hard work," I say. "Mom may not be a big-time fish like Dolphin, but she's a big deal in my world."

Cheryl and Rob agree.

"You're right," Cheryl says. "How can we help?"

"Cheryl, I need you to find out how many extras are staying at the hotel. I know it's a lot but we need a breakdown. Maybe someone's name will stand out when you're looking."

"And what do I get to do?"

Rob has the most important part.

"I need to speak to Dolphin," I say. "So I need you to find a way to buy me time with her."

"And how am I supposed to do that?"

"Rob, I'm almost a hundred percent sure you have a hidden talent," I say. "Something way cooler than the kazoo."

Rob stands up a little straighter.

"I'm on it."

I knew I could count on my friends. It's go time.

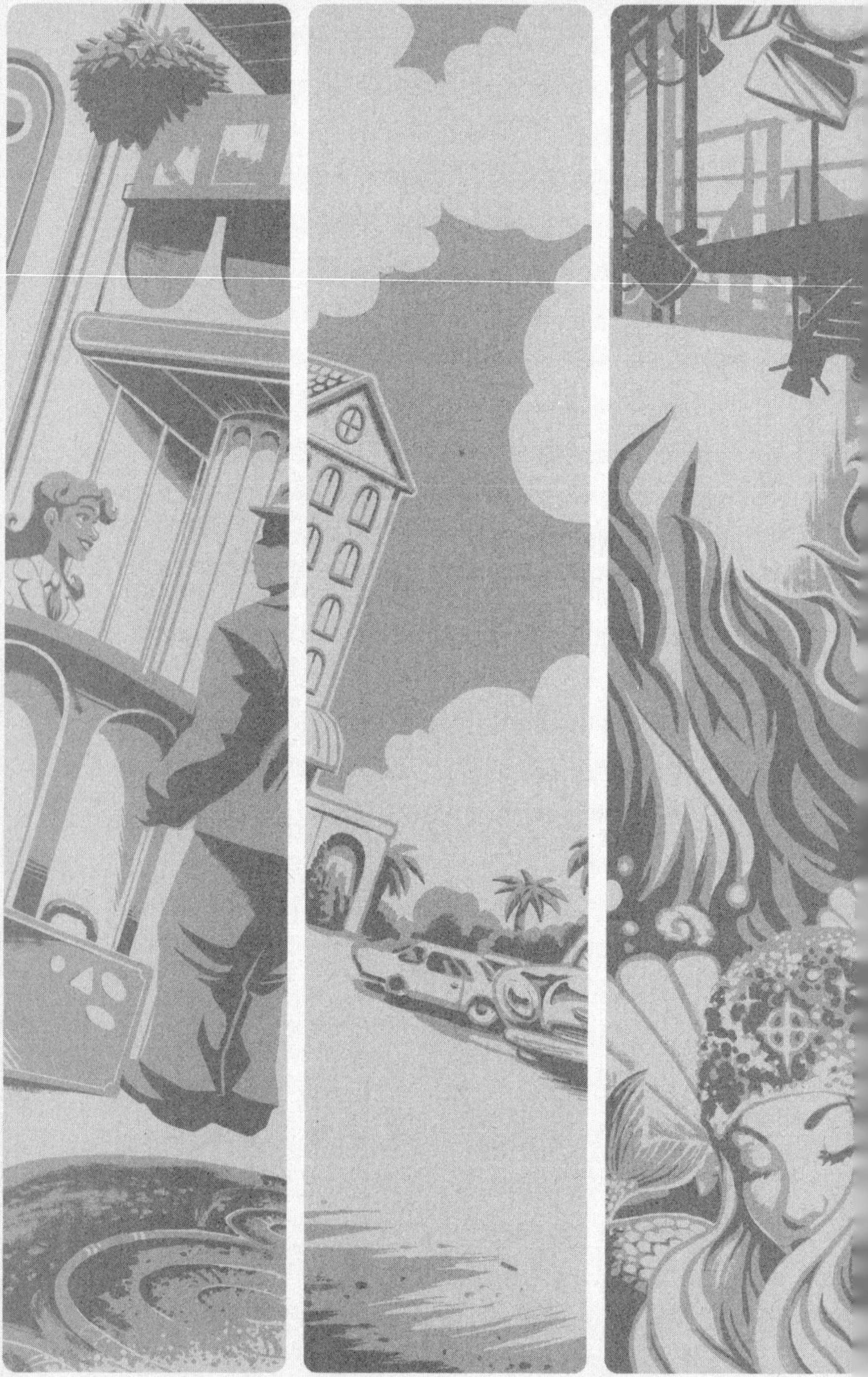

Chapter Thirteen

THERE IS A LARGE CONGREGATION OF SECURITY GUARDS outside of Delphine's suite. Mr. Davenport means business today, and he is not taking any chances. I don't recognize these security guards; they must have been hired by the studio. This means I won't be able to talk my way inside. These burly security guards have mean faces and broad shoulders. They look like one giant wall, but there must be a small crack in there somewhere, just big enough for me to shove myself in. Now to locate the tiny break.

I walk back to Rob.

"Like I suspected. Getting inside to see Delphine is going to be a challenge," I say. "We'll have to move forward with the plan. Are you ready?"

Rob nervously chews on his finger.

"Rob!"

"I'm ready," he says.

"I just need enough time to speak to her," I say. "Ask her a couple of questions. I'm going into position. Count to five, then start."

Rob nods. "Count to five and start," he repeats.

I'm not asking Rob to commit a felony, but from the look of his scared face you would think I was. Rob is a pretty straight shooter. Participating in one of my schemes is a really big step for him. He'll get used to it. I'm almost one hundred percent sure this will not be the last time I ask him for a favor.

"Rob, don't forget. You have to be the maestro in this," I say. "You manipulate the players into going fast or slow."

I wave my hands around like a maestro conducting the world's largest symphony. Rob follows my lead. He's a bit clumsy and is not sure exactly where to position his hands. I place my hand on his shoulder. "Never mind. Count to five and begin. Got it?"

"Got it, Goldie," he says. "I won't fail."

I leave Rob and stroll to a corner. I'm in uniform, and I see that the security guards eyeball me, but it doesn't seem like they find me suspicious. Nobody ever looks at the staff. I'm just doing my job, like any normal day. I start the countdown. Cheryl is by her station waiting for her turn. Everyone is ready.

Five.

Four. Rob walks toward the security guard at a steady clip. Determined. Good face, Rob!

Three. He's in front of them.

Two. I hold my breath. Here's the moment of truth.

One.

"There are two guys over by the golf course!" Rob yells, and swings his arms frantically to get the security guards' attention. "They are armed with a bunch of cameras, snapping pictures at everybody and asking all kinds of questions. You better head over there now!"

The security guards blink a couple of times. They stand stoic like statues.

"Did you hear me or not?" Rob says. "Journalists are out there causing problems."

"Sorry, we can't leave our positions," one of the guards says.

Oh no. How am I supposed to speak to Delphine if this wall does not crumble? Just as I am imagining myself with a battering ram or a horse to gallop inside the suite, Rob does the most brilliant thing.

"You do understand how this ends, right? Everyone at this hotel will have a different tale to tell about the mysterious guest staying in there," Rob says, pointing at the suite. "The reporters will start flooding the news with tons of rumors, and it will get out of control. That's not going to be the big problem. The real problem will be when your boss, Mr. Davenport, finds out you had a chance to stop the stories from circulating, but you chose to ignore it."

Rob shakes his head in disappointment. "*Hmmm.* I wonder how Mr. Davenport will feel about this? Let's find out." Rob turns away from the guards. The men finally dissolve their stone faces and replace them with serious concern, maybe even a little fear.

"Which way did you say you saw them?" one of the guards asks. Rob is elated and so am I! He points toward the golf course. Then he adds a little sugar to the mix:

"One went that way and the other went to the opposite side of the resort. They sure are slick."

Half the security guards follow Rob. The other half run in the opposite direction. Those heading in the opposite direction will be met by Cheryl, and she will point them to another part of the hotel. Hopefully, the guards will become dizzy from walking around in circles.

I could hug Rob, but there's no time for love. I walk up to Delphine's door and knock.

"Yes?" Delphine says, and I enter.

Delphine sits at the table, puttering around with the daisies. There seem to be even more than the last time I was here. Any more and she'll be drowning in daisies.

"Goldie! I'm so surprised to see you here." She quickly walks over to me and grabs both my hands. "I'm so sorry to hear about your mother. Terrible news. How is she holding up? And how are you?"

"I don't have much time," I say. "Delphine, can you tell me a little bit about Edna Blanchett?"

"Edna? Why do you want to ask me about Edna?"

"How long have you been working with Edna?"

"She has been with me since I started working in the studio system," she says. "In fact, she was the very first person I met at Powerhouse Productions when I auditioned for a commercial many years ago. She dressed me in a milkmaid outfit. The milkmaid outfit was way too risqué and Edna found a brilliant way to cover me up."

They have history. This is a good thing.

"Although it may not always look like it to outsiders, Edna has always treated me like a person and not just a prop to position in front of the camera," she adds. "I can always count on her."

"So, she came with you when you transferred over to Baldwin Studios," I say.

"Yes, of course. I insisted."

She insisted. Wait a minute.

"Delphine, you asked Edna to leave her job at Powerhouse to join you over at Baldwin Studios?" I say. "Did she want to come?"

"Well, it definitely wasn't a simple ask. You see, Edna built up quite the costume design department at Powerhouse. The very first of its kind," Delphine says. "She didn't want to leave."

Edna didn't want to leave and yet she did. I wonder if Edna was forced to leave Powerhouse.

"Why did Edna decide to follow you over to Baldwin Studios? Why did she leave behind everything she worked so hard to build?"

"Because I asked her to."

Delphine can't possibly think this is why Edna left. That she would leave a job that she had loved for so long, and an entire department she grew, to go work for a studio she didn't seek out. Where she would have to start over. It doesn't ring true.

"You said she didn't want to leave," I say. "Wouldn't she feel a bit of resentment for having to start at a new job?"

"No, no, no. Edna is not like that at all," Delphine says. She nervously toys with her hair. "She loves the work we are doing. You've seen the costumes. They are truly magnificent. Her very best work to date."

She's got a point. Edna has designed beautiful works of art. And yet, if I go through all the interactions I've witnessed between Edna and Delphine, she always has something nasty to say about Baldwin Studios and the movie.

"Delphine, are you sure Edna wanted to work at the new studio? Is there anything she might have said or done to make you think she's had doubts?"

"Goldie, I think you've got this all wrong. Edna would never do anything to jeopardize her work or mine," she says. "I understand you need to point fingers, but you are looking in the wrong places."

"Mom is being accused of taking the Bejeweled Aqua Chapeau. I have to consider all avenues to clear her name," I say. "I'm not being mean. I'm doing my job. Can you help me? Does Edna wear gloves?"

"Gloves? This is foolish."

"What about the choreographer, Katherine? Would she have any reason to sabotage the movie? How about Mr. Davenport? I mean, you did almost trip from his cigar the first time I met you. What if this is a whole elaborate hoax to cash in on your insurance and—"

"That's enough, Goldie. I've heard enough. I think you should go."

The room suddenly feels cold. I didn't expect this reaction from Delphine. It's hard to think anyone would want to cause her harm, especially if they have been longtime friends. I can't help thinking of what Cheryl said earlier: *Envy is a green-eyed monster.*

"Just because you are surrounded by flowers," I say, "doesn't mean it's all coming up daisies."

Delphine turns away from me. She has a troubled look on her face.

"Good luck with filming today. If you think of anything else, please let me know," I say. Delphine doesn't respond.

At the door is *another* delivery of daisies.

"Another delivery?" Delphine asks. She sounds tired, annoyed even. She briefly looks at the card and tears it up. She takes the bouquet and adds it to one of the many vases in the room.

Leaving Delphine with all those flowers gets me thinking. I'm pretty sure that the daisies are all from Mr. Davenport. He's the only person who technically knows she is staying at the Alcove Suite. And Delphine's reaction to the delivery is clearly one of annoyance, similar to how she reacted to Mr. Davenport when I first escorted her to her suite. If only I got to see that card before she ripped it to shreds.

And speaking of Mr. Davenport... He's a suspect in more ways than one. This may be far out there, but what if he's the one who wants to jeopardize the movie? He wasn't happy filming in St. Pascal. I'd bet more than anything the diamond swimming cap is insured for a whole lot of money. What if he had the cap stolen? Can he still recoup the insurance money? I'm not sure, but it's definitely something to look into. Plus, I found that torn matchbook at the fuse box. I know anyone could have taken Crossed Palms matches, but Mr. Davenport's always smoking a cigar and I haven't forgotten his glove box full of matchbooks.

"*Buenos días*, Ada," I say. Ada is busy working on dinner table displays, tiny bouquets that won't overwhelm the guests' tables but that are beautiful enough to add the right ambience. I've learned a lot of florist talk from listening and watching Ada work over the years.

"*Buenos días*, Goldie. You've been a very busy girl," Ada says while slipping a flower into my lapel.

"Ada, you know exactly who orders flowers at Crossed Palms Resort, correct?" I say.

"Of course. Every flower that leaves this place has been blessed by these hands," she says. "They leave here to give love to another person."

"The daisies. Who ordered the daisies for our special guest staying in the suite?" I ask. Ada completes one of the centerpieces and starts another.

"Someone really loves daisies. I can't seem to keep them in this shop long enough," she says. "In fact, I had to order from my outside vendors to fulfill all the orders. So many daisies."

I carefully place the finished centerpiece inside a box to be delivered to the hotel's restaurants.

"*Es un poquito raro*," she says.

"*Raro?*" This is one Spanish word I can't seem to place. "What does *raro* mean?"

"*Raro* means strange," she says. "The order was a bit strange."

"How so?"

"The person who placed the order is staying right here in Crossed Palms," she says. "I know you're going to say that that's not too strange. Well, what was a little bit *raro* is that they insisted on keeping the order anonymous. So much money for the special guest to never know exactly from whom, especially when the person is staying in the same hotel. Seems bizarre and unromantic to me."

"Wasn't it the *muy importante* man who I met at Walt's office? You know, the big guy with the watch?" I mime pulling out an invisible pocket watch and opening it. Ada shakes her head.

"No. It wasn't him. It was someone else."

Mr. Davenport isn't the person sending Delphine daisies. I would think he would be the only person who would know about Delphine's love of daisies and her special connection to them since she was a child. "Who ordered all those daisies?"

Ada looks around the room, making sure no one is within earshot.

"The only thing he insisted on was for the note to say, *A return to your glorious past,*" Ada says. "He didn't want anyone to find out. A surprise."

The past. Someone from Delphine's past.

A familiar scent of a cigar permeates the air. The sound of stomping shoes draws nearer and nearer.

"Who said anything about reporters?" Mr. Davenport says. I don't want to have any interaction with him. Before I can explain myself to Ada, I duck underneath her table. Mr. Davenport stops in front of the floral shop before banging on Walt's door. But Walt is surely elsewhere trying to find the diamond cap, just like me. "Hello?! Hello?!"

After a few more pounds on the door, Mr. Davenport finally gives up. He walks away in a huff. And when he does, I slowly emerge from under the table.

"*Ese hombre*. He's going to make himself sick with all that rage," Ada says, clucking her tongue. She waves her hand about to get the smoke from the cigar out of the shop.

"He sure is," I say.

"*Pobre flores*," Ada says. "Cigar smoke is never good for flowers."

The flowers are definitely innocent bystanders in this drama. The flowers and my mom. Although Ada may be unable to share the order form, I know someone who might have the information.

Chapter Fourteen

CHERYL IS BUSY GOING OVER THE MANY CLASSES A person can take at Crossed Palms to two young men.

"Cha-cha lessons begin at twelve PM. But perhaps you are looking for a more active workout? Our tennis instructors have played in various tournaments, and I have only heard excellent feedback about their coaching skills. You can also learn horseback riding...."

The couple doesn't seem all that keen to try any of those things.

"What about snorkeling?" The man wears a fedora and a relaxed suit while his partner wears slacks and polo shirt. They are in vacation mode. I hope they will pick an activity quickly. I need to speak to Cheryl. Stat.

"Unfortunately, we are not offering snorkeling because the beach area is off-limits today," Cheryl explains.

"What are they doing over there? Does that have to do with all these sea creatures?" he asks.

"We are not allowed to say, but the beach will be fully available tomorrow. Would you like me to book you a snorkeling package for then?"

"Pierre is the best diving instructor around," I add, to help seal the deal.

The couple nods and Cheryl signs them up for a full day of swimming and snorkeling.

"Cheryl! Do you have a list of the floral orders?" I ask.

"Flowers?" She tilts her head, confused.

"Daisies. A guest staying at the Crossed Palms knows about Delphine's love for daisies. The weird thing is, how would they know to deliver the flowers to the Alcove Suite? I just assumed the daisies were a gift from Mr. Davenport, but Ada said no."

Cheryl digs into her ledger of activities. She locates the floral orders and searches for daisies.

"See. No name," she says, pointing to the order of daisies. "Sorry, Goldie."

I grab the ledger and take a good look myself. Cheryl is right. The person who ordered the daisies did so a day before Delphine was due to check in to the resort. It could have been anyone. I look at the ledger for Katherine, the choreographer, or for any alias that would make sense, but nothing pops out.

"But wait. She just received a new order, like just this second!" I search the ledger and find it. "It's listed right here. Nine AM, order via phone."

Cheryl racks her brain. "Nine AM. I've received *so* many calls today. But wait. Accent. I remember an accent. The person who made the call definitely had an accent."

"Do you remember the person's name?" I say.

Cheryl shakes her head. "Sorry, Goldie."

"No need to apologize," I say. "At least we know it was someone with an accent. I'm getting closer. I can feel it."

A family interrupts our conversation and proceeds to ask Cheryl about restaurants.

"Later, Cheryl," I say.

I have to figure this out. Mom is depending on me. There is no way she will be heading to jail for something she didn't do. No way. Time to go over my clues again.

I walk to the lounge and ask for a glass of iced water. I sit on one of the chairs and pull out my pad. What am I missing? I write this in my pad and underline it three times.

A white glove. Weird footprints. Blackouts. And now a person with an accent, but I must also consider that a thief might use a fake accent to throw everyone off. What am I not seeing? A cold wet nose nuzzles up on my ankle. Clementine, Miss Dupart's poodle, greets me.

"Clementine, do you know who stole the Bejeweled Aqua Chapeau?" I whisper in her fuzzy face. Clementine responds by licking my hand.

"Goldie Vance, how are you doing?" Miss Dupart asks. She's wearing another mint-green ensemble. Mint-green hat. Mint-green slacks and matching sandals. She takes the seat across from me. Clementine jumps on her lap and settles in.

"I've seen better days, Miss Dupart," I say.

"So have we all," she says. "As you can tell, I wasn't asked back on the set today. Too bad for the director and the movie itself. A travesty is what I like to call it."

"I'm sorry to hear that. At least you were able to get some good shots yesterday," I say. I stop and think for a second, and suddenly feel a little sick. I didn't consider it before, but Miss Dupart is definitely a suspect. She was there during the blackouts and when Delphine walked off the set. I've been blinded by the fact that I know her so well. I hate myself for asking, but I have to. "Miss Dupart, when did you last see the Bejeweled Aqua Chapeau?"

"My dear, I've already gone through this with Walter Tooey. He was very thorough with his questions yesterday," she says. "Besides, I believe diamonds can only be given as a gift. These were a gift from my dear friend Frida, a brilliant poet from Chicago." She points to teardrop diamond earrings dangling from her ears.

"How were the other actors on the set? And what did you think about the costume designer?"

"Edna Blanchett. A legend. A legend in wardrobe and design," Miss Dupart says. "Honestly, I was surprised to see she had left Powerhouse to work at Baldwin Studios. She ruled the costumes there."

"Did you ever notice how the chapeau never fully stayed on Delphine's head?" I say. "Didn't you think that was odd? Her job is to make sure it's perfect for Delphine. Right?"

Miss Dupart pats the now-sleeping Clementine, who snores.

"Funnily, I thought they would use a decoy. Most movies wouldn't want to damage such a priceless piece by placing it in the water," she says. "Edna Blanchett tried her best to secure the cap. It wasn't until one of the extras, a Mr. Henri was his name, I believe...Anyway, he suggested using glue. He was such a help. So well versed about the diamond swimming cap, right down to dimensions and quality of stones. Such a funny thing coming from a man in a sea-creature outfit."

Holy Neptune's trident.

"Wait, Miss Dupart. Can you repeat what you just said?"

"This was a gift from Frida," she whisper-talks.

"No, not that part. The stuff about Henri," I say. "The sea-creature extra."

She adjusts her rings.

"Well, Henri was always ready for his close-up," she says, adjusting her hat to protect herself from the sun. "In fact, he was the first in line to take the shuttle to shoot this morning. But Edna Blanchett wasn't very keen about having her assistant be a sea creature. They were arguing quite passionately, in the language of love."

"The language of love?" My heart starts to race out of control.

"Yes, yes, French, of course," she says. "Goldie, you met him. He was right beside your mother and me the whole time we filmed our pivotal scenes. Remember?"

Wait a minute. Images start flooding my brain like a fast-paced movie sequence. A sea creature speaking with a woman with severe bangs on the day I tried to find Miss Dupart's lost ring in the back of her car. Then there was that Grumpy Costume Designer Guy when I was backstage with all the extras. He was there complaining about Baldwin Studios. But he wasn't a sea creature. He was Edna's assistant. But he *was* right beside Delphine before they filmed the water-tank scenes. Delphine thanked Edna for the wonderful work she did on the Bejeweled Aqua Chapeau. French accents!

"What did you say his name was?" I get up, ready to run back to Cheryl.

"Henri. He said he spent his life working in movies since he was a *bébé*. You know the type of man who wants to prove his knowledge by speaking too much?" Miss Dupart says. "That's what Henri is like. A man who desperately wants to tell a story. I, being a gracious observer, always listen."

He *was* super talkative. I was so preoccupied with getting rid of Scoops Malone, I completely overlooked him. The strange webbed footprints. They were sea-creature footprints. A sea creature close to Delphine and well versed in her life, and who knows all about costumes.

It's all starting to makes sense. My brain snaps and revs up like a sports car engine. Why didn't it dawn on me before? The grumpy assistant, Henri, was always right by the Bejeweled Aqua Chapeau. The only time I didn't see him was after the blackout. He wasn't there when we interrogated everyone. He must have slipped out of the club right as I entered, alerting everyone about Scoops. How did I miss it?

"Did he mention anything else about Delphine?"

"He went on and on about his time working at Powerhouse. He called it the *crème de la crème* of making movies," Miss Dupart says. "Personally, I've never been one to stay loyal to just one place. A girl has to keep moving. I don't blame Delphine for doing so. It's all part of the Hollywood game, but this fellow seemed to think Baldwin Studios was beneath them all."

This is a case of the green-eyed monster. Jealousy made Edna Blanchett and Henri want to sabotage Delphine's new movie. They were willing to do anything from causing blackouts to stealing the diamond swimming cap. Scoops Malone was right. I had to look beyond the usual suspects.

A sea creature/costume designer conspiracy!

"Thanks, Miss Dupart! You saved the day!" I hug her, sorry I ever doubted her innocence. I hug Clementine, too, who wakes up with a startled doggie expression.

"Oh my. What did I say?" Miss Dupart exclaims.

"You said it all!"

Chapter Fifteen

TODAY'S SCHEDULED SHOOT IS THE BIG SEA–CREATURE–versus-mermaid battle scene, the climax of the film. Delphine, as the Queen of the Mermaids, will lead the fierce mermaid warriors into the battlefield to save her home. She will come face-to-face with her sea-creature love interest, and she will have to decide right then and there—can love conquer their differences? There will be a ton of action sequences to shoot and an elaborate choreographed battle. I know this because Delphine told us all about it yesterday when she came over for dinner. All the extras will be at the beach, including Henri.

"Quick—Henri," I say across the front desk. "He's an extra in the movie. Did he get on the shuttle heading to the beach this morning?"

Cheryl checks her ledger. The extras who were meant to be on the beach shooting today would have taken the shuttle provided by the Crossed Palms. Mr. Davenport insisted on it. If Henri took that bus, then he is on the set.

"Yes, there he is. Henri. I checked him off this morning," Cheryl says. "I remember him. He was here bright and early. Him and a woman with a French accent have been joined at the hip the entire time. Always huddled together."

"A sea creature, right?"

Cheryl confirms. "You think he has something to do with the bejeweled swimming cap?"

It's all making sense and the pieces are coming together. The more I think of it the quicker my theory takes form. The sea creature and Edna Blanchett must have formed some sort of alliance in order to nab the Bejeweled Aqua Chapeau. I'm guessing Edna sought out Henri. Maybe they have a bond since they speak the same language. He said he's been working on every film with Delphine. He went from costarring in a film as her brother to barely being a sea creature. And I am sure the diamonds were enticing to

Henri. A bit of priceless glimmer can make a person go mad.

"I'm not one hundred percent positive, but if they are at the beach, things cannot be good."

"One more thing. He insisted on boarding the bus with a box. There was no room for it, so I suggested Rob deliver the package later. This man, Henri, he refused and ended up boarding with the box on his lap."

A box? The chapeau?

"Could he have been carrying the diamond swimming cap in the box?"

"I don't know. Could have been just about anything," Cheryl says. "He was very protective of it. Very."

I need to get to the beach as quickly as possible. Who knows what this sea creature wannabe is up to next? Scoops Malone's voice enters my head. There will be more foul play. Oh boy.

"Goldie, wait! I remember one more thing. He had a tattoo on his left arm," she yells.

"A tattoo?"

"Of a daisy!"

Hold on to your blooming buds! Henri has a daisy

tattoo on his arm. Of course. A daisy tattoo and daisies for Delphine. Maybe Henri thought drowning Delphine with daisies would remind her of her past, enough for her to abandon the film. Ha! The flowers are really talking to me now.

"I need to jet," I say.

"Yeah, the beach!" Cheryl says. "Baldwin Studios is mostly filming across the way, but they also set up a whole tent for wardrobe farther down. It's a massive production."

"I'll hit the tent first. Thanks, Cheryl, you're the best!"

Big Blue will not do for this dire situation. I need wheels. Hot wheels!

"Goldie, where are you off to?"

Dad tries his best to keep up with me. "I don't have much time. I have to get to the movie set right now. Lives may depend on it!"

"Now, hold on, Goldie. Don't be rushing off to conclusions."

"Of course not, Dad. Walt has taught me well. Evidence first. And I've got evidence. Now I need confirmation."

"Be careful!" Dad says as I run off to the valet station. I find Rob slumped at his desk, failing to stay awake.

"Quick, hand me keys to the fastest car here!"

Rob shakes his head. "No way. Mr. Maple said no joyrides." He points to a tiny makeshift sign tacked behind the valet station. NO JOYRIDES with three exclamation points. I understand Rob's hesitation, but this is serious business.

"Rob, keys. I don't have time to explain the importance of this." I pound on the desk. "C'mon! I have to get to the beach. My bike doesn't have enough horsepower."

"I can't, Goldie," he says. "Those security guards wanted to throw me in the lake for giving them such a runaround."

"You were perfect. Absolutely top rate. But now is not the time to rehash the past," I say. "The future depends on me securing a fast car."

"A break in the case?" he asks, leaning in. I nod. "Hot diggity." Rob smacks his head. "A break is a break," he says while handing me keys. "The Metropolitan, in parking slot four. Need me for anything else?"

211

"Thanks, Rob, you're the greatest!" I say. "And if anyone comes looking for me, you'll know what to do."

"I'm a pro!"

I run to the compact Nash Metropolitan with a cool red stripe. Dire situations call for dire actions. I shift gears. One light touch on the gas pedal, and *zooooom*. I'm off to the races.

BALDWIN STUDIOS IS FILMING AT THE BEACH RIGHT across from the Crossed Palms Resort. This strip of gorgeous, pristine shoreline allows guests to feel as if they have entered their own private oasis. The water is crystal blue. What also makes this location perfect for Baldwin Studios are the large rock formations that bookend the strip. The rock formations are massive and look both futuristic and ancient. An ideal setting for a sea-creature movie.

Wow. This Metropolitan purrs like a kitten. This car is small and fancy with a capital *F*. I push the pedal to the metal. Just like the engine, my mind races. I think about how I was trying to pin the drama on Scoops Malone. I should have been paying way more attention to the costume department. Sometimes the clues are there, and it's just a matter of honing in, like setting the magnifying glass just right so you see what's really going on.

When I become a world-famous detective, I'll need a car like this one. And leather driving gloves. And a whole driving ensemble. Oh yes, a tiny red car to buzz through the streets of St. Pascal like a professional. Okay, I need to quit with the driving fantasies and concentrate. Once I arrive, I'll need to find a way to sneak in. Mr. Davenport will have super-duper, extra-tight security at this location after everything that has happened. Infiltrating the set is first on my list.

Because the beach is closed off, I take side streets along the coast until I find the right spot to park the car. There is a concealed access point to the beach that few would know about, unless you live in St. Pascal. I make it my mission to be familiar with every access point there is. Time to go stealth mode.

Massive crowds are milling about. Sea creatures and mermaids alike. The tents are situated exactly how Cheryl described. The actors appear to be exiting the tents and making the trek over to where the cameras are, but it doesn't look like they've begun to shoot yet. A string of security guards are stopping anyone from entering the beach. This is going to be a challenge. But I love challenges. They are like puzzles waiting to be solved. And the pieces all exist; you just need to put them together. It's time to see if I've put all the pieces of this mystery in their correct slots.

Chapter Sixteen

THANK GOODNESS I'M SMALL. THIS GIVES ME THE ability to take light steps. And thank goodness I know St. Pascal inside and out. I crouch down as close to the ground as possible and inch my way toward the dunes.

Four security guards are mere steps away from me. They're so close that I can hear one of them chewing gum and blowing bubbles. Not quite security-guard protocol in my book, but so be it. With each pop of his bubble gum, I am able to move closer to my destination.

"I'm starving," the guard blowing bubbles says to the group. "I read somewhere chewing gum can help stave off hunger."

"What are you talking about? That's a bunch of baloney," another guard responds.

Bop! He blows another bubble and I move.

Only a few more yards. Lucky for me, there is a loud commotion happening just across the way. Movie mayhem is in full effect. I keep crawling, leaving the security guards behind and finding refuge in a wooden scaffold nook. I nestle in between boxes. With so many people rushing about trying to make sense of the chaos, I have a clear view. Undetected.

"Stay on your marks, people," the director says into a megaphone. How do you corral hundreds of extras in one spot? The answer: by yelling, illustrated by Mr. Davenport, who just grabbed the megaphone from the director.

"This is costing us thousands of dollars. Do not waste a shot."

Even on the beach, Mr. Davenport wears a suit. He pulls out his watch and shoves it back in his front pocket.

Now that I've made it this far, I don't really have a plan of how I'm going to stop production of this movie, but I need to find Henri and the box he is carrying. I scan every extra walking around the set. It's not an easy task when there are so many, but I take my time and really concentrate. Patience. Hawk eyes, don't fail me now.

There he is. A sea creature holding a box. Way to not be obvious, Henri. I wouldn't be surprised if Edna Blanchett is the brains behind this diamond cap theft. While everyone on the set is being told to stay in place, Henri slowly walks away from the crowd. I keep my eyes on him. He heads toward the large tent, totally against the grain. I have to follow him.

Hmmm. It dawns on me.

The pile of boxes concealing me right now contains a box that looks like others on set; I can use it to pretend I'm delivering something to the tent. I grab a box and hoist it upon my shoulders. I walk with purpose, flipping the box from shoulder to shoulder in order to avoid making eye contact with anyone.

"Hey, where you going with that?" a crew member yells at me. I just point and keep moving. Lucky for me, another person distracts him with a question. When I finally reach the tent, I wait by the entrance, using the flap to conceal myself while I listen.

When I finally reach the tent, I wait by the entrance, using the flap to conceal myself while I listen.

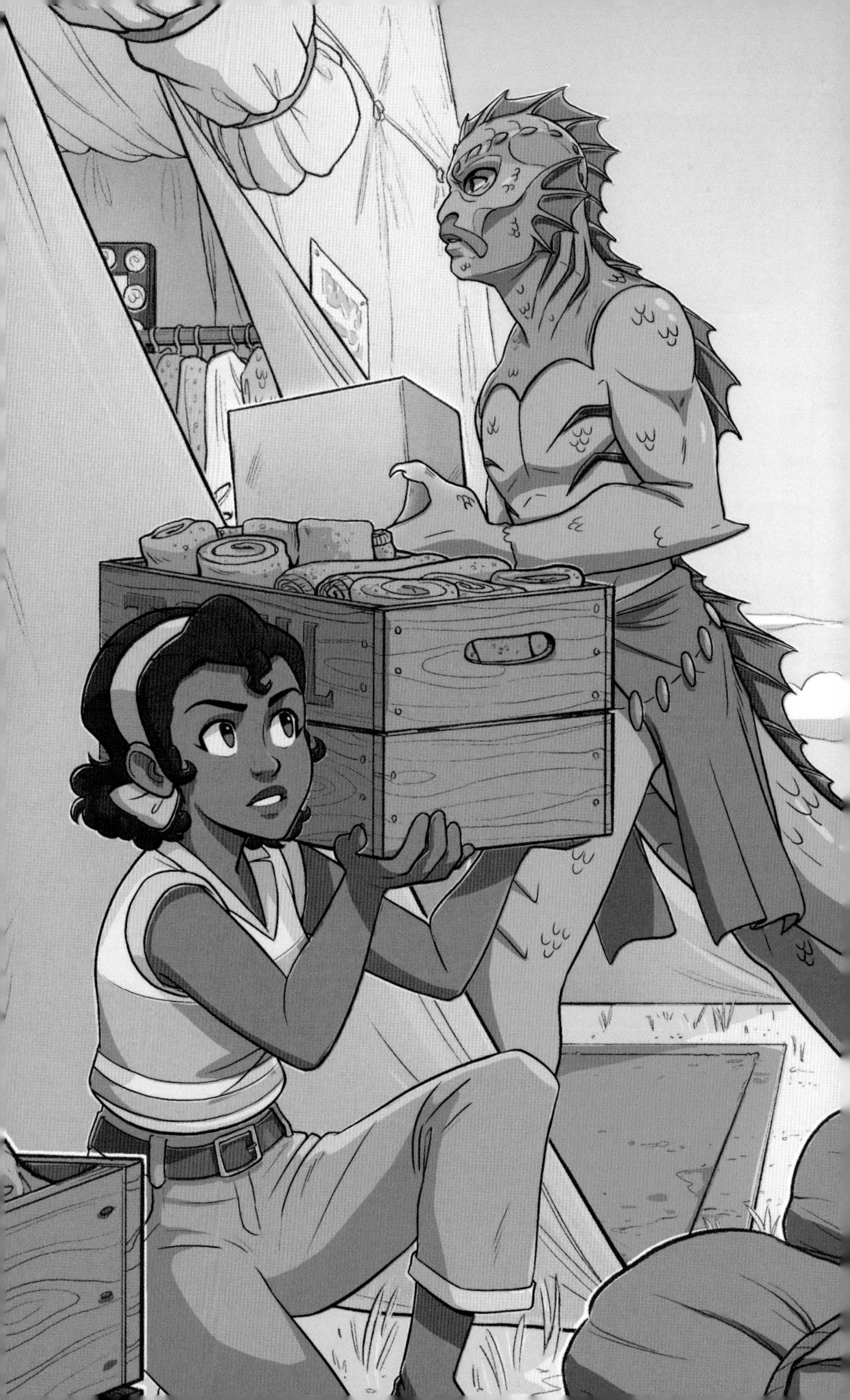

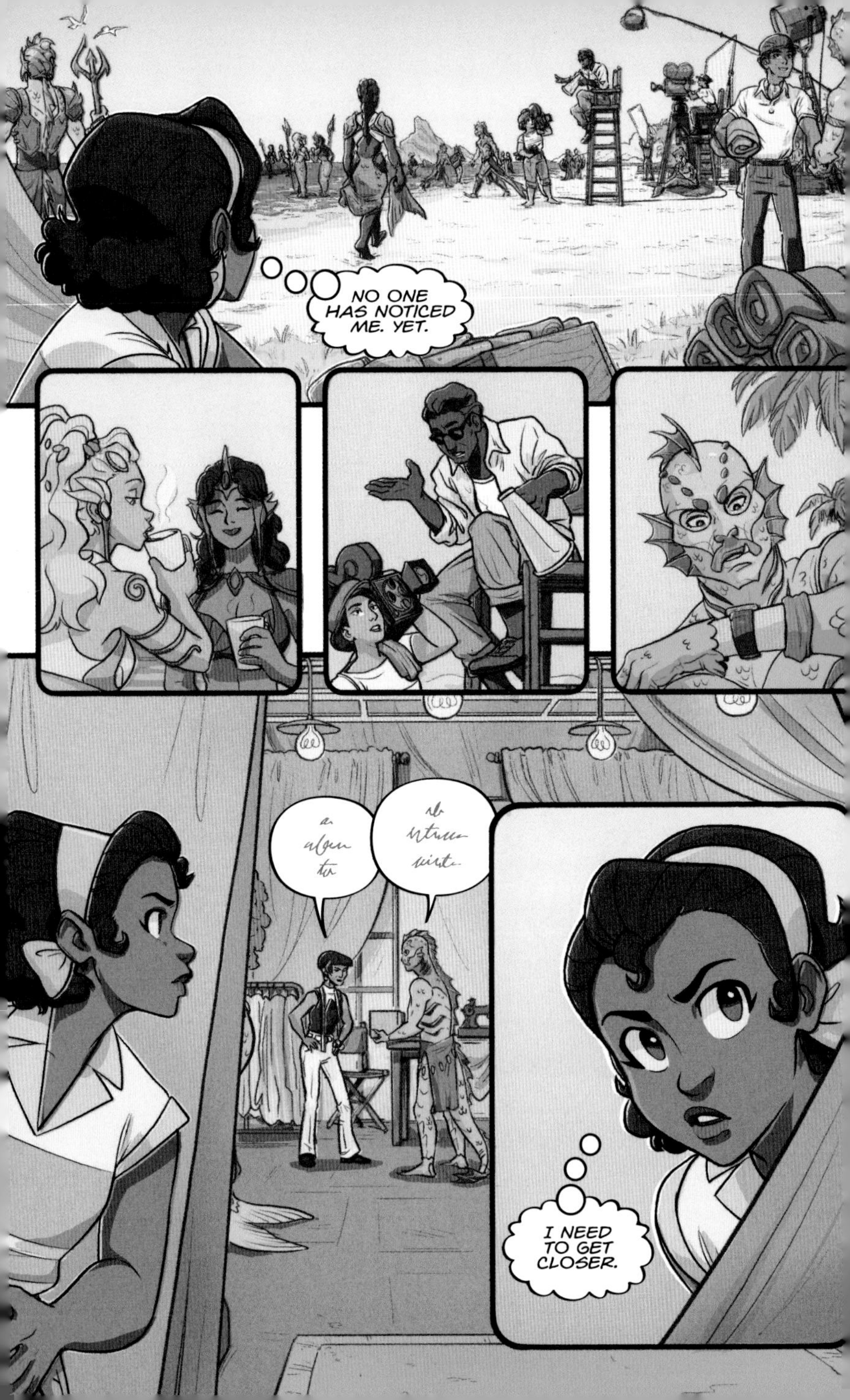
NO ONE HAS NOTICED ME. YET.
I NEED TO GET CLOSER.

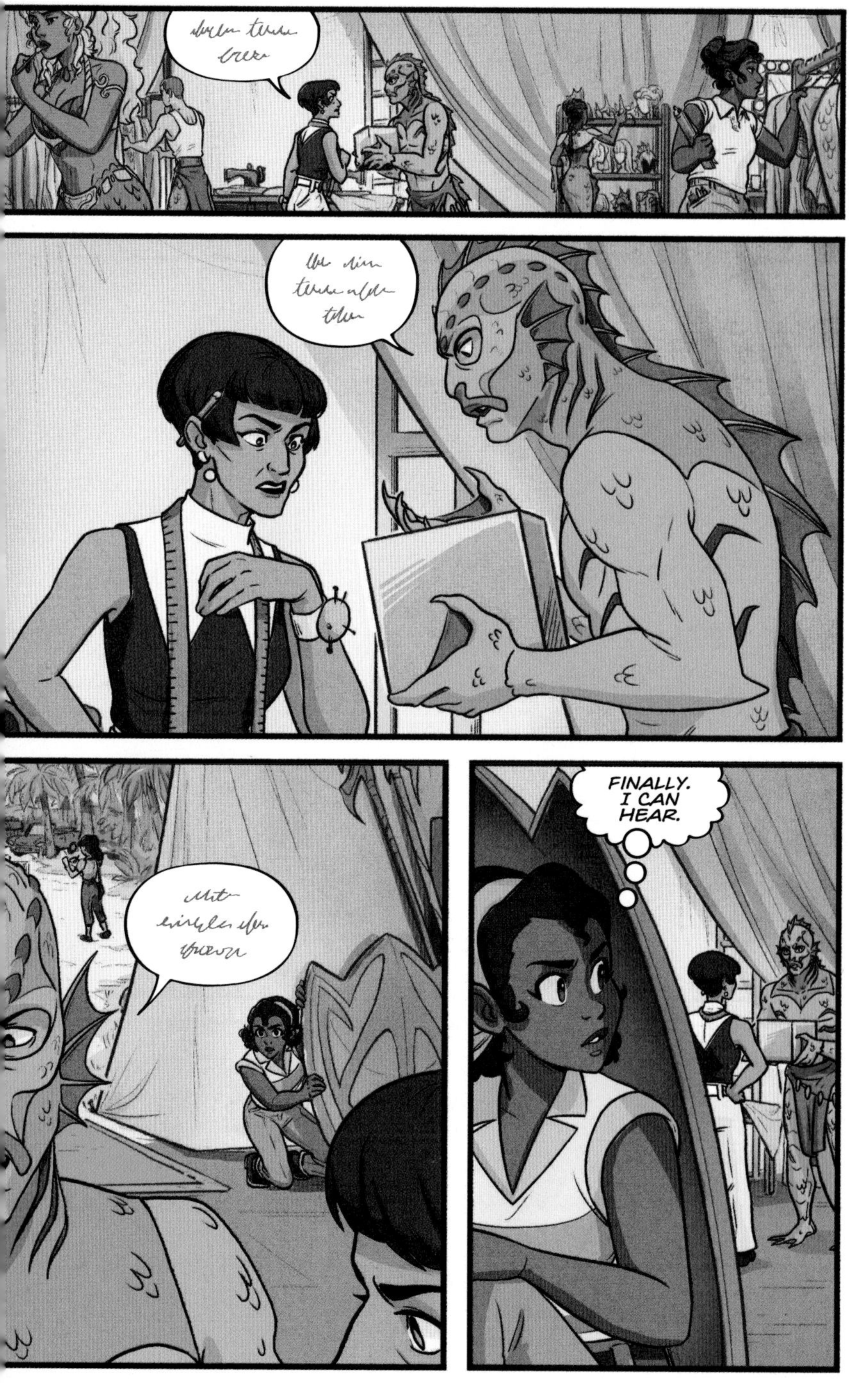
FINALLY. I CAN HEAR.

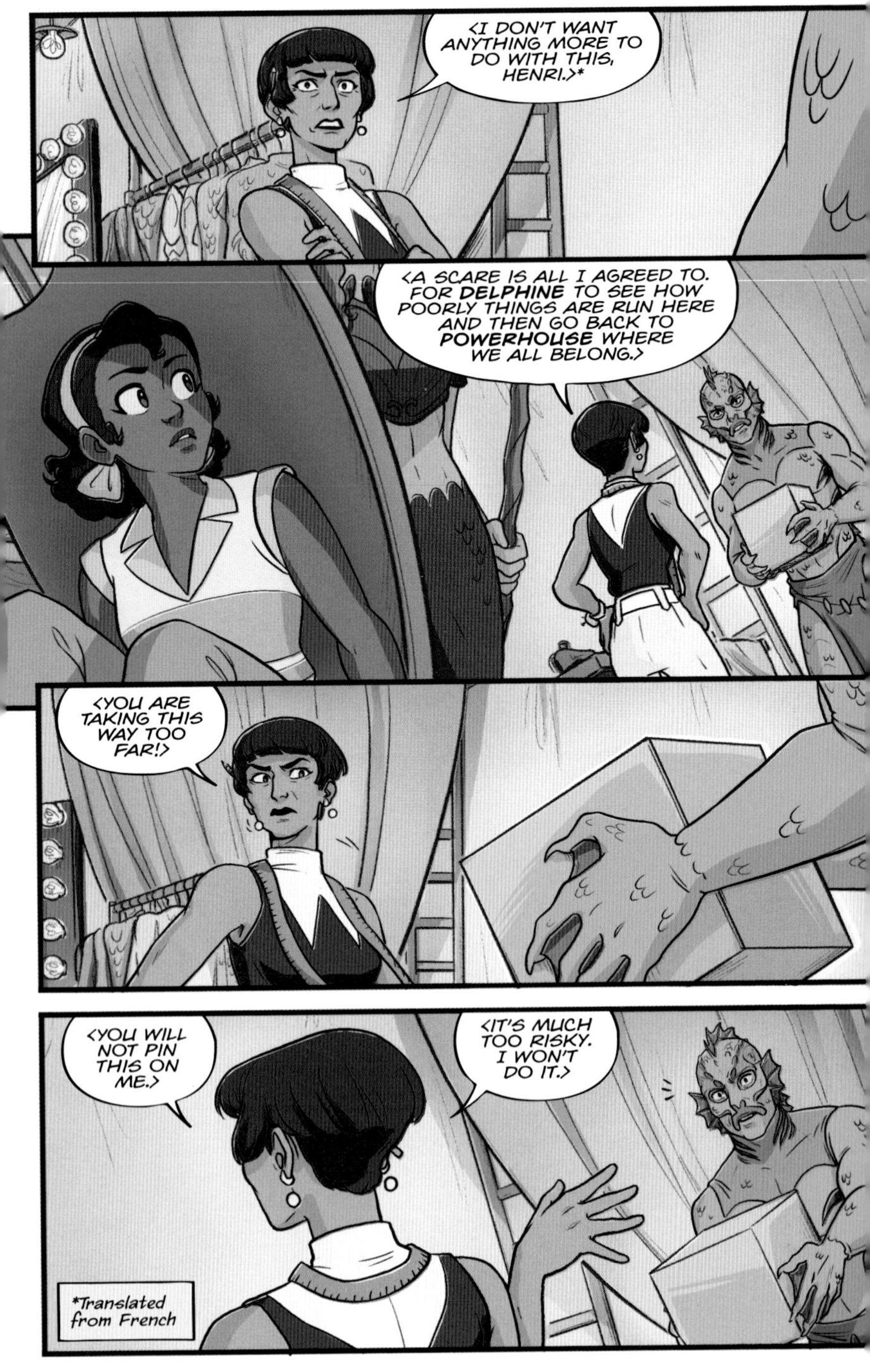

<I DON'T WANT ANYTHING MORE TO DO WITH THIS, HENRI.>*
<A SCARE IS ALL I AGREED TO. FOR DELPHINE TO SEE HOW POORLY THINGS ARE RUN HERE AND THEN GO BACK TO POWERHOUSE WHERE WE ALL BELONG.>
<YOU ARE TAKING THIS WAY TOO FAR!>
<YOU WILL NOT PIN THIS ON ME.>
<IT'S MUCH TOO RISKY. I WON'T DO IT.>
*Translated from French

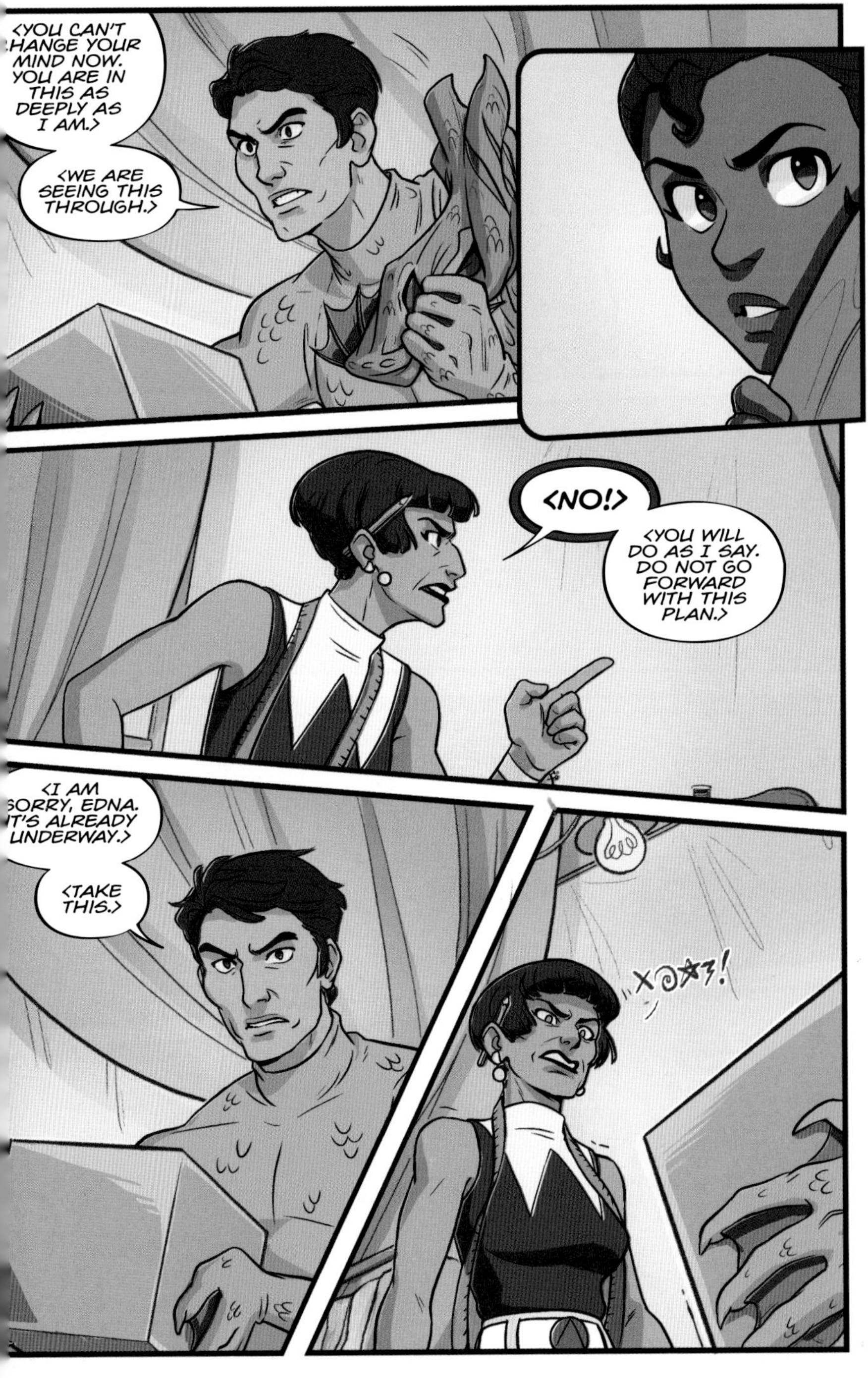
<YOU CAN'T CHANGE YOUR MIND NOW. YOU ARE IN THIS AS DEEPLY AS I AM.>
<WE ARE SEEING THIS THROUGH.>
<NO!>
<YOU WILL DO AS I SAY. DO NOT GO FORWARD WITH THIS PLAN.>
<I AM SORRY, EDNA. IT'S ALREADY UNDERWAY.>
<TAKE THIS.>

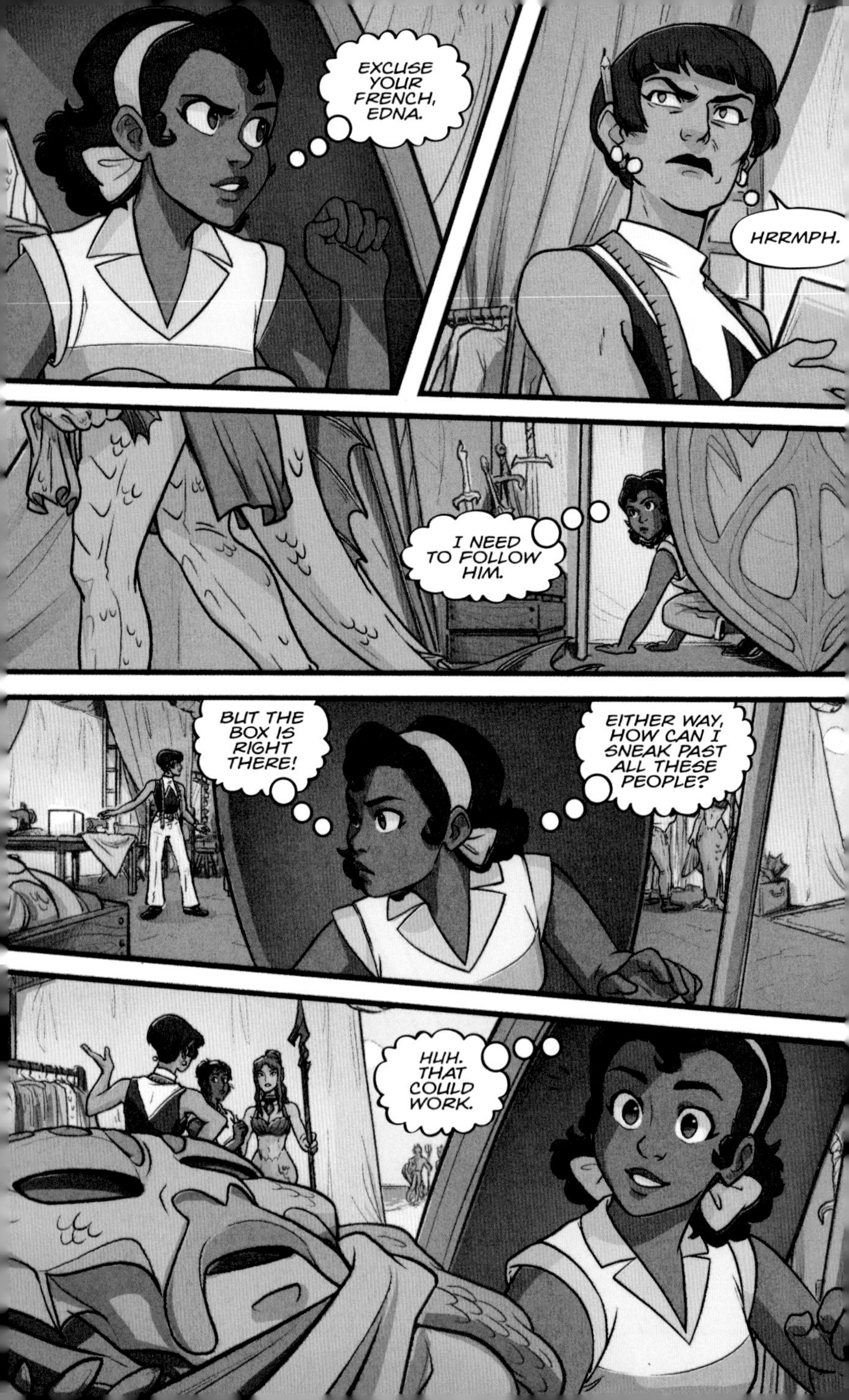
EXCUSE YOUR FRENCH, EDNA.
HRRMPH.
I NEED TO FOLLOW HIM.
BUT THE BOX IS RIGHT THERE!
EITHER WAY, HOW CAN I SNEAK PAST ALL THESE PEOPLE?
HUH. THAT COULD WORK.

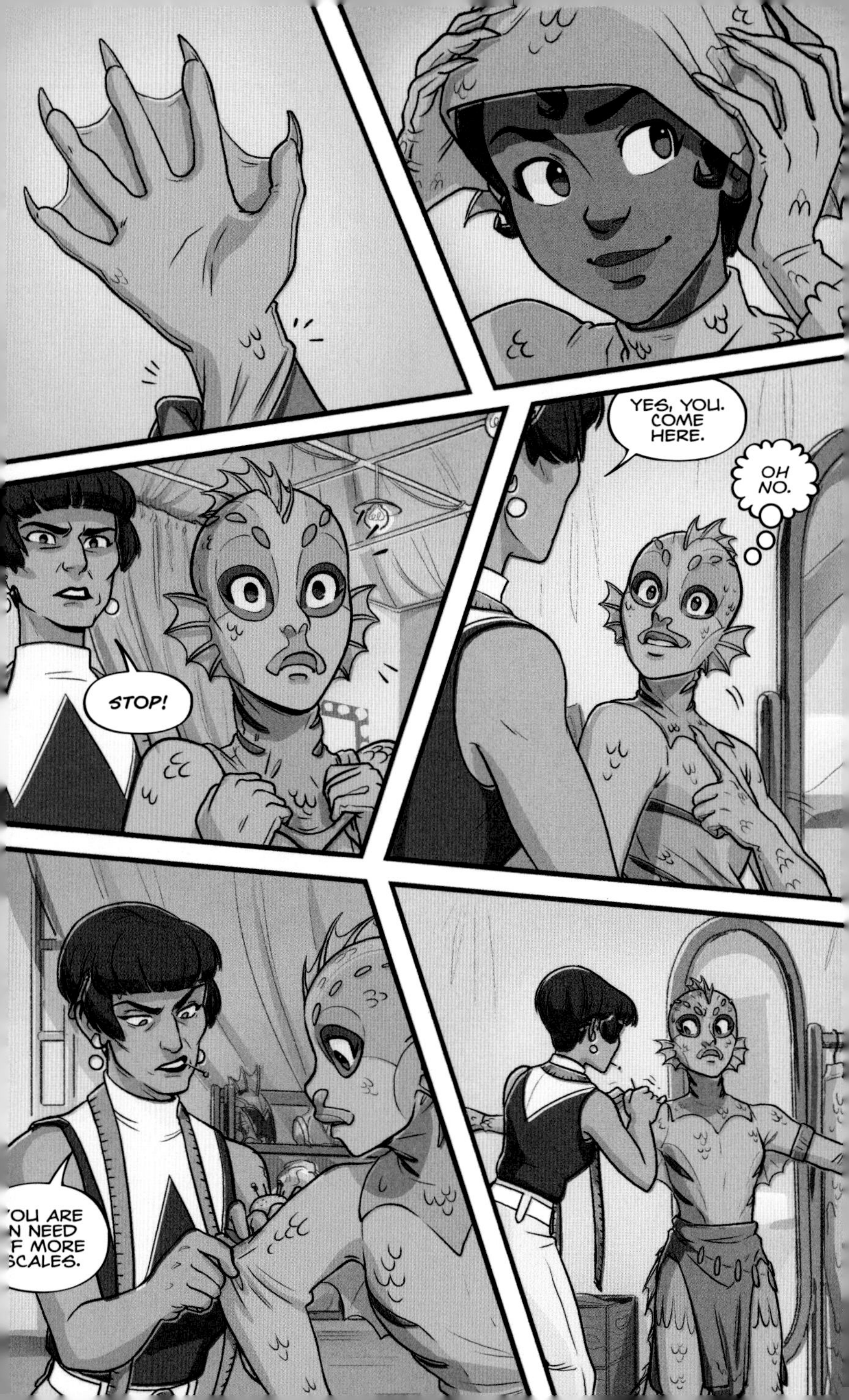
STOP!
YES, YOU. COME HERE.
OH NO.
YOU ARE IN NEED OF MORE SCALES.

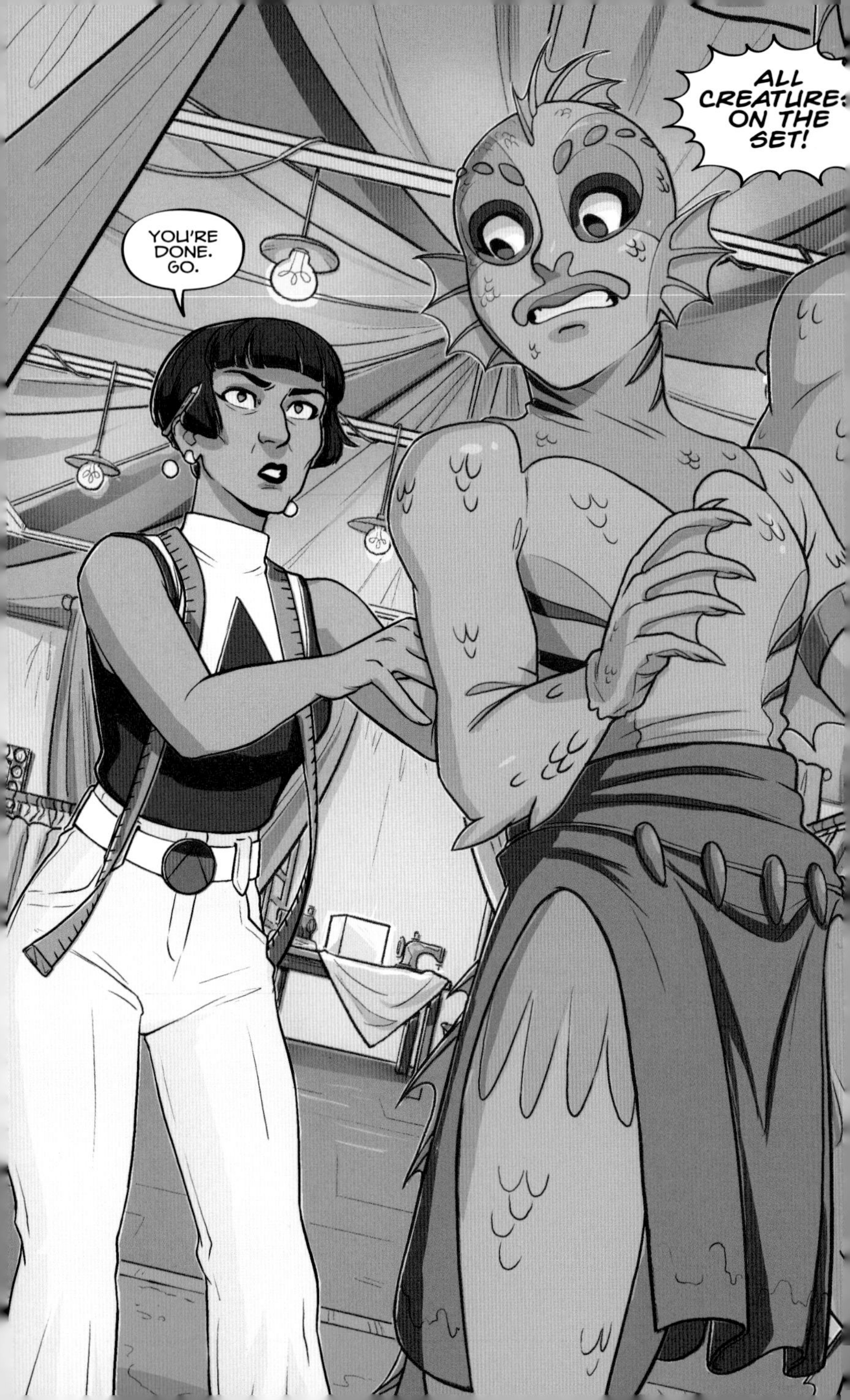
YOU'RE DONE. GO.
ALL CREATURES ON THE SET!

I hesitate. The box is right there. What would Edna do if I just grabbed the box and ran? No, that won't do. Henri said something about a plan being underway. Foul play? I have to follow Henri. The box will have to wait. I am swept away in a wave of sea creatures. I might be the shortest in this army, but no one seems to mind. I guess when it comes to this fantasy war, it's every man, woman, and *child* to the forefront.

Delphine stands atop an elevated stage, looking like a true mermaid goddess. Her costume is various shades of greens, yellows, and blues. People from miles away could easily spot her. She is a majestic vision.

I wobble around until I locate Henri and stand beside him, but he starts to slowly inch his way to the back of the crowd. He's about to do something. I can feel it in my bones.

"You there—stay in position," Mr. Davenport yells into the megaphone, but he's not talking to Henri. He's talking to me. Sorry, Mr. Davenport. I just can't listen to you. I need to follow Henri. I stand still, but as soon as Mr. Davenport turns to yell at someone else, I take at least two or three steps toward Henri.

"Baby sea creature, stop moving!" the leader of the

sea-creature army, the costar of this film, says directly to me. It's amazing how the makeup artist is still able to preserve his good looks *and* incorporate a sea-monster face. Now, that's talent.

"But where's my daddy?" I say, making sure my voice sounds a little bit deeper than usual. Can't have them find out I'm a girl underneath all these scales. Apparently in this film, sea creatures are boys and mermaids are girls. So silly. "I need my daddy."

I point to Henri, who is trying to act casual while also sneaking toward Delphine's elevated platform. The assistant to the director runs over to Henri and leads him right back by me. Much to his chagrin, I take hold of his hand just in case he thinks he can get away. Whatever Henri had in mind is going to have to wait until we finish shooting this scene.

"Action!"

"I don't want war. I don't want to see our brothers from the sea fight with us," Delphine declares. "We can get along. I know this because..."

All I hear is the crashing of the waves against the rocks and the thumping of my heart as I hold tight to Henri's hand. He is definitely trying to let go. He's going to stick by me if I have to put glue on this sea-creature hand to keep him from whatever diabolical plans he may have.

Delphine continues with her monologue. "I have known true love from across the ocean. I've seen it with my own eyes. It is possible for mermaids and sea creatures to live peacefully together.

"We have loved before, haven't we?" she says, imploring the handsome leader of the sea creatures. "We've known love."

"Yes, we have," he says. "I love you."

I can't help rolling my eyes. Let's get on with it. Even Henri is twitching next to me.

"And I love you."

Gasps all around. Or at least that is what we were told to do as extras.

"And cut! Beautiful work, everyone. Let's take a break. Stay close to your positions. Delphine, let's go over the lines again."

Henri pulls away from me. I take his hand anyway. He pulls again.

"We should stay in character," I say with my deep voice. Henri tilts his head.

"No, thank you. I won't be taking notes from *un garçon*."

How rude! He walks away from me. I figured I couldn't keep him nearby forever. I've got to stop him. *Think, Goldie, think.*

Walt! Walt is the perfect person to help me out. Lucky for me, he's off to the side surveilling the crowd. I run to him.

"Walt! I've got no time to explain, but you need to follow that sea creature," I say. "I think he's trying to sabotage the elevated stage."

"Who are you?" he says, squinting his eyes.

"Walt, it's me, Goldie! Your assistant!"

"Goldie, you're in there?"

"The guy walking away in the sea-creature costume. Him!" Henri walks with purpose. "Follow him. I'm going toward the dressing room and securing the Bejeweled Aqua Chapeau."

Walt runs toward Henri. Back to the dressing room tent I go.

I stop at the entrance of the tent. Edna is still in there. I need her to leave or be distracted, so I can grab the box before Henri is found out.

"There's a fashion emergency," I say. "It looks like the tails on some of the sea creatures are falling off.

They're all loose. You better bring your equipment and check them out."

I show her how loose my tail is. It isn't, but I wag it back and forth like I'm about to break in two. Edna examines the tail.

"Sea creatures," she says with disgust. She grabs a bunch of things and something that looks like a wardrobe designer tool kit and heads out of the tent. *Phew.*

Now to find the box. It's no longer on the table. Where did she hide it? I look under the tables, behind boxes. There are so many pieces of fabric everywhere. I dive into some clothes hanging on a rack and come up with nothing. Then it dawns on me. There is only one place a wardrobe designer like Edna Blanchett would conceal a box.

At Jim's Emporium, they have a section filled with fabrics. Spools upon spools of fabric are stacked against the wall. Those who work there can find customers the right material for whatever dress or Halloween costume their hearts desire. I suddenly remember how every single piece of fabric is usable in the eyes of a designer. No scrap is ever thrown away. The seamstresses would cut the amount of fabric needed and toss the remaining scraps into a large bin or box. A scrap bin would be the perfect place to hide a box. I'm almost one hundred percent sure that's where Edna has buried the bejeweled cap.

"Hello!" I say. The bin is overflowing with scraps of sea creature and mermaid materials, vibrant greens and bright-red fabrics galore. I shove my hands in the bin and get to excavating. Soon enough, pieces of fabric go flying in the air. I'm making quite the mess but the box must be in here somewhere. I keep digging until my whole body is practically in the bin.

Yes! I found it! I pull the box from the bin and place it back on the table. Now for the moment of truth. To see what's inside.

"What are you doing here?" Delphine says just as I am about to open the box.

Chapter Seventeen

"DELPHINE, I CAN EXPLAIN EVERYTHING, BUT FIRST I need to figure out what's inside this box."

She shakes her head. "No, I don't think that's a good idea, Goldie. Let go of that box. It's property of Baldwin Studios. I think you've done enough."

Does Delphine really believe I had something to do with this drama? She is breaking my heart. I thought she trusted me.

"Whatever is in this box will explain exactly what's been going on."

I open the box and what is inside is *not* what I expected. Not at all. Oh my goodness. This is a true movie tragedy. No cliffhanger here. No hope for Delphine and her army of mermaid warriors saving the day. The Bejeweled Aqua Chapeau is no longer the

Bejeweled Aqua Chapeau. Someone has plucked every single diamond off the cap. The cap is completely bare.

"This is terrible," Delphine repeats. "What did you do?"

Wait a second. She can't possibly think I had anything to do with this?

"No, no, no. Not me. It was Edna Blanchett and her assistant Henri. I'm telling you, I've been unraveling this case and it was them. They stole the diamond swimming cap."

Delphine shakes her head. She doesn't believe me.

"Edna? No. It's not possible. Why would she do such a thing?" she says. "She loves me. We've worked together for so many years. She wouldn't do that to me or to the director. She wouldn't want to sabotage the movie."

"Think about it. Maybe she wouldn't do it to *you*, but do you really think she doesn't have any resentment toward Baldwin Studios? You told me yourself she didn't want to leave Powerhouse and she did," I say. "She doesn't seem all that happy to be working on this movie. And neither does Henri. She wants to get you back with Powerhouse. How else to do that, but by sabotaging you and the movie?"

Delphine is losing all faith in me. I can see it in her

face; she isn't reacting to anything I say. Just when I am about to continue my case, Edna Blanchett walks into the dressing room tent. She stares at the box and then back to Delphine, her lips pressed in disappointment.

"The box," Edna says, as if it's the box's fault for showing its contents.

"Edna, what is this all about?" Delphine asks.

Edna slowly walks over to us. She thrusts her pointy chin up.

"The swimming cap was ugly. It was always ugly. Diamonds on a swimming cap," she says. "What is the word Americans love to use? Tacky."

Delphine is as stunned as I am. I would never describe the Bejeweled Aqua Chapeau as tacky. A bit over-the-top, sure, but perfectly fitting for a mermaid queen in my humble opinion.

"You hated the cap enough to do this? To sabotage the whole movie?" Delphine says. "I don't understand why you would do such an awful thing. After all we've been through."

Edna looks down at the cap with a scowl.

"A mermaid queen wears a crown, not a swimming cap," she says.

Can't blame her on that. A crown would have been

really nice. Honestly, Delphine can wear anything and make it look empowering. Who cares? Cap, crown. Toe-may-toes, ta-mah-toes.

"It's not what you wear, but how you wear it," I say, trying to cut the tension. It doesn't work, since Edna sends a scowl my way, too. Her mean mug makes me feel as if she's pricked me with one of her sewing needles. Ouch.

"What is the meaning of this?" Delphine points to the unraveling, plucked cap in disbelief. "You voiced your opinion on the cap and it didn't go your way. That didn't mean you had any right to destroy it."

"My designs. My work."

Delphine shakes her head in disappointment. "Making a movie isn't a one-person job. It's a team effort. What you did is so wrong."

Edna presses her thin lips.

"I don't like it here. I don't like Mr. Davenport. I don't like sea creatures. I don't like anything!" She raises her hand and motions to the tent.

"But, Edna, you could have just told me. Why ruin the swimming cap? Why?"

Edna laughs. Not a mean laugh, just a sad, quiet chuckle.

"You no longer listen. It's all Mr. Davenport this, Mr. Davenport that."

Delphine's face drops. I feel bad, both for Delphine and for Edna. It seems their friendship has fallen apart.

"But to do this." Delphine lifts the sad-looking cap. "I don't understand."

Edna takes her measuring tape from around her neck.

"You are more than this," Edna says. She closes the lid of the box. She places her hand on the top of the box. "We are more than this."

Delphine places her hand over Edna's. "Movies are my life. Each person who joins me on this journey does so because they want to entertain. It's not about me or us," she says. "It's about the people we provide an escape for as well as moments of joy, laughter, sadness, or empathy."

"Movies are my life, too. I left a job that I built from the ground up with my own sweat and tears. Everyone respected me in this industry. A silhouette made by the Oscar-winning designer Edna Blanchett meant something," Edna says, quietly shedding her angry demeanor. "But now all I'm doing is gluing scales onto bodies for some horrible monster movie. You promised me movie productions of value, extravagant period pieces, dramatic costumes for serious roles. Instead, here we are on a beach."

"I didn't know," Delphine says. "I guess I was foolish to think making a movie or having a steady job was enough. Does Henri feel the same?"

"Ah, now you remember my son."

What?! Henri is Edna's son. I can't help gasping. I mean, I feel as if I were literally watching a movie right now, and we've reached the revealing climax.

"The only thing Henri wanted more than anything was to play your leading man in a Powerhouse picture." Edna has tears in her eyes. "And when that was taken away from him, you didn't even bother to get him a decent role in this. What choice did we have?"

A sudden commotion is heard outside of the tent.

"Maman!"

Walt stumbles into the dressing room with Henri in a disheveled mess.

"Henri!" Edna says, rushing to her son.

"I caught this one trying to rig the platform," Walt says.

I shake my head. All this just because they didn't like their new jobs? I mean, they could have just quit.

"Enough is enough," Edna says. "Listen to this man, Henri. We have caused enough damage."

Mr. Davenport runs into the tent, completely out of breath. It's the cigars. Just saying.

"What in—?"

Before Mr. Davenport starts screaming, Delphine walks to him and tilts her head sharply.

"No more screaming," she says. "We need to talk to Edna and Henri. A normal conversation, not a shouting match."

I take the box with the naked cap and head out with Walt, giving them the privacy they will need.

"The sea creature, Henri, had this." Walt shows me a wire cutter.

It looks as though I was right all along. Henri had plans to screw around with the rising platform. What a terrible thing to do.

"So much drama. And the true tragedy in all this: the Bejeweled Aqua Chapeau. Take a look," I say.

Walt takes a peek inside. "All that work," he says. *"Oof."*

I close the lid. "So sad," I say. "And I didn't even get a chance to try it on. A diamond swimming cap would have really upped my game here at Crossed Palms.

Take my already awesome fashion sense to a whole other level." *Maybe even get the attention of Diane,* I think.

In the distance I can hear the sound of a police siren. The cops are on the way.

Walt and I wait to meet them.

Chapter Eighteen

AN EARLY BREAKFAST AT CROSSED PALMS RESORT means I get the dining room all to myself before the hustle and bustle of the guests. Ernesto, one of our servers from Mexico, places a big ol' plate of scrambled eggs in front of me.

"¡Buen provecho!"

"¡Gracias!"

Most of the movie crew and actors packed up and checked out yesterday. The rest are due to leave today. Cheryl mentioned something about a busload of shoe salesmen arriving soon for their shoe convention here at the hotel. Shoes, shoes, shoes! Well, I will miss the Hollywood glitz and glamour, but we could use a bit of a change. It's just been sea creatures, sea creatures, and more sea creatures. As usual, whatever is going on at the Crossed Palms, I'm ready to perform my house detective duties. A pair of diamond-encrusted heels could easily be making an appearance at Crossed Palms, and if they do, I'll surely be well versed in how to handle such a priceless *objet d'art*.

I eat the last of my eggs and head over to Walter's office. Ada the florist is off today. She told me she likes to spend her days off working in her garden. *You must shower your flowers with love every day, Goldie*, she once said. I wave to her assistant and cross over to Walt's door.

A familiar scent of cigar wafts through the air. I press my ear to the door. Yup, Mr. Davenport is in there. It's kind of early for business, but then again, Mr. Davenport is business twenty-four seven.

I don't do my usual storming in. I actually knock.

"Come in," Walt says, and I do.

Mr. Davenport sits opposite Walter, and to my surprise, they are also joined by Delphine.

"Good morning!" I say.

"Good morning, Goldie. I'm so glad you are here," Delphine says. "We were hoping to run into you before we head back to California."

For once, Delphine is dressed casually in pants and

no makeup! She's still so beautiful. Mr. Davenport is in his usual suit.

"Mr. Davenport here was just saying what a great and thorough job Crossed Palms Resort did," Walt says proudly. I can't believe it. Mr. Davenport actually had nice things to say. I won't believe it until I hear from him.

"You were! What else did you say?"

Mr. Davenport shifts uncomfortably in his seat. I like this side of Mr. Davenport. A bit speechless for once. Then he suddenly stands up.

"Goldie, I've already personally apologized to your mother, but I would like to apologize to you. I was wrong when I doubted you, and I was wrong in accusing your mother. I was also wrong for treating you like a child."

I wait for him to insert a *but* in there. The silence starts becoming a little awkward. I guess he won't be amending his apology, and I'm *amazed*. He thrusts his hand out for me to give it a handshake. Delphine looks on with a slight smile. I grab Mr. Davenport's hand and give him a hearty shake. I didn't know I was going to get so much love and appreciation this morning. I'm soaking it in.

"Good instincts. Focused. And above all else, unwavering work ethic," he says. "Goldie Vance, you will no doubt be quite the detective. Look me up in ten years if you're interested in a job in Hollywood."

"Oh no, Mr. Davenport. I would never, ever, ever leave St. Pascal or the Crossed Palms Resort. This is home!"

"We should be heading out. I have a bit of a drive," Delphine says.

"You're driving?" I ask.

"Oh yes. I think I'm past due to visit my old stomping ground. A little detour to see how the five-and-dime is doing. And maybe even a dip in the pool."

"If she insists!" Mr. Davenport says. "I'll be flying to California. This movie won't get finished unless I'm there."

I can already picture Mr. Davenport pointing at random suits with his stinky cigar. I guess some things never change. At least Delphine is going on an adventure.

"Good for you, Delphine. I bet it will be fun to go home," I say.

"Actually, you can call me Josephine. My closest friends do," she says. "Before we go, I have a little something for you."

She pulls out a little statue of a mermaid. It's a winking blue mermaid. "I thought you might like this."

"It's so cute! I know exactly where to put it in my room." I give her a hug. "I love it!"

Mr. Davenport and Josephine say their good-byes.

"Oh wait, I have one more question," I say.

Walt lets out a moan. He doesn't want me to mess up this beautiful moment. Sorry, Walt. I need to know.

"What's going to happen to the Bejeweled Aqua Chapeau? All those diamonds. All that hard work," I say. "Will it ever be put back together?"

Mr. Davenport furrows his brow. "It was a beautiful piece. But we can't justify re-creating it for the movie," he says. "If there are reshoots we'll use the prototype."

It's too bad. The original diamond cap was breathtaking.

"Well, I'm glad I was able to see the original."

"Me too," Josephine says.

The two finally leave and Walt breathes a sigh of relief.

"I'm sure going to miss them," I say.

"What? The number of times I thought I was losing my job…" he says while counting his fingers. "Too many times."

Walt isn't looking on the bright side. He didn't lose his job. We solved the mystery of the missing bejeweled swimming cap, and Mom is back working at the Mermaid Club. All is well, just as I knew it would be.

"I, for one, had no doubt. In fact, I'm surprised I didn't solve the mystery sooner," I say. "My takeaway on all of this: You can never have enough undercover costumes. What are your thoughts about creating a wardrobe of disguises? We can convert a closet. A detective should always be ready to change at the drop of the hat. What do you think?" There is a pause. "I can find us some threads, no problem. What's your size, Walt?"

Walt grimaces. He may not be hip to the idea now, but I'll convince him. It will take time for him to see things my way. He reaches for his suit jacket.

"I don't think we'll need costumes."

"Hear me out, Walt—"

I list five reasons why my idea is the best. He listens patiently as we exit his office and walk toward the lobby.

"Okay, okay, Goldie. I'll think about it," he says. "Good job. Now that the movie business is behind us, I'll need you to focus on the new day. Deal?"

"Deal!" I stare at the mermaid statue. "This statue may not be an Oscar, but it's close enough." I clutch the mermaid to my chest and begin. "I would like to thank the Deep End for making the best brain food around. And I couldn't have solved the case without the help of my true friends Cheryl and Rob. A big kiss to my parents for being the very best parents a girl can have. And last, I owe it all to Walter Tooey, house detective extraordinaire."

I take a lavish bow and a twirl, just like Josephine did when she wore the beekeeper outfit. Walt claps, which I so appreciate.

"Cars are waiting," he says.

"Yes, sir!"

Walt goes one way and I head toward the valet station. But before I reach the valet station, I take a sharp right. There is an empty shelf in my bedroom that will make the perfect home for my mermaid.

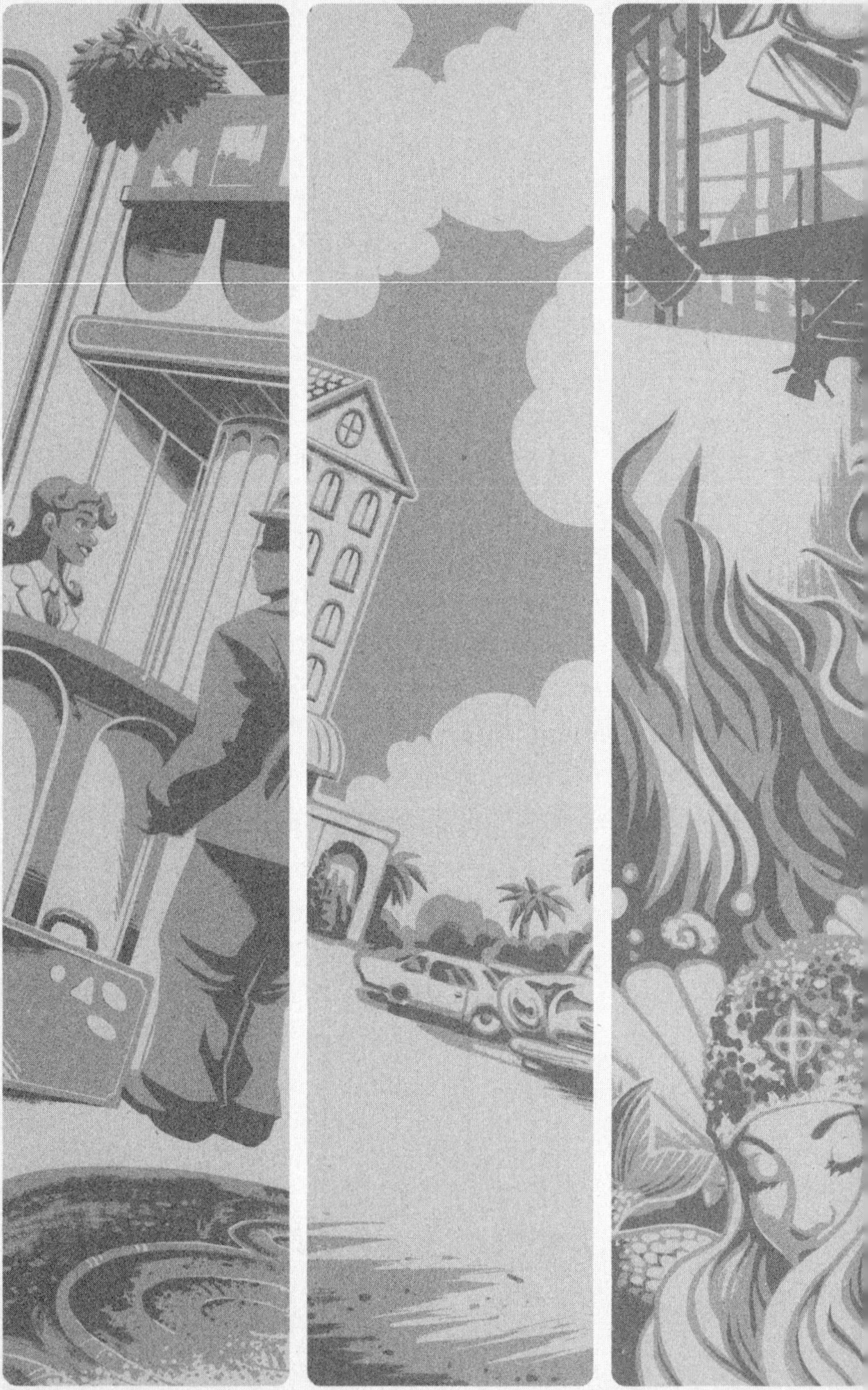

Chapter Nineteen

THE DOORS TO THE MERMAID CLUB ARE CLOSED. IN A couple of hours, they will be open for business. I place my bike against the front door and head to the secret entrance. An electrician is working on the fuse box. I guess after all the blackouts, it's time for the club to get an electrical checkup. Hopefully there will be no more lights out in the club's future. Or mine.

Mike leans over the bar, writing in his tiny notebook. His face looks intense. Across from him, Angie unloads a box of bottles as she hums a tune to herself.

"Hey, Mike. Are the words flowing today?"

Mike doesn't answer, but he gives Angie a nudge. Angie in turn pulls out a glass and fills it with bubbly water. Mike then slices a lemon and tucks in a tiny umbrella. "Here you go. A little treat to quench your thirst."

I take a good look around. The Mermaid Club is no longer the land of sea creatures and mermaid warriors. The battle is officially over. Gone away are the vibrant corals, the textured walls, and the majestic throne. You would never even know that a big movie studio had taken over the Mermaid Club. All the cozy tables are back facing the tank of water. No more blinding spotlights or wires. And no more Mr. Davenport yelling in the megaphone. In fact, the club is quiet.

"Wow. It's hard to believe the Mermaid Club was once ruled by a queen," I say.

"What makes you think the Mermaid Club still isn't ruled by a queen?" Angie says, hauling a box over to the kitchen.

"You miss it? Because I sure don't," Mike says. "I like to know what to expect during my day. I've also missed your mom and our customers. I won't lie; I miss making money, too."

He laughs and looks at the empty tank.

That is the one thing I missed, too. Mom doing what she does best. Mom as a magical mermaid.

"Funny. I never did find out who owned this glove."

I pull out the last of the evidence. Everything else checked out except for this. Walt said someone must have just accidentally dropped it.

"Where did you find it?" Mike exclaims.

"Huh?"

"Angie's been looking everywhere for it. What with the movie business, I thought for sure we lost it." Mike takes the white glove and pulls out the matching one from under the bar. "She must have dropped it with the blackouts. Thanks, Goldie!"

I can't believe it. The owner of the gloves happened to be the one person I forgot to ask. I can't stop laughing. I grab my glass and head to the dressing room.

"Hey, before you head back there. Thought you might want to see this." Mike pulls out the latest issue of the *Daily Gazette*. "Look who made the front page."

Well, how do you like those seashells? I'm on the front page of the *Daily Gazette* with the headline LOCAL GAL UNCOVERS DIAMOND HEIST. Byline by none other than Scoops Malone. Walt is also in the picture, as are Mr. Maple and Mr. Davenport. The interview happened a couple of days ago.

"Cool! Can I keep this?"

"Of course you can. We already have, like, ten copies back here."

I may not have gotten a promotion but Mr. Maple can't deny my skills, not when it's printed in black and white for all to see. I might have to frame this. Maybe hang it right alongside my pictures with Mom and Dad. I mean, I cannot believe Scoops wrote this:

"Budding house detective Goldie Vance…"

Now that's the scoop right there! And he never once divulged how Josephine Walters was filming here. He kept his promise that all he would publish was an exclusive on the missing diamond swimming cap. Scoops may have had questionable working ethics, but he turned out okay. He'll never be someone I think of as a mentor, like Walt, but I appreciate his drive. We both love uncovering the truth. We just have different ways of approaching it.

I knock on the dressing room door three times.

"C'mon in, babe."

Mom faces the vanity mirror, applying purple eye shadow.

"Hi, Mom! Did you see who made the front-page news today?" I say. "Me!"

"Look at you. Your name in print. Why do I feel like

this won't be your last piece in the news?" She hugs me and I sit next to her.

"Actually, to be a great detective, it's probably best not to be in the spotlight. A great detective stays behind the scenes. It's the only way to gather the best information," I say. Mom nods, listening attentively. "I made an exception because I wanted printed proof of Mr. Davenport's apology."

Mom laughs.

"Did you see his other gift?" Mom points to a bouquet of flowers. Beautiful red roses. Their fragrance fills the room. "In his note, he said if we ever want to make it in Hollywood to look him up."

"Hollywood can't compare to St. Pascal. We've got everything we need here. Right?"

"Don't worry, babe. I don't think I'll be paying Hollywood a visit anytime soon," Mom says. "Especially not when I have rehearsal in less than twenty minutes."

I'm so glad Mom is right where she's meant to be, doing underwater flips with such grace and wonder. I hand over her fin and she puts it on.

"Have you ever thought of incorporating a crown?" I ask.

Mom shakes her head. "I know I'm royalty. I don't need a crown to prove it."

The other dancers enter the room. They greet me with hugs and applause for my newspaper article. It feels good to be acknowledged for a job well done.

I think today's Mermaid Club show is going to be extra special. I'll be sitting in the front row, eager to watch.

Chapter Twenty

CHERYL'S FACE IS DEEP IN AN ENGINEERING BOOK. (Yup, not only is she into science, she's also a wiz in math, mechanics....) Now that Baldwin Studios has officially shipped out all their things and everyone is checked out of the hotel, Crossed Palms is back on familiar ground. It's a little strange walking through the lobby and not running into a mermaid or two or a cluster of swamp things. I kind of miss it. But I don't miss Mr. Davenport and his cigar smoking. I do miss his sweet ride.

"You never take a break, huh, Cheryl?" I say. "It's time to leave!"

"I still have ten minutes left in my shift and so do you," she says, pointing to the big clock hanging on the wall. Ugh. I'm just itching to take off my valet uniform, and I have no desire to head back to my station. Besides, there's no point. In my mind, I have checked out of valeting and checked in to my house detective duties, even for my last ten minutes. "How about heading over to the Deep End? Celebrate surviving this week and not losing our jobs. What do you say?"

"Sounds like a plan," she replies. "Yum, french fries. Now that the case is closed, how's life in the quiet lane?"

I flip through Cheryl's engineering book until she closes it and tucks it underneath her desk. "A little boring. I keep expecting Mr. Davenport to come out from somewhere barking out orders," I say.

"No thanks. I won't be missing that."

"I'll miss having to prove him wrong," I say, laughing.

"Who doesn't like doing that?" Cheryl says.

"Goldie."

I turn to see Dad.

"Hey, Dad—I mean, Mr. Vance. Cheryl and I are having a really intense conversation about how much we are going to miss Mr. Davenport and Baldwin Studios."

As much as Dad wants to hide his smirk, I can see it forming. It's right there.

"We were lucky to have Baldwin Studios grace our hotel. When the movie comes out you'll be able to see a little of St. Pascal," he says. "That's something to look forward to."

I totally forgot that about it!

"Hey, maybe I'll still make the cut as a baby sea creature," I say. Picture that. A fifty-foot Goldie on the big screen. Whoa.

"Goldie as a sea creature," Cheryl says. "I can't wait to see that!"

"You might have to wait at least a year," Dad says.

"A year?!" Cheryl and I both scream.

"Movies take a long time," Dad replies. "Editing, coloring, music, sound. Reshoots. Who knows what else they'll have to do?"

Movies. They are way too much work for me. I prefer my action right here and right now.

"Things have been slow. It's okay for you girls to head out a little early," Dad says. "We'll see you tomorrow, Cheryl."

Yes! Cheryl gathers her things. The Deep End is calling! French fries, here we come!

THE DEEP END IS ALSO DEVOID OF MOVIE EXTRAS, directors, and mermaids. Ho-hum. But the regulars are all back and it's busier than ever. Cheryl and I grab a booth and order milk shakes to start us off.

"Hey, guys, what's cooking?"

Rob strolls over with freshly pomaded hair and a nice polo shirt. He's all spiffed up. He must have changed right after I left him at the valet station. Cheryl notices, too.

"You're pretty dressed up, Rob," I say. "Where are you off to in such stylish duds?"

Rob's face turns completely red. Oops. I didn't mean to put him on the spot. I'm just doing my thing, getting to the bottom of a mystery.

"Just came to eat fries. That's on the agenda, right? Fries?"

Cheryl chuckles. Her face is a little red. They're both hard-core blushing. It's kind of cute.

"Fries are definitely on the agenda," I say.

I sip on my milk shake while Rob hems and haws. He wants to say something, but instead of cutting the tension, I sit back and enjoy watching him get so flustered around Cheryl. Cheryl is just Cheryl. Super smart and beautiful.

"I was thinking, Cheryl. Not sure if you've got plans. But I was wondering…"

Cheryl looks down at her milk shake. She's nervous, too. I'm just glad I've got a front-row seat to this. I lightly kick her under the table. *She* could at least help Rob out a bit. He looks like he's going to faint.

"Yes, Rob?" Cheryl says.

"Want to go see a movie? There's a double feature tonight: Dracula and Frankenstein."

Scary movies.

"Okay, Rob. I'll go to the movies," Cheryl says, and Robs smiles the biggest smile ever witnessed by humankind.

"Want to join us?" Rob asks.

Oh no. I don't want to be a third wheel. Besides, I have plans of my own.

"No thanks. I've got a thing I have to do."

Cheryl looks at me quizzically. "I thought the mystery behind the diamond swimming cap has been solved. Aren't you off duty?"

I grab a couple of fries and leave a few bills on the table. "I am. I think it's time for a new adventure," I say. "Have fun at the movies. And look out for Miss Dupart. She stars in the Dracula film!"

No more driving ritzy cars today. It's back to my Big Blue, which is fine and dandy with me. I can truly appreciate St. Pascal when I cruise around on my bike. I once again watch families take their evening strolls. Couples getting ice cream. Jim of Jim's Emporium waves a hello. He's about to close up shop soon.

There's one shop that will stay open for a few more hours. I park my bike and head into Wax Lips. As I enter, Diane is nowhere to be found. Bummer. I wonder if she has the day off. Go figure. The one day I get the courage to actually try and talk to her, she isn't here.

"Looking for anything special?" the owner asks, and I shake my head. *Oh well. I tried. I guess it's not meant to be.*

"No thanks."

I head to the door.

"Oh, hey, Goldie!"

Diane comes out from the back of the store with a stack of albums in her hand. I'm literally beaming. She's wearing a striped shirt and cropped denim capris. She's so cool.

"Hi! I thought you weren't working today," I say, walking over to maybe give her a hand.

"Nope, I'm here. Just unpacking new orders. Check this out."

She puts the stack down and walks over to me and shows me an album I've never seen before. "Her name is Eartha Kitt."

Eartha Kitt is wearing a beautiful, poufy dress on the cover. She's looking directly at the camera with such assuredness. Boldness. She's a little different from the other singers out there. Something about Eartha Kitt reminds me of Josephine when she first stepped out in her Bejeweled Aqua Chapeau and sequined mermaid outfit. Fearless and magnificent.

"I was just about to pop this on the player," Diane says. "Want to listen?"

A big band sweepingly plays while Eartha Kitt sings "C'est si bon" with a purring quality. I'm loving it. I'm also loving how much Diane gets into the music.

"Do you know what she's saying?" I ask.

Diane shakes her head.

"I don't know every word, but *c'est si bon* means it is so good."

"*C'est si bon.* It *is* good!"

We both sway to the music.

This is it. I have absolutely nothing to lose. What was the thing Mom always says? I shouldn't let fear stop me from doing what I want to do.

"So, Diane," I say.

"Yes?"

"I was thinking of taking a walk by the beach. Collect some seashells. Want to come with?"

"Seashell hunting, like explorers," Diane says. "I like that."

She said yes! A simple ask and she said yes. Why didn't I do it sooner?

"Yes, an adventure," I say, my smile wider than ever before.

Diane and I listen to the rest of the Eartha Kitt album. I like when Eartha Kitt rolls her words. Diane and I take turns imitating Eartha Kitt until we can't stop laughing.

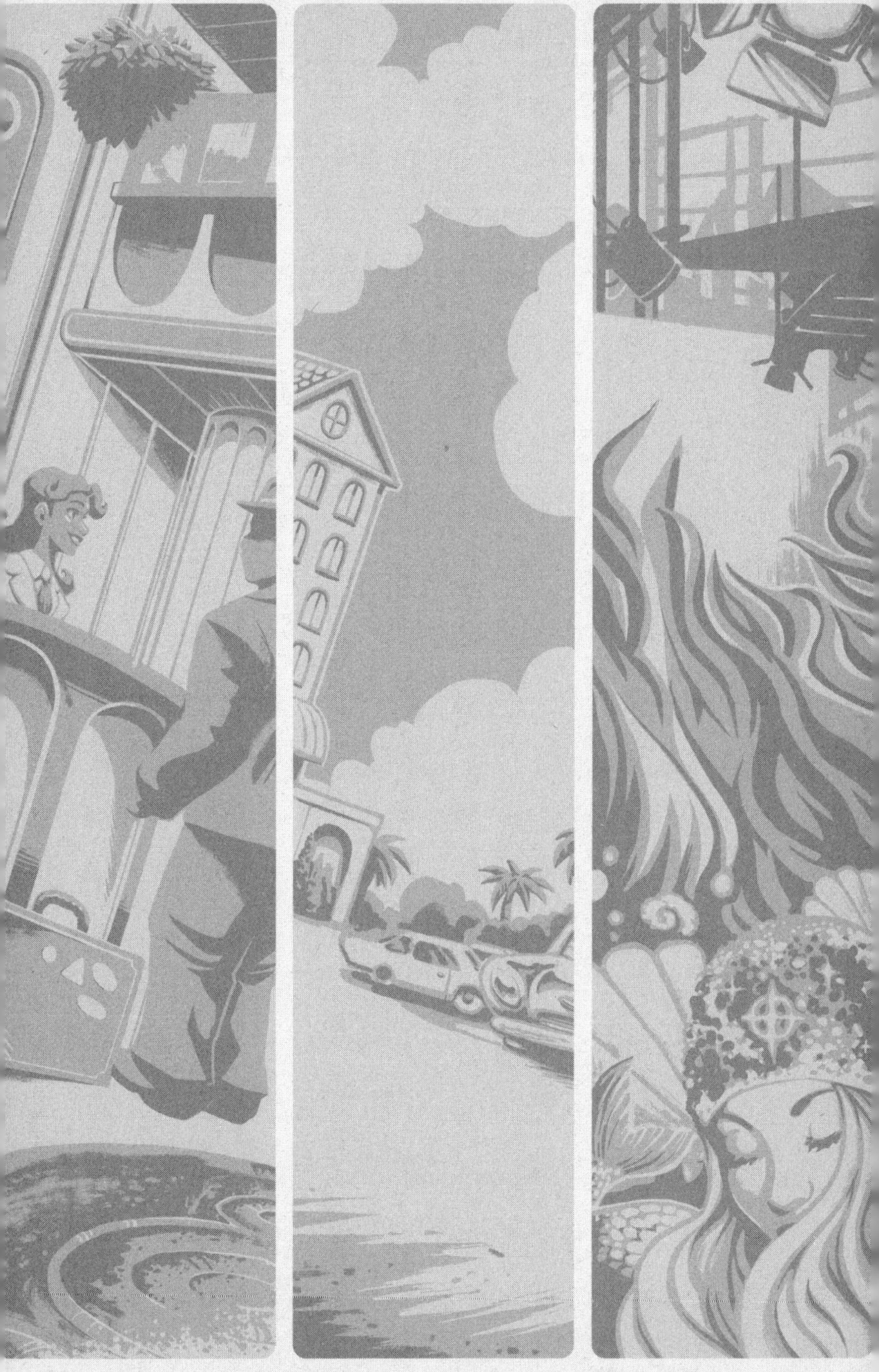